THE BILLIONAIRE'S MATCHMAKER

AN INDULGANCE ANTHOLOGY

D1445101

DRIVING MR. WRONG HOME

SHIRLEY JUMP

Entangled Publishing, LLC
2614 South Timberline Road
Suite 109
Fort Collins, CO 80525
Visit our website at www.entangledpublishing.com.

Edited by Shannon Godwin and Libby Murphy
Cover design by Libby Murphy

Ebook ISBN 978-1-62266-217-3
Print ISBN: 978-1493783717

Manufactured in the United States of America
First Edition October 2013

To Barbara, Susan ,and Jackie, three of the most spectacular authors, friends, and people I know. I couldn't have asked for a more gifted—or giving—team to work with on this book. Thanks for the laughs and the friendship.

Chapter One

Gabby Wilson had perfected the art of covering up the things she wanted to forget with a few brushstrokes of burnt sienna and emerald green. In a painting or a photograph, she could frame a whole other version of who she was, and she had been doing exactly that for damned near eight years. She didn't want the people in Chandler's Cove to remember the impetuous, rebellious girl she used to be, the one who had made the pages of the *Chandler's Cove Gazette* twice—not for scoring a last-minute goal or writing an award-winning essay but because she'd been the youngest resident to get a free ride to jail, courtesy of the sheriff's department. One more time, the sheriff had joked, and she'd get her own plaque on the wall.

She wasn't that Gabby anymore. Now she was an artist with an affinity for mixed digital media, blending her love of photography with her penchant for quirky expression. A respectable, tax-paying citizen who stayed out of trouble.

Well, mostly.

Still, a part of her missed the old days. Maybe just the thrill of them, the unexpectedness that each day brought.

Unexpectedness—yes, that was what it was. Maybe that explained why she was striding up to her reclusive neighbor's massive stucco monolith on a brisk winter afternoon in Chandler's Cove. Earlier today, she'd received a mysterious message from Mr. Bonaparte's butler, asking her to come by.

She had just about reached the granite steps when a familiar six-foot-two figure emerged from the house. A piece of her past, here, of all places.

"Well, well, if it isn't Gabby Wilson," he said.

"T.J.?" she said.

T.J. Shepherd took off his sunglasses and grinned. Something went hot and dark in Gabby's gut. "Hi, Gabby."

She hadn't seen T.J. in almost a decade—not since high school. They'd grown up in the same area, gone to the same schools, but it wasn't until they'd been paired up in a chemistry lab freshman year that she got to know him. The T.J. she'd remembered had been nice, funny even, but way too into computers and technology. He could drone on and on for hours about megabytes and RAM and stuff that bored her to tears.

That T.J. had been a bookish, quiet guy who rarely loosened the leash on his life. His reticence and caution had intrigued her in those days. But the man standing before her now had done a complete one-eighty. He had a dangerous sexiness in the way he stood, the smile playing on his lips.

"What, uh…What are you doing here?" Gabby said, the syllables a little harsher than she intended. T.J. Shepherd's appearance on the doorstep of the Bonaparte mansion was about as incongruous as a hippo in a ballet.

Not that he looked anything like a hippo or anything that would belong in a ballet. Heck, if it hadn't been for his eyes, those ocean-colored green-blue eyes of his, she wouldn't have believed it was really him. He didn't look one bit like the nerdy guy she remembered from high school. She shook her head, and found her wits again. For Pete's sake, this was *T.J.* She'd known him practically from birth.

"I had an appointment with Mr. Bonaparte," he said, interrupting her wayward thoughts. He thumbed toward the door.

"But…I thought you lived in Boston or something."

The boy she had known and the man she saw now were two different people. The one who had left Chandler's Cove for college had been a scrawny guy with glasses and an affinity for buttoned-up polos. In a weird way, she'd liked that buttoned-up side of him. It seemed to dare her to figure out what it would take to get T.J. to *un*button.

The man standing before her now was as far from buttoned-up as he was from the moon. Taller, broader, and more defined, as if Channing Tatum had morphed into T.J.'s body. He still had the same eyes and sharp, lean features she remembered, only now they danced with hidden secrets and a sexy tease. And when he'd smiled at her—

Well, she wasn't here to think about that. Not at all.

"I'm sort of between residences," T.J. said, and once again she reined in her runaway thoughts. "I'm meeting with Mr. Bonaparte about a…potential job. I've been here for a few days, visiting my grandma at the same time, and I thought I'd take the opportunity to call on Mr. Bonaparte. Since he travels so much he's pretty hard to catch."

T.J.'s explanation made sense but a part of Gabby thought there was a piece missing to the story. He'd been gone a long time and his return felt, well, sudden. Maybe because seeing him had hit her with a hot, fast rush of something that sure as heck wasn't nostalgia.

"What about you? What are you doing here?" he asked.

Oh yeah, back to the reason she was here. Which had nothing to do with ghosts from the past. Ghosts who had cut off all communication, at a time when she was hurt and vulnerable.

"I had a message that Mr. Bonaparte wanted me to come up and see him. Even though he's lived here for years, I've never met him. I'm hoping he wants to commission me for some artwork or something. I don't know. The message wasn't really specific. Anyway, I'm...here." God, she was rambling. What was wrong with her? She never rambled.

It had to be her nerves. A lot rode on this appointment. Sure, she had that gallery in Chicago that wanted to take a look at her work, but that was far from a done deal. Especially with Gabby's reputation hanging in the balance after that stunt she'd pulled last year. She'd grown up a lot since then and had a whisper of a second chance. She couldn't let anyone or anything distract her, or she'd be forced to go back to that job working in her mother's lingerie store. Helping a woman in her eighties wrangle her way into a set of Spanx wasn't quite how Gabby envisioned using her creative skills.

T.J. took a step closer. She swallowed hard. Reminded herself to breathe.

Maybe she was just hormonal, because she'd *never* reacted to him quite like that before, or maybe it was just that he had filled out, in a lot of ways and in all the right places. Or maybe it was because he had this confidence, a demeanor that said he owned this little space of the world, and that was intoxicating as hell.

"We should get some dinner, get caught up," he said.

His proposal sent a trickle of temptation through her veins. "I…I can't. I'm leaving for California tomorrow. A cross-country art journey kind of thing." *Journey* was an understatement. This road trip was a chance at an art show that could take her career to the next level.

"That's too bad."

"Yeah. Maybe next time."

"Our timing was never right, was it?" he said.

She shrugged. "We were two different people then."

"Sometimes opposites attract—"

"And sometimes they repel. That I remember from chemistry class." And from past history with T.J. He might be sexy as hell now, but she would bet dollars to gigabytes that he was still as technology focused as ever—even more so since it was his livelihood.

She was no longer the girl who'd talked him into skinny dipping in Geraldine Martin's pool. Or the one who had convinced him to make them fake IDs so they could go bar hopping during junior year.

She was finally on the right track, rather than getting derailed by bad decisions. And she had no plans to entangle her world with T.J.'s, not after the way he had let her down years ago.

"Is that all you remember from chemistry class?" he asked.

No, she also remembered his patience in explaining

the complex theories. The way he'd answered her every question, never making her feel stupid for not understanding chemistry. The hours he'd spent after school helping her study. How she'd begun to notice him and wonder about him, and want more time with him. But then when he had finally asked her to go out with him, she'd panicked and told him it would be better if they just stayed friends. Was that why he had let her down years later?

"That was all a long time ago," she said finally. "Anyway, I need to get to my meeting with Mr. Bonaparte."

She started to brush past him, but he put a hand on her arm. Just a whisper of a touch, but it jolted her. "Are you going by yourself to California?"

"I put up an ad, looking for a co-pilot. You know, someone to split the driving and the cost." Babbling again. For Pete's sake, what was wrong with her? Since when did a touch on her arm turn her into a chattering fool? She nodded toward the door. "Anyway, I better get to my appointment with Mr. Bonaparte."

T.J.'s gaze held hers for a long time, as if he wanted to say something else. Then he slipped on his sunglasses again and gave her a nod. "Maybe another time."

She almost agreed—a polite, auto response—then she stopped herself. Years ago, T.J. used to be her good friend, the person who had helped her survive puberty and high school and her mother's constant chaos. But after T.J. left for college and Gabby stayed behind in Chandler's Cove, they had lost contact and their friendship. She'd sent him a couple of emails, left him a voicemail when she'd needed him more than ever, and there'd been…nothing in return.

He completely ignored her efforts at staying in touch.

That had hurt. T.J. had been the one person she'd truly, completely trusted, the only one who knew the real Gabby. And when her life had crumbled and she'd needed him most—

No response. Nothing.

"No, T.J. I don't think so," she said. "You've never been much for staying in touch, and I'm not about to chase you for a return phone call."

"Gabby, I need to explain about—"

She put up a hand. "It's over, in the past. And so are we."

A taxi pulled into the drive and honked. T.J. waved at the car then turned back to her. "I have to go, but I will be in touch. I promise."

She just nodded and turned away. She waited until she heard the crunch of the taxi's tires on the drive before she let out a long breath and refocused on the door of the mansion and her most important goal right now.

Her career. Mr. Bonaparte's message, sent via his butler, could be her big break, and she intended to nail it down before she left town. This could be her chance to finally break into the competitive high-ticket art world. With Mr. Bonaparte's connections, she could be designing pieces for corporations, other billionaires, maybe even city planners. She'd be taken seriously finally, rather than seen as a flighty, flaky artist who had made a mockery out of her career.

The criticism the art critic had written in the *Tribune* last year still burned in her mind. Even now, she kept the article in her wallet, a daily reminder to try harder, reach further. Not to let people down. She'd ruined that Chandler's Cove mural, thumbed her nose at the people who had hired her to beautify the town, and that giant mistake haunted her still.

She climbed the smooth granite stairs of the Bonaparte mansion and rang the doorbell. A muffled gong boomed a low bass melody inside the house. A moment later, the door opened, and Cyrus, the elderly butler, peered down his pointy nose at her. The white-haired man wore the sour, exhausted look of overworked mortician. "Ah, Miss Wilson."

A bundle of brown and white fur wriggled past the butler's black pants and barreled into Gabby's arms. She laughed at the warm and furry greeting. "Hey, Charlie," she said, giving the terrier a friendly hug. "You getting into trouble again?"

The Jack Russell looked up at Gabby, wagged his tail, and raised his pert snout to let out a happy yip.

"*That dog* makes trouble a full-time occupation." A pained expression formed across the butler's tight face.

"Oh, he's not so bad. Are you, Charlie?" She gave the dog a pat, then lifted her gaze. "I got your email, Cyrus. Is Mr. B…Mr. Bonaparte here?"

"Mr. Bonaparte is busy, preparing for his extended trip to Europe. He asked me to talk to you in his stead. The job he is offering requires the ultimate in attentiveness and care."

Yet not so much that Mr. B would take a meeting? How had T.J. managed to secure a face-to-face when she couldn't? "It's usually helpful if I talk to the client directly," she said. "It's best to get his input on the type of art he's commissioning."

Something that could have been a smile flickered on the butler's face. "Art piece? Mr. Bonaparte didn't ask me to call you here about artwork. He has a different offer for you." The pseudo smile blinked on the butler's lips again. "He would like you to watch his dog while he's in Europe for the next several months."

The words hung in the cold January air. Gabby shook her head, sure she had misheard. "Watch Charlie? For months? This isn't some kind of a practical joke?"

The butler across from her, who had the tottering frame and slow movements of a hundred-year-old man, just nodded. If the cold bothered him, he didn't display so much as a shiver. "Mr. Bonaparte is not a man given to humorous pranks. He is serious about his job offer."

She reached in her pocket and tugged out the email that Cyrus had sent. Read it again. A short message, sent via the contact link on her webpage, something Cyrus used from time to time when he wanted to thank her for returning Charlie. No specifics, merely a mysterious missive to come to the house about an important job. The email was as much of a puzzle as Mr. B himself. Not that she had ever met her reclusive neighbor, but it was the impression he gave. A wealthy enigma, that was Mr. Bonaparte, dubbed Mr. B by Gabby and her friends. Hiring her to—

Watch his dog.

She'd known Charlie ever since Mr. B moved into the mansion some time ago. The dog had a habit of escaping the mansion's grounds and traveling into town. She'd heard that Mr. B made a hefty donation to the local animal shelter, and that made the animal control officer turn a blind eye to the determined Houdini of a dog who often slipped his leash and yard. Thankfully, Charlie steered clear of the traffic heavy areas of town, and nine times out of ten, he ended up at Gabby's studio, preferring to take his afternoon nap in the sun-dappled renovated warehouse space she shared with a pizza parlor and a dry cleaner. At the end of the day,

Gabby would walk Charlie back to Mr. B's house and hand him back to the butler, something that had become a bit of a ritual.

Charlie dashed away and started rooting in the shrubs beside them. His paws flew in furious intent, shoveling away snow, then bare dirt. "St. Clair Charles Osgood Bonaparte!" The butler waved his hands to no avail. "Stop that this instant!"

Charlie jerked his head up, a tennis ball in his mouth and a *who, me?* look on his face. His tail wagged once, then he charged back into the house, past the butler, leaving a muddy trail of footprints on the front stoop, the white marble entryway—and the elegant cardinal red Aubusson rug.

"Not the Aubusson!" The butler paled. Behind him, the maid dove for Charlie, but the dog barked and outran her in furious fast circles on the rug. Gabby could swear Charlie was smiling.

The maid cursed like a truck driver, reaching for and missing the wily puppy. The butler dabbed a folded handkerchief against his temples and ashen cheeks, looking like he might stroke out in the well-appointed hall. "Oh God, oh God, the Aubusson."

"Hey, Charlie, come here, buddy," Gabby said. She patted her thigh and made a kissing sound.

The dog stopped circling and trotted over to Gabby, his whip-thin tail beating a furious pace behind him. He plopped down on the stoop, as innocent-looking as a red-handed burglar.

The butler glared at the brown and white terrier, then reached into the breast pocket of his black suit and exchanged the handkerchief for a slim piece of paper. "Mr. Bonaparte trusts you will find this amount adequate recompense for watching St. Clair Charles Osgood."

Gabby's brain stalled, trying to process the zeroes on the end of the check. She was the typical starving artist, living in a third-floor walk-up in a renovated Victorian a couple blocks from downtown Chandler's Cove, renting a drafty studio because her one-bedroom apartment was too small for anything more than a double bed and a fridge. She drove a Toyota nearly as old as she was, had forgotten what the word vacation meant, and maintained a savings account bordering on anemic. "This is a *lot* of money. Just to watch a dog?"

"Mr. Bonaparte wanted his dog in the hands of someone he trusts while he travels to Europe. And…" Cyrus lowered his voice, "that dog is a…spoiled handful. If he was left here, I rather suspect the staff might do something that might… well, let's just say *annoy* those PETA people."

Gabby bit back a laugh. True, the little dog did have a penchant for getting into trouble, while Mr. B. seemed to be an indulgent owner who didn't mind his dog's wild antics. Charlie was like a two-year-old on a perpetual sugar high. But when he calmed down and laid his slim body at Gabby's feet, he could be positively lovable. Plus, she had to admit she kinda liked his company.

Not to mention the check would mean she wouldn't have to drive a complete stranger across the country. Soon as she left Mr. B.'s, she was taking that ad down. "Okay, I'll do it. I'm going out of town for a couple weeks but I can take Charlie with me if that's okay with Mr. Bonaparte."

"I'm sure whatever is convenient for you will be fine with Mr. Bonaparte. Let me just say, on behalf of the entire staff, that we appreciate you accepting this job." Relief loosened the butler's stiff features. "Thank you again, Miss Wilson." Then he shooed the dog out of the house and shut the door.

"Wait! Is there any special—"

The door opened again and the butler plopped a crystal studded leash, several outfits, a porcelain dish and a bag of dog food into her arms. "Enjoy your time with *that dog*." The last two words sounded like a curse. Then he shut the door again. Fast.

"Looks like it's just you and me, kid," Gabby said. Charlie barked in agreement then fell into place beside her, eager, happy and ready for whatever path they chose. About the same way Gabby felt right now, with the check in her pocket and a second chance at her career lying just down the road.

But in the back of her mind, the mysterious reappearance of T.J. lingered, like taffy stuck on the roof her mouth, daring her to take a taste.

Chapter Two

The woman who had stolen T.J. Shepherd's heart at the Andrew Jackson High School Sweetheart Dance stood outside the Shop 'N Save market, a Jack Russell terrier parked at her feet, and that sweet mix of frustration and confusion he had seen before all over her face. He knew exactly where that look came from, because he'd caused it. More than once.

Heck, he'd seen it earlier today when she'd stared at him like an alien. He knew he'd changed in the years since he'd left Chandler's Cove, but he didn't think he'd changed *that* much.

But Gabby—

Wow, she still looked incredible, but with that adult edge that added a bit of sass to her lithe figure. Despite the January cold, his body warmed at the sight of her. Gabby Wilson. The one person he'd never forgotten.

He hadn't seen her in seven—no, eight—years, not since

graduation when she'd dashed his hopes and broken his heart by making it clear he was a good friend, nothing more. He had high-tailed it for college on the west coast, determined to forget her. He'd gotten a hell of a tan and a hefty student loan tab, but his mind had never left Chandler's Cove, or Gabby.

She'd been right about how he had let her down. Every man had his regrets, and that topped T.J.'s list. Seeing her again had him wondering if he could set things right between them and maybe push the envelope to open the door to something more.

That was why he'd returned to Chandler's Cove. For Gabby. And a second chance—or a final good-bye. He'd spent too many years looking to fill the hole her absence had left in his life, when really only one thing would do. Gabby herself, and her wild, tempestuous spirit.

In high school, he'd been too buttoned up, too cautious, too afraid of risk. He'd learned since he left Chandler's Cove and the heavy thumb of his father's rules that risk was the only way to get what he wanted. Which was what had brought him here, back to the town he vowed to never see again, to pursue the one woman he'd never forgotten.

After he'd left Mr. Bonaparte's house earlier, T.J. had an idea for how to get that time with Gabby he wanted, those uninterrupted hours to answer the question of whether she was the missing piece to his life, the one person who truly knew him and cared about him, rich or poor, nerdy or not, or whether his mind was clouded by the passing of time. So he'd come downtown, figuring this would be Gabby's next stop. He'd been right.

"Looking for something?" T.J. said.

She whirled around, letting out a little gasp of surprise. "God, you scared me. You're popping up everywhere I go today."

"Almost like it was meant to be?" He cocked a grin at her.

"Or just really bad luck."

"I wouldn't say I'm all bad, Gabby."

Her green eyes danced. "That's a matter of opinion, Mr. Shepherd."

Even in a thick winter coat and jeans that ended in zebra striped boots, she was beautiful. The cold bloomed pink in her cheeks, and her long blond hair peeked out from beneath a white fleece hat, a look saved from being ordinary by one rebellious streak of hot pink mixed into the blond and a chunky tri-colored necklace made out of recycled metals. No one would ever describe Gabby as traditional or dull.

She'd been his polar opposite, a woman who challenged him to live outside the box and color the world with aqua and fuchsia instead of black and white. It was part of what had scared the hell out of him and at the same time, drew him in like a fly to a gossamer spider web. Even now, even after all these years apart and all these murky waters between them, he still wanted her as much as he had years ago. He'd been fooling himself, thinking he could forget her, because he hadn't. Not one bit.

"I almost didn't recognize you earlier," she said. "You look so different. So…" The pink deepened in her cheeks. "So grown up."

"I hope that's a good thing."

"Um, yes." Her gaze swept over him again, and her voice

dropped to almost a whisper. "Very good."

Tension coiled in the space between them. T.J. took another step closer. The space between them heated.

He had never forgotten her, never stopped wanting her. But did she want him? She had told him a long time ago they'd never be more than friends, but could he change that? There was only one way to find out. Take a risk. In the end, he'd either make a colossal fool out of himself or have a final resolution between them.

"You know, after we talked, I got to thinking. I've got this job interview in California in a couple weeks." A small lie, but no lightning struck him down, so he plowed forward with the story he'd concocted on his way over here, "and after my car died the other day, I've been debating how to get out there when I thought about you and your trip. So I came down here, and found your ad." He held up the index card he'd pulled off the community bulletin board a few minutes earlier. "Right between Ernie Youngclaus's 'Good Manure Wanted' and Henrietta Vincent's 'Handmade Lace Doilies for Sale.'" He shot her a teasing grin. "You're in good company."

She reached for the ad, but he pulled his arm back. "Hey!"

"Did you find someone to," he dropped his gaze to the words, "'head off on an interesting adventure across the country, complete with a stop at the 'world's largest ball of popcorn'?"

She darted forward and plucked the paper out of his hands. "No. Yes. Well, sort of."

She seemed disconcerted, which surprised him. The Gabby he'd known had brimmed with confidence and self-assurance. He'd always been the one off-balance around her, until now. "Yes, no, sort of?"

"Charlie is going with me."

A quick flare of jealousy mixed with disappointment rose in T.J.'s chest. Damn, he was too late. She'd found someone else, something he'd expected. Women like Gabby didn't come along every day. Any man worth his salt wouldn't let her get away.

Well, T.J. had. But the circumstances had been... complicated.

In his mind, his plan to reunite with Gabby had gone a lot better than this. Now he was unsure and hesitant, as if he was fourteen again, standing in the decorated high school cafeteria while a DJ spinned dance music. T.J. had stood in the room at that dance, brimming with desire for her, a desire he'd been afraid to express, afraid of risking rejection. Then four years later, when he'd finally gotten up the courage to express those feelings, she'd made it clear she didn't feel the same and dismissed him like a pesky door-to-door salesman. Maybe returning to Chandler's Cove had been a bad idea.

Didn't mean he hadn't missed her like hell, though. He'd missed being with the one person in his life who knew him as he was—not as the mayor's son, not as the workaholic CEO. As just T.J., plain, simple T.J.

He had come to this town to see if that connection still existed. And he'd be damned if he'd let some guy named Charlie stand in his way. "It makes sense for us to travel together," T.J. said, "since we're going to the same place. Why don't you let Charlie get his own ride?"

She smiled. "I can't exactly do that."

"Why not?"

"It's…complicated."

He came another step closer, the ad still in his hands. "Ah, but that was always the best part about you. That you were complicated."

A shimmer of amusement shown in her eyes. "Why do you need a ride to California? Why not fly?"

An opening, a chance. Not a big one, but he'd take her question as a possibility she was considering his offer. He could tell her the truth now—and risk losing her all over again—or finish the fib and pray that she understood later. The lies churned in his gut, but he thought of those simple days by the creek, the afternoon visits to the museum, all those times with Gabby, and forged forward with the rest of his fabricated story. "The, uh, interview isn't a sure thing. It's a…risky venture."

"You? Embarking on a risky venture?" She laughed. "That's not the T.J. I knew."

"I've changed, Gabby. A lot." He grinned. "I'm a regular adrenaline junkie now."

She laughed. "That I'd have to see."

"Then maybe we should go together to California. Catch up a little, save some money." He pressed on, ignoring the twinges of guilt pinging in his gut. "I could fly, but my funds are limited and you know how expensive those last minute airfares are. Plus my grandmother loaded me down with some family mementos to truck with me."

She nibbled at her bottom lip, a gesture he'd seen a thousand times when they were younger. Now, though, the sight of her biting that tender flesh made him bite back a groan. "Well, I *could* use help driving."

"What about Charlie? If he's along for the ride, surely

he'll help with the driving?"

She laughed. "He can't drive. For one, he doesn't have opposable thumbs and for another," she gestured toward the space beside her feet, that laughter lighting in her green eyes, dancing on her face, "he's a dog."

Dog? Then TJ made the connection with the terrier waiting patiently by Gabby's side. Behind the dog, on one side of the store was a painted mural of a bucolic park scene, which somehow seemed apt for the Jack Russell. "This is Charlie? Your dog?"

"Not mine. Mr. Bonaparte's. I'm dog-sitting for a few weeks. That's what he hired me to do. That meeting wasn't about art after all."

T.J. exhaled with relief. He hadn't realized until then how much he'd been counting on Gabby being available and willing to make this trip with him. For months, he'd been feeling this longing to return to his roots. No, not his roots— the unfinished business he'd left in Chandler's Cove.

Unfinished business named Gabby.

All these years, he'd left that one story incomplete, a loose end that threaded through his thoughts. Had he missed his chance with her years before because he hadn't taken a big enough risk? If he tried again with Gabby, would the results be different this time? There was only one way to know.

"I'd love to hitch a ride with you. It'll be just like old times," he said, taking a step closer, and thinking that was the last thing he wanted was old times and the way things used to be, "you and me together, walking on the wild side."

She raised her chin and met his gaze. "I don't do that anymore. I'm a respectable tax-paying citizen now."

"Pity," he said, while the urge to kiss her and be with her, to be part of her world again, raged inside him, "because you being rebellious was the highlight of my days."

A smile curved up one side of her face, a smile that told T.J. there was still hope, still a connection, and maybe a little of the old Gabby left after all. "Well, I'd hate to disappoint you, but I'm not planning on ending up in jail on this trip."

"That's okay," he said, meeting her deep green eyes with his own. "Neither do I. I told you, Gabby. I've changed."

She gave him a long, assessing gaze. "That remains to be seen."

T.J. figured he had hundreds of miles to change her mind about him, and to make up for letting her down in the past. He could only hope they didn't run out of road before he could make everything right again.

Chapter Three

Gabby regretted the decision to let T.J. ride along almost the instant she agreed. This was the guy who had disappointed her, hurt her, the one who used to be her best friend then proved the opposite. Why was he back in town? Why this sudden interest in her? And why was she alternately dreading and anticipating the next few days together?

They were opposites. Always had been, always would be. Wild, unpredictable Gabby and nerdy, practical T.J. They might have been friends once but anything more than that would be insane. Then why had her body reacted with the instantaneous ping of a coin with a metal detector?

She flicked a glance at T.J.'s profile, outlined by the sun and white snow-covered landscape seen through the passenger's side window. Damn, he was handsome. Sexy. Desirable. How had she never noticed it before? Was it because he'd ditched the glasses and opted for contacts?

No, it was more than that. It was the way he carried

himself with self-assuredness. The geeky, shy kid she knew in high school, the same one who had tempered her wild side with his voice of caution and restraint, had been replaced by a man who knew his place in the world. That kind of confidence was…intoxicating. It had her looking at T.J. as a man, not as an old friend from high school. And the part that noticed him as a man…

Well, that part kept her pulse racing and a simmering heat brewing in her gut. More than once since she first saw him outside of Mr. Bonaparte's mansion, she'd had to push aside the image of him kissing her, touching her, taking her to bed—

This is T.J., she reminded herself. *Plain old T.J. About as exciting as buttered bread.*

No, that wasn't exactly true. T.J. might have been practical and bookish, but he'd always had this edge to him, as if there was a door he was keeping shut. It had intrigued her and attracted her and driven her to get him to open up, to let her in. But when he'd wanted more, wanted a real relationship, the scared rebel in her ran.

Truth be told, he'd always been more exciting and attractive to her than she'd admitted to him, or to herself. She'd missed him over the years. A lot. But she'd be damned if she'd admit any of those things to him now, especially after the years of silence.

Charlie had his little head propped between the bucket seats, his tail thwapping a happy beat against the leather while T.J. scratched him behind the ears. Clearly, T.J. already had the Charlie stamp of approval.

"He doesn't like men too much," Gabby said. "You're one of the few I've seen him warm up to."

"He must be an outstanding judge of character." T.J. grinned.

"Or a sucker for potato chips." She gestured toward the bag T.J. had opened a little while ago. "Mr. B would have a heart attack if he knew you were feeding Ruffles to St. Clair Charles Osgood."

T.J. rubbed Charlie's head. "We'll keep that between us, won't we, buddy?"

Charlie yipped and pressed his head against T.J.'s arm. His tail tap-tapped agreement.

"If all it takes is some fried potatoes to warm up to me…" T.J. said, tipping the bag in her direction, "would you like some potato chips?"

The scent of salty chips teased at her senses. She dipped into the bag, popped a couple of chips into her mouth, and tried not to picture warming up to T.J. over a lot more than a snack. She cleared her throat and focused on the road. "If you're not careful, I'll eat the whole bag. I love chips."

"Oh, I remember, Gabby."

A few words and she was whipped back in time, to a spring afternoon, when the scent of fresh cut grass hung in the air and the skies were filled with hope and possibilities. She had stayed after school, just her and T.J. in the chemistry lab, while he tried to explain the intricacies of balancing equations. "Who would have thought back then you could make chemistry understandable with a bag of chips?"

He chuckled. "Well, it would have gone better if you hadn't kept eating them. I'd put down two for oxygen, then turn around to only find one left."

"I wanted to keep it balanced." She grinned. "But seriously, if it wasn't for you, I never would have passed that class. I'd probably still be in high school today."

"You don't give yourself enough credit. You always were smarter than you thought you were."

She shrugged off the words and turned her attention to the road. Her nose twitched, and something burned behind her eyes. She lowered the window and let the rush of cold air whisk the emotion away. She refused to be softened by him. Maybe in the old days, but not now, not with the disappointments that had followed. He had let her down once before—he could easily do it again.

Her friends in Chandler's Cove would be reminding her to be cautious if she was at their weekly coffee meeting today. Marney, Mia, and Jenny provided more than just friendship—they were often her second compass, a way of reminding her what was important. She was going to miss those women, that was for sure. Their supportive texts and Facebook messages had sent her off on her journey with a hearty "good luck." Gabby hadn't mentioned T.J.'s presence—maybe because she wasn't quite sure what to make of it herself.

"Once we cross the state line, do you want to stop for lunch? There's this barn I want to photograph with a building-sized version of the *American Gothic* painting on it. I think it'd be perfect for my exhibit. You know, a slice of Americana on a trip across America."

"Sure." He shifted in the seat to look at her. "Tell me about this exhibit you're working on."

"Well, it's not an exhibit yet. All I got was an "I'm interested" from the gallery owner in Chicago. He wants me to send him digital images of what I'm planning before he makes a commitment." She explained the concept—

mixed media representations of quirky stops along the road between Illinois and California. "The pieces are all going to be displayed in halves, because I'm calling it One-Half of America, and if it does well, I'll do the other half of America next year."

T.J. nodded his appreciation. "So these will be like three-dimensional photographs?"

"Yup. And I'll layer them with items endemic to that area, like poker chips for Nevada and prairie grass for Wyoming."

"That sounds cool."

"Thanks." The praise warmed her. She slid another glance in T.J.'s direction. He'd always been supportive of her art, the only person she knew who "got" her, even with all her quirks.

She remembered the two of them hitting museums on the weekend. T.J. would tell Gabby he could see her art hanging there someday and she'd brush off the encouragement. One time, he'd lingered in front of a painting of a father and son fishing. And in a quiet, somber voice he had told her about a father who never encouraged, only criticized, a father who had mapped his son's path from birth and allowed zero deviation from the plan.

It had been one of the few times he'd talked about his father, but it had explained everything about T.J.

Maybe that had been half the reason she'd kept trying to get him to join her on her crazy adventures. To force T.J. to see there was a world—and people—outside the expectations of his father. It had been a constant challenge to get him to loosen up, to step outside the boundaries he placed on himself, coupled with the rules and expectations of his stern, cold father. And maybe a part of her had wanted to spend time with T.J., the one person who used to balance her, and who made her crazy world make sense.

An hour later, they had grabbed some sandwiches from a deli and pulled up outside the barn. A two-story image of Grant Wood's iconic painting stared back at them, the serious couple with the pitchfork seeming to watch the passing traffic with slight disapproval. Gabby got out of the car, her camera in hand, and positioned herself on the other side of the fence. A soft blanket of white snow covered the hillside and the barn's roof, giving the building a stark but ethereal feel. She settled into the shot, feeling the moment ease into her mind, her heart. Here, creating art, was where she was most at home. Where she found peace.

She had missed that feeling. She'd lost it the day she'd painted that crazy, offensive mural—angry caricatures of town officials who she'd seen as trying to box her in as an artist, rather than being adult enough to recognize the mural was a job, not a chance to thumb her nose at the world and at the power of the haves versus the have-nots in town. Ever since, she'd been trying to get that feeling back. And here, finally, she'd found it.

Or almost. Something nagged at her as she framed the image then snapped a few photos. The scene didn't feel quite right, even with the perfect composition and lighting. Something was missing. But what? Behind her, she heard T.J. and Charlie exit the car and join her.

"Aren't you going to get closer?"

She shook her head. "The owner doesn't let anyone on the property." She gestured toward the No Trespassing signs posted every few feet. Charlie scrambled underneath and stood on the other side, prancing in the snow.

"And when has a little sign stopped you before?"

"T.J., I—"

Before she could explain, T.J. pushed down the fence and climbed over it. "Come on, Gabby. Let's get closer."

"I can zoom—"

He pushed down the wire fence again with one hand then extended his opposite hand in Gabby's direction. "Come on. Live dangerously."

His voice had dropped into a deep, dark range that stirred something inside her. Something that hadn't been stirred in a really long time, that tempted her to take chances, to step off the path, to climb over the fence and into whatever adventure waited on the other side.

Before Gabby could think twice, she put her hand in T.J.'s and broke a law for the first time in years. Not the one warning people away from the property, but the no trespassing wall she'd been trying to keep around her heart ever since T.J. had shown up on Mr. B's doorstep.

Chapter Four

They didn't stop laughing until they reached the interstate again. Even Charlie joined in, yipping and barking his excitement about the adventure. T.J. drove, zipping Gabby's Toyota down the road. The light mood wrapped them all in a bright cloud. T.J. liked that. A lot. "That was close," he said.

"I thought they were going to call the cops. I haven't run that fast…well, since the last time someone called the cops on me." She laughed, and shook her head. "I never thought I'd say this, but you are a bad influence, T.J. Shepherd."

"Me? I'm the brainy, sensible one." He grinned then flicked on the turn signal when he noticed a sign for a rest stop.

"Maybe years ago, but now…"

He glanced over at her. "Now what?"

"Now you're living on da edge, dude." She grinned.

Maybe Gabby was seeing him differently now and his plan was working. He wanted to apologize for the past, but worried that if he brought it up, it would burst this happy bubble. Later, he decided. They had miles to go yet. "You ain't seen nothin' yet, baby. So, are you going to admit I was right? That a little bit of trouble is fun?"

"Okay, a little. But no more." She wagged a finger at him. "I'm working hard to repair my image, and the last thing I need to do is to get arrested."

"You? Repair your image? What was wrong with it?" The girl he remembered had broken the rules, yes, but she was that daredevil everyone wished they could be. Especially him. Gabby had tempted him, then and now. It wasn't just because of how different she was, it was because she still saw the real him—the only person who hadn't cared about his political connections or his bank balance. For a long time, she'd been just his friend, but now he wanted more. "You were always badass and cool."

She shook her head and her voice dropped, softer, sadder. "I'm just not who I used to be."

"Me either, Gabby. Me either." He sensed she didn't want to talk about it, so he let the subject drop. T.J. parked the car in the rest stop parking lot then dropped the keys into Gabby's palm. "Come on, let's get some fresh air."

The three of them climbed out of the car. T.J. grabbed the bag of sandwiches and drinks and gestured toward a picnic table sitting under an awning to the right of the main building. No one else was around, and the entire pavilion was covered with a pristine, white, snow blanket. "Lunch al fresco?"

"It's January." She shivered in her coat. "We'll freeze to death."

"It'll be an adventure. A more legal one this time."

She looked dubious, but T.J. trudged up the snowy hill, spread their sandwiches on the wooden surface, and set down their drinks. As soon as he was released from his leash, Charlie bounded off, excited to have some room to run and explore. The dog stayed close, circling out and back around, leaving a trail of tracks peppered into the snow.

"Mr. B would kill me if he knew Charles Osgood was outside without his little wool coat on."

"He *is* wearing a coat," T.J. said. "The one God gave him."

She laughed. "True. Well, I won't tell if you don't."

He made a motion of zipping his mouth closed. "My lips are sealed."

That drew her attention to his mouth and to thoughts of kissing him. Damn, he looked good, with the dark hair she remembered, now a little longer and with a wave that swung across his forehead. She had the strangest urge to brush that hair back, to let her hands tangle in the locks, to draw him closer to her, to—

Kiss him.

Instead, she talked, keeping her mouth busy with something other than T.J. "What's with you and this adventure thing? You used to be the one I had to convince."

He mouth quirked. "Do I detect a little surprise? At not being in control?"

"I can turn the tables on you so fast, your head will spin."

He leaned back on the bench, crossed his arms over his chest, and smiled. "Oh yeah? I'd like to see you try."

The challenge roared inside her, awakening the old Gabby. It spurred her to stand up slowly while T.J. watched the movement. Even in jeans, boots, and a thick winter coat, she knew how to shift her hips to draw his attention. His smile grew wider as she closed the distance between them, propped a hand on either side of him, and then leaned in close, a breath away. She waited until his brows arched in surprise, and his smile faltered, like in the old days when he stuttered, unnerved by her in a miniskirt or a racy suggestion. Oh, she'd show him who was in control, and maybe he'd stop trying to prove otherwise.

She brought her lips to his and whispered against his mouth. "The tables are turned, Mr. Shepherd. What are you going to do about it?"

"Turn them back in my favor." He cupped her head and drew her closer.

"Wait? What?" Her eyes widened and she readied a protest, but it died on her lips the moment he kissed her. It was no ordinary kiss, nothing like what she might have expected out of the T.J. she used to know. No, this was a prelude to sex, a long, hot sensual kiss that slid across her lips with delicious precision, igniting a fire within her. The heat shimmied through her veins, burned deep inside her, and made her think of tangled sheets and hot nights.

His tongue teased hers and his fingers awakened the nerves in the back of her neck. Her thoughts swirled, her heart raced. The world closed in to just them, this moment, this kiss.

Too soon, T.J. drew back. Gabby took a second to catch her breath, to gather her thoughts and clear her head. She hadn't been prepared for a kiss, especially not one from T.J. And especially not one so...hot and sweet. "What...what was that?"

"If you don't know, maybe we should go back to sex ed

class." T.J. grinned, then swung his leg over the bench and got to his feet.

She put a hand on his chest. "Not so fast. What the hell was that?"

"A kiss, Gabby. Nothing more."

"Why?"

"Why what?"

"Why kiss me? I mean, it's not like we have a romantic history. We were just friends in high school, and then you…"

"Left." He'd been waiting for this question, for the elephant to make an appearance in the room.

"Yeah. No contact, nothing for all these years. Now you pop back into my life, go on this cross-country road trip with me. Then you kiss me. What is going on, T.J.?"

He sighed, and his gaze went to some place in the distance, some place far from her. She got the feeling he was hiding something, but she wasn't sure what. "I never meant to let our friendship die when I left, Gabby. I just needed some time away from here, away from everything that came with Chandler's Cove."

"Meaning your father."

He nodded. "I needed an opportunity to see if I could make it on my own. Without his influence or his name or his demands." T.J. released a long breath and focused his gaze on hers. "Out of all the people in the world, you are the only one who knows what he was like, what living with him was like. And I hope that means you can also understand why I just needed to…shut myself off, I guess, from all of that when I left for college."

"And from all reminders of what used to be."

"Yes," he said. "And I'm sorry now that you and our

friendship were caught in that."

His cutting her out of his life had been a side effect of his determination to shed Edward Shepherd's influence. T.J.'s father had been a beloved mayor, a successful businessman, a charity darling—in public. Behind closed doors, Edward had been a tyrant, a man who expected perfection from his family. Second place didn't exist in Edward's mind, and he pushed T.J. to excel in everything, to maintain a straight A average, to be the smartest, brightest, most organized student. T.J. came home at the end of every school day to a silent, pristine house where dust didn't dare to settle. Gabby had always tried to ease that weight hanging around his shoulder, to help him forget his father's rules and expectations. "When I was with you, it was my only chance to cut loose, to be someone else. But then I had to go back home, right into that suffocating house again. When I got to college, I wanted to see what would happen if I relied only on me. So I told my father I didn't want his money. I'd do it on my own."

Her brows furrowed. "How did you pay for school?"

"I got a few scholarships and paid for the rest by waiting tables. Delivering pizzas. And I started a small business on the side that did pretty good." He ran a hand through his hair. "I got so consumed by my determination to make my own way that I let everything in my past go. Including you. I'm sorry."

She'd heard rumblings around town that T.J. had done well after college. But she hadn't listened. He'd cut her off; in her hurt, she'd done her best to excise him from her thought and her heart.

"That's okay." She shrugged as if it didn't bother her,

but it did. A lot. T.J., the one person she'd thought she could always count on, had let her down. Even though a part of her—okay, the majority of her—was attracted to this new T.J., the sensible side threw up caution flags, warning her if he had let her down once, he could do it again. He tipped her chin until she was looking at him. "It was a mistake. I didn't realize how big of one until I saw you again. And then I knew what I had lost."

Her eyes filled with tears as a mixture of hurt and hope coursed through her. She shook her head, closing off her emotions to him. Was she that weak that a couple of sentences and a tender touch could make her forget that T.J. hadn't been there for her when she needed him?

If he had truly cared, he wouldn't have left her behind.

"We better hit the road," she said. "We have a lot of miles ahead of us."

"Gabby—"

Charlie came running at Gabby's whistle, waited while she reclipped the leash, then bounded along at a happy run beside her. Gabby tossed the trash into a nearby bin and headed back to the car, trying to calm the riot of emotions awakened by one very simple kiss and one honest apology.

Both had come too late. T.J. had left Chandler's Cove to leave his past behind, and as soon as this trip was over, she was going to do the same.

Chapter Five

Almost ten hours after they left Chandler's Cove, Gabby and T.J. pulled into the Pioneers Park in Lincoln, Nebraska. T.J. was back behind the wheel, with Charlie tucked against Gabby in the passenger's seat. The dog had slept a good portion of the trip, content just to ride along with them. For a moment, T.J. allowed himself the luxury of imagining he and Gabby were married and this was their dog.

The wild Gabby he had known in high school was as far from domestic bliss as someone could get. She'd changed over the years, become not just more adult but also more self-assured and...solid. Yes, that was the word for it. A part of him was still figuring out this new Gabby and whether they were still the match he'd envisioned.

Either way, in the back of his mind, he knew this family-on-a-trip moment would end. He had started this trip on a lie, and eventually he was going to have to come clean to

Gabby.

At the time, the lies had seemed like a good idea, a way to convince her to let him come along on the cross-country drive and at the same time rekindle the closeness they had in the past. But as the miles passed, he began to wonder if he should go ahead and tell her the truth—he wasn't a struggling salesperson trying to get to California for an interview but, in fact, was the founder and CEO of his own successful software company.

Even now, all these years later and after that mind-blowing kiss, he risked her rejecting him again. The memory held firm, a wall. T.J. telling Gabby at the school dance he wanted to be more than a friend, then leaning in for a kiss, only to have her turn away and sputter something about not wanting to screw up a good friendship.

When he'd left town, he'd vowed to put Gabby from his mind. He'd dated several women, even come close to marrying one, but none of them had been Gabby.

When his fiancé turned out to be just after his money and the life it could buy her, T.J. had started thinking about the old days. Before the money, before the company. All those days came attached to a memory of Gabby.

Lord knew he'd tried to forget her, but Gabby had been… unforgettable. So here he was, in her Toyota, answering the question once and for all. Was Gabby just a friend, a sweet memory from the past, or was she more?

He glanced at her, remembering their kiss earlier today. A rush of desire roared through him all over again and he knew why he'd come back to town, to try again with Gabby. She had taken off her coat in the warm interior of the car, leaving her in the simple attire of a V-necked T-shirt and jeans. On any other woman, it might look boring or dull, but Gabby's curves made the V an enticing peek at her cleavage, while the jeans outlined strong thighs and sweet hips.

Gabby was sweet danger and hot temptation. That— mingled with her being the only person he'd ever opened up to and allowed a glimpse into his true self—gave them a connection he had tried like hell to deny and couldn't anymore. Every time he looked at her, he wanted her, not just in his bed but in his life.

"Watch out. You almost hit the curb there."

He jerked the wheel back, overcompensating for the near miss, and sending Charlie sliding across the back seat. "Sorry. My mind wandered for a second."

"Fantasizing about gigabytes and RAM again?" She grinned.

"Something like that."

"Is that what you did for a side business in college? Computer stuff?"

He chuckled. "I thought you hated when I talked about hard drives and programming codes."

"I did. I was being polite." She grinned.

"Okay, I'll tell you. And leave out all the boring parts." He paused a second. "There. Story done."

She laughed at that. "So I take it if you're traveling to California for a job, then the small side business is no more?"

He could tell her the truth, that the small side business had grown into a giant, multimillion dollar firm, but if he did, then he'd have to admit he could easily afford a trip to California, which would take away his excuse for being with her. So instead, he fudged a little white lie. "It's definitely not a small side business anymore."

"That's too bad. I'm sorry, T.J." She pointed toward a paved lot on the side of the road. "We're here."

Perfect timing. He parked the car and they got out. Charlie tugged on his leash, eager to explore, to try on this new world. He kept peeking over his shoulder, as if making sure both of them were following him.

"This park is amazing," she said. "Almost seven hundred acres of prairies and woodlands. And that, over there, is the remains of an old federal treasury building. It's so unique, especially in this setting. I think I'll start here," Gabby said, dropping her camera bag and tripod on the ground then pointing toward a quartet of concrete pillars that looked like second cousins to Stonehenge. Two stood complete, with Grecian style caps, while two others had lost part of their height, as if some giant had tripped over them on his way toward the pond, leaving the stony remains scattered on the ground below.

Gabby brought her camera up and sighted the pillars. Her face took on a serious cast, her mouth an all-business line. He'd always loved this side of her. She became determined and somber when it came to her art, her concentration only on her creation. He respected that about her. He always had loved to watch her work.

Charlie strained at the leash, barking and nipping at her leg. She waved a hand at him. "Charlie, quit it, I want to get this shot."

The terrier jerked left suddenly, yanking the leash out of T.J.'s hand. Charlie scrambled down the trail, disappearing around a curve, the crystal studded leash trailing like a kite. T.J. took after the dog, while behind him Gabby cursed and got to her feet, grabbing her camera case. The two of them hurried down the path until they spied the brown and white terrier. They called out to him, but instead of coming back, Charlie turned back, let out a little bark, then ran off again, picking up speed this time. "What's with this dog? It's like he wants us to go somewhere special."

"Yeah, the road that leads to Drive-Us-Crazy."

T.J. laughed. "No, look at his path. No diverging to hunt a squirrel or peek under a shrub, straight on to his destination."

She groaned. "I don't have time for this. I have a schedule to keep and a whole lot of pictures left to take. The gallery wants unique representations of Americana, not the brown and white rear end of a—"

Charlie's paws were propped against the side of a giant statue of a bison. A long white strip of flat, pristine, snowy lawn ran behind the statue, flanked by dark green pines lining the sides. The sun was starting to set, casting the sky in rich hues of blue, offset with puffy white clouds. A unique representation of Americana. Charlie was either one smart dog or one lucky puppy.

"This is perfect," Gabby said.

"I think it just got better," T.J. whispered. He pointed toward the tree line.

A real bison stood to the edge of the trees, watching them, wary, as still as his bronze counterpart. Gabby moved slow and easy, setting up her camera, framing the shot of the fake and real animal. Just before she pressed the button,

Charlie scrambled up onto the bison statue, and laid down between the bronze animal's massive forelegs. Gabby clicked the picture, then tried to call Charlie down from the statue, but the dog stayed, resolute.

"Seems he's a bit of a ham," T.J. whispered to her. He was close behind her, watching her work, mesmerized and intoxicated. The moment seemed magical, with Gabby composing her shot, Charlie holding his pose, and the air crisp and fresh with possibilities.

"One more shot of him and then hopefully he gets down. I want to get this before," she pressed the camera button again, "the real bison leaves."

As if he'd heard her, the massive animal shifted his weight, then headed back into the woods. Gone. Gabby cursed.

Charlie jumped down from the statue and trotted over to Gabby's feet. He plopped his little butt down and looked up at her, happy with himself. T.J. bit back a grin.

"You are trouble," she said. "Now stay and let me see if that bison comes back."

Charlie stayed, the leash firmly in T.J.'s grip this time. Gabby and T.J. waited, her camera at the ready, but the bison never returned. The sun sank behind the trees and the shot was lost. Gabby finally admitted defeat and packed up her stuff. "That darn dog keeps getting in the way. If I was at home, I'd have my photo editing software and I could airbrush him out of the shot, but all I have is my laptop with me, and it doesn't have all the bells and whistles."

T.J. stopped in front of her and placed a hand on her arm. "You have great instincts. I was watching you work, totally in awe."

She scoffed. "I took a few photos. It's no big deal."

"No, you created magic. I saw what was on the camera's screen and it was…amazing." She glanced away, and shifted her weight.

"You make me sound like a cross between Picasso and Ansel Adams."

He kept his touch on her arm, wanting to hold her and shake her at the same time until she saw what he saw. "Why don't you believe in you like I believe in you?"

She exhaled. Charlie pulled at the leash to nose around a shrub, his tail wagging at whatever he'd discovered in the snowy space beneath the greenery. "In my line of work, it's easier to believe the negative stuff. I'm working through it, though. Or trying to."

He could see the doubt and fear in her eyes, those twin demons to so many artists. She'd always been so reluctant to trust in her gift, and most of all, to trust another person. "Don't be so afraid to take a risk, Gabby."

"Me?" she scoffed. "I'm not afraid."

"Maybe not afraid of breaking a couple property laws or taking on a challenging art piece. I'm talking about life. Love." He shook his head and closed the distance between them. "I know all about being afraid to take a risk."

"You? What risk did you ever take? Everything you've ever done has worked out, T.J. You had straight A's, went to college—"

"Tried to date you."

She glanced away. "T.J. that was a long time ago. I was young. Immature. I didn't know what I wanted."

"What about now? Do you know what you want now?"

She didn't meet his gaze. "I just want to finish this trip and get my career on the right track."

"And after that? Will you still be taking risks?"

She laughed. "Art is all about risk, T.J."

"I'm talking about another kind of risk. The one…" he said, raising his hand to her cheek, aching to kiss her again, "with me."

• • •

The dog had impeccable timing, T.J. had to say. The minute the words had left his lips, Charlie interrupted them by shaking the snow on his fur onto their legs. Gabby had used that as an opportunity to head back to the car, punch in the GPS coordinates of the motel they were staying at that night, and get back on the road.

She'd started chatting as soon as the car was in gear, spouting facts about the state of Nebraska, the sites she hoped to see as they made their way to California, her excitement about the possibility of having a show in Chicago. In short, she talked about everything *but* what had happened earlier that day when they'd kissed or what he'd said moments before.

Every time he tried to circle the conversation back to the two of them, Gabby detoured into small talk. She was avoiding something but T.J. wasn't sure what or why. The years apart had left him with a few pages missing from the book of Gabby. Maybe this trip hadn't been such a good idea. Maybe he was too late and their friendship would never be what it was—or become what he wanted it to be.

That kiss had been something more, and he knew he hadn't imagined Gabby's reaction to his touch—a decidedly more heated reaction than the one he'd gotten years ago. Still, her hot/cold reaction today had him wondering if this was going somewhere or if he was just grasping at straws.

They pulled into the motel's parking lot around seven. A hip-roofed diner sat next door, with a blinking orange neon sign in the window advertising HOT EATZ. Between that and the dilapidated motel, T.J. opted to look at this as a chance to experience a little something outside his comfort zone.

He glanced again at the rundown building, with its blinking VACANCY sign hanging askew in the front office.

Okay, a *lot* out of his comfort zone.

He thought of offering to pay for a room at a nice hotel in a big city, something with multiple stars, then remembered he was pretending to be poor. In truth, T.J. could afford to not just put them up at nice hotels during the trip, he could afford to *buy* those hotels. Could have taken the corporate jet to get him from Chicago to California. Could have taken this trip a hundred other more comfortable and faster ways.

Ever since he'd made his first million, he'd realized something. The more money he had, the less satisfied he felt. He'd worked hard to get from where he had been to where he was now, yet still he found himself craving those simple days by the creek with Gabby. The two of them watching crawfish dart through the shallow water while they tried to count the silver minnows winking beneath the soft ripples of the gurgling brook.

Every time he'd picked up the phone or clicked on an

email to contact her, he remembered that night at the dance and how long it had taken for him to get over her rejection. He'd told himself to move on, to leave his past where it was, to find someone else. But every time he'd tried to do that, it was Gabby's smile he saw and Gabby's voice he heard.

After this trip, he vowed, he would know for sure if they had a chance or if he was a hopeless idiot. Either way, he'd move on and forget about Gabby and those days they'd spent together. This motel was no babbling creek, and he doubted the diner sported any minnows in the décor, but Gabby was here and for T.J., that was enough for now.

"Looks like a decent place to catch some sleep before we head to Wyoming tomorrow," Gabby said. She shut off the car and reached for her purse. "Let me just get the rooms—"

"I'll take care of it," T.J. said.

Gabby's hand covered his and something warm ran through his veins. "Hey, I understand what it's like to be watching your pennies. I don't mind paying for the rooms. I was planning on doing it anyway. Plus, I got this check from Mr. B. that I totally didn't expect. I'm practically rich, or at least my version of rich. I'll never be one of those wealthy elitists and that is totally cool with me."

He bit back a wince. How would she react when she found out about his success? He'd become one of the members of the "haves," something Gabby had never much cared for. "I don't feel right making you pay for me. It's the least I can do to thank you for letting me hitch a ride with you."

"Okay, if you insist, but dinner's on me." She withdrew her hand and a shiver of disappointment replaced the warmth.

The protective instincts in him wanted to take over, to make this road trip easier and more enjoyable for Gabby. He could buy her a car that ran instead of shook its way down the road, take her to a five-star restaurant, and put her up in a hotel that offered hot stone massages and butter-soft sheets. But he knew Gabby wasn't a woman who would be impressed by those things. She liked the simple life, uncomplicated and ordinary, where she could get paint on the floor and set up an easel in the kitchen because the lighting was better. That was part of what he had liked so much in high school—when he was with Gabby, it was like he was home. Comfortable, and at ease.

So he stuck with his plan—find out if the Gabby he remembered could fall for the man he was now and still see the man he used to be beneath the success. The real T.J., not the one with a hefty bank account attached to his name.

In Chandler's Cove, he'd been invisible. People in that town still talked about his father, adding T.J. as an afterthought to the conversation. T.J. had never wanted the public accolades his father had and had managed to keep his own success mostly off the radar by limiting media interviews and keeping his name out of press releases. All good choices, it turned out, for his cover story with Gabby. But he knew the lies would be that much more hurtful when he finally came clean.

What had seemed like a good idea a few days ago now soured in his gut. Damn.

"T.J.? Does that plan work?"

He jerked his attention back to her and tried to stuff the

guilty feelings away. "Sure, sure. Sounds great."

She smiled, and a part of him warmed deep inside. Damn, she had a nice smile. One that lit her features from within, sparkled in her eyes. For the hundredth time, he was glad he'd gone on this trip with her. However it all ended, he'd have the memory of her smile. "Deal."

A few minutes later, T.J. returned to the car. "Good news and bad news. There's some big convention in town and every motel and hotel in a thirty-mile radius is booked."

She made a face. "What's the good news?"

"They had one room left." He dropped a keycard into Gabby's palm.

She turned it over. "One room? But…but…we can't… Where will you sleep?"

"I'm not picky. I'll just stay here." He indicated the Toyota's passenger seat.

"T.J., it's January. In Nebraska. You can't sleep in the car." She closed her palm over the key. "Listen, why don't you share with me? We should be able to share a bed for a night and not have…anything happen."

"Even after that kiss?"

Her face reddened and her gaze flickered away. "Well, we just won't do that again."

"Because we're grownups. Right?"

"Exactly." Gabby climbed out of the car and grabbed her backpack and overnight bag from the backseat. Charlie hopped down beside her, waited for his leash to get clipped on, then followed her to the room. T.J. trotted to catch up to them and held the door for Gabby after she unlocked it. "Thanks."

"Anytime."

"You know, you don't have to play the gentleman thing with me," she said. "I've known you forever."

"That doesn't mean you don't deserve to be treated with a little chivalry."

"It's been so long since I've seen any of that, I thought it was extinct." She flashed him another of her smiles as she brushed past him and into the room.

T.J. stepped inside and shut the door before the cold invaded the space. Typical motel room—decorated in Early Depressing. Tan carpet, threadbare tan quilted bedspread, and a framed print on the wall that was supposed to be of happy red carnations and orange mums but had faded to colors that blended with the rest of the desert-colored décor. The air smelled of old buildings mingled with something like gym sweat. "Well, I'll give you one thing. It's better than sleeping in the car."

"Not to mention the great company you'll have." Her lips curved, and something in T.J.'s gut flipped.

"There is that." And it was a nice bonus, he decided.

Gabby set her things on the faded mauve armchair in the corner, then shrugged out of her coat and kicked off the zebra boots. She stretched, arching her back, which thrust out her breasts and hips and sent T.J.'s mind down a thought train that began with foreplay and ended with fantasy.

"I'm so glad to be out of the car," she said.

"Me, too." He tried not to stare at the enticing cleavage exposed by the V in her T-shirt. His mind flashed an image of her beneath him, her body slick with sweat, skin soft and warm, as she arched her back and he slid into her—

"Do you know Mr. Bonaparte well?"

Her question jerked him back to reality. They were two friends sharing a room. Platonic. Well, *almost* platonic. Not after that unforgettable kiss. "I don't know Mr. Bonaparte very well," he said, remembering his ruse and the reason he'd given Gabby for needing a ride. He was supposed to be poor, unemployed, on his way to a job interview. Not meeting with wealthy men to talk about providing them with customized computer security solutions. "I've been thinking of getting into the security software industry, and he said if I was in the area to stop by and he'd talk to me about anti-hacking protections."

"Anti-hacking? Does he work for the White House or something?"

"Defense contractor, I think. I don't usually ask."

"My friends and I are always speculating about that billionaire on the hill. He's definitely a topic for gossip around town." Gabby perched on the edge of the seat. "What's he like? Mr. B.?"

"Haven't you met him?"

She shook her head. "He's lived in town for a few months now and no one I know has met him. He's…reclusive, like he's a hunchback living in a tower."

T.J. chuckled. "I can attest to one thing. He's definitely not a hunchback. But I don't really know much more than that. I dealt mostly with Cyrus. While I was at the house, Bonaparte only put in a brief appearance. He stuck to the back of the room and stayed in the shadows. Almost like he was—"

"Reclusive," they both said at the same time.

Gabby laughed then slid onto the floor. Charlie scrambled into her lap, pressing his head against Gabby's chest, happy and content. "Hey, Charlie," she said.

Envy flickered in T.J. Ridiculous. How could he be jealous of a dog? But he was. He wanted to be the one welcomed into Gabby's arms. He wanted to kiss her again, damn it, but every time he tried to get close, she shifted away.

"I need some air," he said. "I'm going to go grab us some food at the diner."

"Sounds good. And I can get some work done while you're gone." She reached for the wallet she kept in her backpack. "Let me —"

"I've got it, Gabby." He ducked out of the room before he got into a battle for her affections with a twenty-pound dog.

Chapter Six

Two seconds too late, Gabby realized her mistake.

Her hands still hovered over the keyboard on her laptop, as if sheer will could recall the email she'd sent. She cursed, then cursed again, loud enough that Charlie hopped up and let out a bark. "Damn it," she said to the dog. "How could I be so stupid?"

There was only one area of Gabby's life that she had learned to keep organized and detailed—her career. Ever since that debacle with that controversial mural she'd painted, she'd kept a detailed appointment log, made daily To Do lists, and always followed up on calls and emails. She'd seen too many artists let their creative side rule the business, which made for a chaotic approach and ultimately ticked off clients and gallery owners. Something she had been guilty of for years because she'd been too cocky, too brash, to play by the rules of grown-up life. But quirky, creative, disorganized artist didn't equal smart and successful businesswoman, nor did it help build a career. She was still working on juggling her creative and sensible sides. And today, she'd failed.

Damn.

She'd been distracted by that damned kiss and the changes in T.J. He'd been on her mind all day and even more so once he had left her in the room.

The single room. That she'd offered to share with him. Even as her body hummed at the prospect of sharing a bed—*oh yes, a bed*—with him.

Ever since that day at the dance when T.J. had asked her out, Gabby had wondered what it would have been like if she'd said yes. That O-M-G kiss they'd shared today had raised all those thoughts again, only now they had a very adult edge to them.

One room. One night. Just her and T.J.

Gabby's fingers went to her lips. What if tonight she acted on those feelings she'd held back for so long? What if she took advantage of the bed, the privacy, the temporary togetherness? Would she regret it—or savor the night as a wonderful sweet memory?

Then she glanced at her laptop and chided herself. Getting any more distracted by T.J. would detonate her comeback before it even got off the ground. T.J. was only along for the ride, and at this point in Gabby's life she needed roots, permanence, direction.

The door opened and T.J. stepped inside, holding a bag. "I wasn't sure what you wanted, so I—" He stopped talking and took another step forward. "What's wrong?"

She let out a laugh that sounded more like a sob. Despite all the years that had passed and everything that had happened, T.J. could still read her emotions as plain as a sheet of paper. It showed that he was still one of her closest friends and right now, she needed that. Needed him.

"I screwed up. When I sent the email of today's images to the gallery, I accidentally sent the wrong photos." She moved to the computer on the desk, pivoted the screen toward T.J., and showed him the two photos of Charlie—one with him in front of the *American Gothic* barn, and the other of him laying at the feet of the bison statue. "It's not a big deal, and I sent the right ones immediately afterward, but it *feels* like a big deal because this job was so important to me."

"It'll be fine, Gabby. I'm sure."

She shook her head. "I sure hope so. I've never worked with this gallery before, and I hate to give a bad first impression. I've worked so hard ever since—"

"What?"

She lowered her gaze. Bit her lip.

"What?" he repeated, softer this time.

She dropped into the chair. Maybe if she told him, she'd feel better. In the old days, talking to T.J. had always eased her burdens, from difficult classes or to the tough days when her parents fought like warring armies. "After you left for college, things kind of got off track for me. I mean, I had my friends, and they were great, but my family was pretty much gone. My parents got divorced. My dad moved to Portland and my mom went to Florida, leaving me in Chandler's Cove. I always had this wild, almost self-destructive side of me, and that just brought it out more."

"I always liked that part of you," T.J. said. "You encouraged me to break all those rules that put a straightjacket on my life."

"Sometimes, T.J., rules are a good thing." She crossed

her hands on her knees and met his gaze. "I just took a little longer to learn that lesson. About a year ago, the Chandler's Cove Convention and Visitors Bureau hired me to paint a mural downtown. It was supposed to showcase the town's attributes. How it was family friendly, a great community, etc. They invited the media to watch me paint it live, a whole 'local girl brings the town to life' thing."

"Sounds like a great opportunity."

"It was. But I blew it when I got into an argument with the head of the committee. Do you remember Richard Wilkins? He thought his money gave him power, and he kept dictating what he wanted me to do. I got all indignant and rebellious, and instead of painting what they wanted and I...I painted a mural that didn't exactly put the town or the Convention and Visitors Bureau in a flattering light. I painted Wilkins with a pile of empty beer cans, Mark Napier with his mistress on his arm, and Joe Sampson wearing a dress."

"Oh. Oh wow. That is pretty daring."

"No, pretty stupid. I was angry and blasted that in public, rather than being professional and doing the job I was hired to do. I just felt like Wilkins was trying to control me with all that money. Plus, my grandma died the week before, and I think I was just not in a good place after losing her, because she was more of a mom to me than my own mom. The critics crucified me, and for a while there I thought the town council might run me out of Chandler's Cove."

"What did you do?"

"Holed up in my apartment, ate a lot of ice cream, and watched a lot of movies. I figured I was done as an artist. I'd blown it, let my idiocy and my stubbornness take control.

Then I got an email from a gallery owner in Chicago who had seen the image on the web. She said that my work was exciting. Different. She wanted more. I finally took a good hard look at myself and I grew up, got a clue, and realized what I'd done. I went down there and repainted the mural. Turned it into an image of a park. With a creek."

"Our creek," he said.

She nodded, but didn't hold his gaze. "Our creek."

He took a step closer. "I saw it. That day I went downtown to grab your ad. It's a beautiful mural."

"Thank you."

"So you regrouped, made it right," he said. "That's good."

"Yeah, but I'm still worried about messing up again, which is why sending the wrong email got me so upset. It was a small thing, and I need to learn to chill a little better. I'm sure it'll be okay."

He helped her to her feet, then tipped her chin until she was looking at him. "On a scale of one to expelled…"

That made her smile. "I don't think I can get expelled anymore."

"Then it's all good. And fixable. It'll be fine, Gabby."

A little laugh escaped her and lit her eyes. Gabby cocked her head and studied him. "How can you still do that?"

"Do what?"

"Make me forget. No matter how bad my day was or how awful I was feeling, you always had this way of making me forget. Forget what's bothering me. Forget what scares me. Forget…" She shook her head and let out a soft curse. "In a few words, you have this way of making it all…okay."

"That's what friends are for." Though he wanted more

than that and had for a long, long time. He wasn't on this trip with Gabby to see if he should forget her. He'd come to see if she loved him like he'd always loved her.

"Is that what we are?" she asked. "Friends?"

"Are we?"

The two-word question hung in the air. Hell, the question had sat between them for years, ever since the day they'd met. There'd always been this magnet that drew him to her, a magnet he'd attributed to her being so different from him, so wild, so unpredictable. When really, what he wanted more than anything was Gabby herself.

"I think we've always been more than that," he said. He reached up, let his hand trail along her jaw. Her eyes widened, and her pulse leapt in her throat. "Don't you?"

"T.J...." She turned away. "I don't think we should take this any further. I just don't think it's a good idea."

"Okay." He lowered his hand.

A heartbeat passed, another. The temperature rose, heating the space between them. She caught his hand with hers, her fingers warm and tight against his. "I want you," she said softly. "But I'm so afraid. Of a thousand things, of making a mistake."

"Oh, Gabby." Her name slid from his lips, part groan, part whisper. "Don't be afraid. I'm here and I'm not going anywhere."

A long slow smile curved across her face. She splayed her fingers, pressed her hand on his chest. Her touch trailed down the front of his shirt, skipping over the buttons, dancing along the ridges of muscle beneath the cotton fabric. "You've changed."

"We both have. We've grown up." His attention drifted

to her curves and the desire that had been on a slow simmer began to burn hotter, brighter.

She laughed, a deep, throaty sound. "I don't know if I have. But you have grown up. In very nice ways." A flush of pink invaded her cheeks, nearly as bright as the streak in her hair.

"I'm not that geek you remember."

"No, T.J., you definitely aren't. But underneath it all, I think you're still the same guy. You're down to earth and honest. At your core, you're the T.J. I remember. I've missed that person a lot."

"You missed me?"

"More than I realized. You've always...tempered me. Brought out the best in me."

The words filled him with joy. She saw who he was underneath. She always had. "And you're still the same person who pushes me to step out of my comfort zone, to take chances."

"I could say you've turned the tables in that department this week." Her gaze softened when she looked at him.

"Maybe we should take this beyond just a road trip. To something more." He'd said nearly the same thing years before. Back then, she'd rejected him. But this time, he sensed the undercurrent of attraction, the simmer of want, warring with whatever battles Gabby had inside her.

"But..." She got to her feet, and shook her head. "We're just traveling together for a few days. It wouldn't be smart to complicate that. What's going to happen when we get to California? You stay there, I go back to Illinois? We have something long distance?"

"Honestly, I don't know what will happen then." He

wanted more, wanted it all, but to have that, he had to tell her the truth about who he was…about why he stayed away all these years.

Gabby nodded and bit her lip. The air in the room shifted from warm to cool. "Neither do I, T.J. Which is why I think we should just play it safe."

They faced one another, not touching. Charlie had woken up and pranced around their feet, panting and yipping, as if confused by the change. T.J. shook his head. "You used to be fearless, Gabby."

She snorted. "I used to be a lot of things. I'm sorry, T.J. As much as I want…" she waved between them as she took a step to the right, "this, I know it wouldn't be — "

Just then Charlie pounced on Gabby's legs, knocking her off balance. She stumbled forward into T.J.'s arms. Fire erupted in his gut, and the world stopped spinning.

"It wouldn't be…" But she didn't finish the sentence, and he didn't leap to fill in the blanks.

For that moment, all he knew, all he felt, was Gabby in his arms, the only woman he had ever really wanted but never stood a chance with. Her lips parted but no words came out. She looked up at him with those big green eyes. "Damn it, forget what I said. I do want you. A lot."

Before he could think, she rose on her tiptoes, grabbed his head, and hauled him to her for a hot, searing kiss.

His arms circled her, and Gabby's body melded into his, her sweet breasts pressed against his chest, her pelvis ground against his erection with delicious temptation. He slid his hands between them, reaching for the hem of her T-shirt, tugging the soft cotton up and over her head. At the same time, she worked at the buttons of his shirt, parting the panels in a feverish rush.

He tugged off her jeans and then his own, kicking the denim to the side. The TV played the muted soundtrack of a movie in the background, but all T.J. heard was the skip of Gabby's breaths, the whisper of her hands against his skin and his on hers. He slid his fingers under the satin straps of her bra, dragging them down her shoulders, watching as the fabric dropped, inch by inch, to reveal the swell of her breasts. The clasp released, the bra dropped to the floor, and T.J. lowered his head to follow the trail with his mouth. He kissed the curve of her breast, then teased along the edge of her nipple. She arched beneath him and he sucked the sensitive nub into his mouth.

"Oh, God, T.J."

The sound of his name slipping from her lips nearly sent him over the edge. T.J. scooped Gabby into his arms, crossed the tiny room in three strides, and then laid her on the bed. He stepped back and paused.

She smiled. "What are you doing? Taking a break already?"

"Taking a second to think how damned lucky I am."

"That you're welcome to do. As long as you're quick about it." The smile widened, and she opened her arms and beckoned him into the bed. He slid into the space beside her then watched her lift her hips, slide off her panties, and toss them aside.

"You are absolutely beautiful," he said.

"And you are going to make me blush."

"Which only makes this part more attractive," he trailed his hand down the center of her chest, "and this part," he danced his fingers over her nipples, "and definitely this part."

He finished with a long slow slide down her abdomen, then between her legs and finally, inside her. She gasped, rose up, and clenched against his fingers.

God, she was wet, eager, and hot as hell. It was all T.J. could do to take his time, to stoke the fire within her with his fingers and his mouth, moving down from her breasts to her delicious core, spreading her legs and tasting her in long, fast licks of his tongue, while Gabby groaned his name and tangled her hands in his hair.

"T.J., God, please, just please…" She bucked against his face. "*Please.*"

That was all it took. He paused only long enough to retrieve a condom from his overnight bag and slip it on, and then he positioned himself above her and slid inside her delicious warmth. She grasped at his back and his ass as he drove into her with long, hard strokes. She matched him move for move, and his brain stopped functioning. All he knew was this hot, fast, incredible moment. The vanilla notes of her perfume danced under his senses and mingled with the scent of her sex, and when she called out his name again in one drawn out syllable, he drove harder, faster, until the world exploded.

After a moment, T.J. rolled into the space beside Gabby and drew her against him, then tugged the thin comforter over their bodies. She rested her head on his chest, one palm on his heart. The movie had ended and a beer commercial flickered on the television. From outside the room came the sounds of traffic passing on the highway, punctuated by the staccato of horns.

Music to fall asleep by, T.J. thought, just before he drifted off with the most amazing woman in the world in the last place he'd ever thought she'd be…

His arms.

But sleep remained elusive, his mind filled with the knowledge that in the morning he'd have to tell Gabby the truth—

And risk losing her forever.

Chapter Seven

Gabby paced outside the motel room, blowing clouds into the cold January morning. She'd been up early, before T.J. woke, trying to work out what was bothering her about this whole trip. T.J. was holding something back, leaving some detail out, she was sure of it. He kept clamming up when she asked about his job, and redirecting the conversation. It didn't make sense. Maybe a little Girlfriend Therapy would help. She'd missed having her friends as sounding boards over the last few days.

Charlie nosed around on the snowy ground across from the parking lot, picking out his morning bathroom location. Gabby clutched her cell, muttering "come on, come on, answer" while she waited on the dog.

"Gabby!" Marney's warm voice filled the connection. "How's your trip going?"

A simple question, but oh, such a complicated answer. "Not how I expected."

"In a bad way? Or a good way?"

"Both." She sighed. "I don't know what to think. I need some advice."

"Well, you called at the right time, because I'm here with all the girls at coffee. Want me to put you on speaker?"

"Sure. Speakerphone is great. It'll almost be like being there."

Marney, Mia, and Jenny had become her best friends a few years back when the four of them connected at the same coffee shop in downtown Chandler's Cove. Each of the women brought something different to the group—pragmatic Jenny always had a word of advice, while witty Mia offered a snarkier view of life's events. Marney was the steady one, the one Gabby relied on most for a sensible shoulder. She thought of her friends, gathered around the scarred wooden table at the back of The Cuppa Cafe, chatting and laughing over lattes and muffins. She missed them, especially now, with her world in turmoil and her heart in a tangle.

"Except without all the calories." Marney laughed. "They made chocolate chip muffins today. I know I'll be paying for that later. I'll just work it off, putting in extra hours to pay for that crazy mortgage."

Gabby laughed. After a pause as Marney switched the phone to speaker, then Gabby heard the trio of voices saying hello. "Hi, everyone! Wish I was there!"

There was a chorus of agreement, then Jenny's warm voice came over the phone. "I hear you're having more fun than all of us. With a certain sexy passenger."

Gabby laughed. She knew exactly who'd been peeking out of her lace curtains when T.J. had gotten into Gabby's car. "Let me guess. Mrs. Perkins called you to tell you that I was canoodling with a strange man."

"Actually, she used the word *cavorting*. She wanted to make sure I knew, in case you ended up on 'Dateline.'" Jenny and the others laughed.

"There's no chance of that," Gabby said. "He's not a stranger. It's T.J."

"Really? T.J. from high school? The guy you used to like so much?" Marney said. Of the other three, Marney was the one Gabby had bonded with the most. They'd spent hours talking about exes and mistakes, including Marney's divorce and Gabby's missed chances with T.J. "I thought you said he was the classic studious type."

How did Gabby begin to explain that her attraction for T.J. had always gone beyond the physical? That it was about the way he brought out the best in her, something she didn't fully realize or appreciate until after he was gone and out of her life.

"He was. But now he's all grown up, and well...hot." Speaking the words sent a little fissure of desire down her spine. Even now, even after two amazing times last night.

She told the girls about the mistake with the pictures and the night with T.J., leaving out the intimate details. "I just get the feeling that I'm missing something and this whole relationship is going to blow up in my face. Or maybe I'm just overthinking things and worrying for nothing."

"Sounds to me like you did nothing more than have a good time and take a couple risks," Mia said. "You've been playing it safe too long, Gabby."

"Safe keeps you from getting hurt," Jenny put in. "I think she's being smart."

"The important question is, was he good?" Marney asked.

Gabby laughed. Leave it to Marney to get to the heart of the matter. "Yes, very. But—"

"There is no but," Marney said. "Do what Mia said and take a risk. Isn't that what you're always telling me good art is about? Well, the same applies to good artists."

"And true love," Mia added. "You can't find Mr. Right if you're too afraid to jump in with both feet."

Charlie twined his leash around Gabby's legs and plopped down at her feet. She leaned against the exterior wall of the motel and exhaled a long breath. She hated it when her friends were right. "I'm going to remind you all of this down the road."

"Hey, if a Mr. Right ever comes knocking at my door out here in the middle of nowhere, feel free," Marney said.

The women laughed and gabbed a bit more, and then Gabby caved to the cold and ended the call. She and Charlie ducked back into the motel room. The bed was empty and the sound of running water could be heard coming from the bathroom. A part of Gabby—okay, the majority—wanted to go in that bathroom, slip off her clothes, and step into the warm shower with a naked, soapy, and sexy T.J.

But that would wrap her up with him all over again, and she wasn't ready. Her mind was still reeling from last night. T.J. Shepherd, her one-time best friend and now, something more. Someone she could fall in love with.

Fear mingled with excitement in her heart. Fall in love with T.J.?

You can't find Mr. Right if you're too afraid to jump in with both feet.

Yeah, but what if she was still afraid that he would let her down? That this was all some temporary thing, gone the minute they hit the California state line? The Gabby she was today wanted stability, dependability. And T.J. had proven to be the opposite in the past. But a part of her longed to be with him again anyway, to be wrapped up in his blue eyes and his warm touch.

On the other side of the bathroom door, Gabby could hear T.J. singing a classic rock song in his deep baritone. She smiled and warm happiness spread through her like honey.

Yes, she could definitely fall in love with T.J. Maybe she already had.

Maybe she always had been.

Focus, Gabby, focus. Work *had* to come first. She was on this trip to resurrect her career and she needed to keep her eye on that. But as she waited for the computer to boot up, her mind wandered to images of T.J.'s muscular back, his hard ass, his tight legs. Her rebel mind pictured the soap running down the planes of his chest, following the light V of chest hair, then slipping between his legs—

"Work, Gabby. Work." But even her own stern self-lecture didn't stop the thoughts.

Charlie parked himself at Gabby's feet. His tail thumped against the floor, as if he agreed.

Emails started pinging into her inbox. Gabby skimmed them until she saw one from the gallery owner. Her heart stopped and she said a quick prayer before opening the message.

I know you wanted me to use the second set of photos you sent but once I saw the images with the dog, I changed my mind, the email began.

Damn. Gabby took a deep breath, steeled her nerves, and kept reading.

There's something engaging about that dog, something I think people will relate to. If you can deliver more material like that, featuring the dog, I'll slot you in for a September show. Let me know if that works for you.

Gabby exhaled. A rush of triumph ran through her. She'd done it. Well, she and Charlie had done it. She bent down and scooped the terrier up, nuzzling his soft neck. "You are the smartest dog in the world, do you know that?"

Charlie licked her face, his tail slapping against her arm as if telling her, *yeah, I know.* Beside her laptop, a buzzing started. It took Gabby a second to realize the sound was coming from T.J.'s cell phone. Funny, he'd never taken out his phone during their drive. Most people she knew were glued to theirs. The shower had stopped running so Gabby scooped up the phone to take it to T.J., in case the message was something important. Then she hesitated as those nagging doubts returned. Who kept their phone tucked away for hours on end? The phone buzzed again, and her gaze dropped to the screen.

Hey, T.J., Forbes called. They're doing next year's profile and wanted to know your avail. Call me back with a time for interview.

Forbes? As in *Forbes* magazine? What would they want with T.J.?

The suspicion she'd had for days that T.J. was keeping something from her exploded into full-blown mistrust. She thought of all the times he'd changed the subject, or avoided talking about his job. She spun back to the computer, brought up the search engine, and typed in *Forbes + T.J. Shepherd.*

In an instant, the words "tech wunderkind," "software genius," and "global leader" sprang onto the screen. All of them followed by one word she never would have seen coming.

Billionaire.

Gabby stared at the screen for a long, long time, while her heart broke and she faced the truth. Her best friend, the man she had once again fallen for and trusted with her heart, had lied to her—

And played her for a fool.

Chapter Eight

Silence.

T.J. had come out of the shower, his heart light, a smile on his face. Today, he'd vowed, he would tell Gabby the truth and let the chips fall where they may. She would understand, he was sure of it. "Gabby, I—"

The dingy room was empty, the bed unmade, Gabby's backpack and Charlie both gone, replaced by a note sitting beside his cell phone.

Charlie and I are back on the road. I'm sure you can afford your own way out there, Mr. Forbes.

Shit. He picked up his phone, saw the text message that had undoubtedly led to the note, and cursed. He'd thought he was doing the right thing. Thought he was embarking on some grand test to see if she could love him for who he was, not what he had become. He'd wanted a few days to rebuild the relationship they'd lost without the distraction of his wealth. Just her and him, like in the old days.

Instead, he was the one who had failed the test by lying. And in the process, lost the only thing that truly mattered to him.

. . .

Gabby drove, while Charlie lay on the passenger's seat, his head on his paws. Gabby could swear the terrier was sulking. "Don't give me that face," she said to the dog. "He was lying to us. To me. And to think I took pity on him and offered to pay all his expenses."

Charlie shifted in the seat and placed a paw on her lap. The anger eased in Gabby's heart, and she gave the dog a tender pat. "Just you and me, buddy. For a gazillion miles."

She had twenty hours of drive time and four states to go. It would probably take her three days to cover that much ground and work in the destinations and photo shoots along the way. The worst part about driving was how the endless miles made her mind wander. She kept trying to focus on why she was on this trip but all she could think about was T.J. The man she thought she knew—and clearly didn't.

She chided herself, forced her focus back to the approaching exit. Her work would eventually take the place of the hurt.

Why had she thought they could make this work? She should have known T.J. would just leave her behind while he went on his next adventure. Except this time, he'd be doing it in a Lear jet.

Focus on work. Not T.J.

"Charlie, ready to be the star again?" The dog's tail slapped against the seat, and he popped to his feet. Gabby pulled into a parking lot, grabbed her camera bag, and got out of the car, shading her eyes against the bright winter sun.

A few hundred yards away sat her photo destination for the day, a rough-hewn, dune colored pyramid. Hand built in the 1880s, the pyramid stood as a tourist stop for railway passengers. It had been dubbed the Ames Brothers Pyramid, after two men who worked for the rail company. The railway had long ago been shut down, and today, held no tourists, save for Gabby. A long dirt path wound up a low hill and around to the structure. The wind cut across the empty Wyoming plateau surrounding the pyramid with a low, lonely howl. "Seems like an appropriate place to be, huh, Charlie?"

The dog didn't respond, just walked along beside her, quiet and somber. If she didn't know better, she'd say he was depressed that T.J. wasn't with them.

She reached the desolate pyramid and looked around at a whole lot of nothing. Okay, so maybe she should have picked someplace happier. Perkier. But this place, with its solitary existence, mirrored the emptiness in Gabby's heart.

She sighed. "Back to work, Charlie."

Gabby lay on the hard earth, raised her camera to her eye, and waved at Charlie to go ahead. The dog did as she asked, dashing up to the stone building then turning back to face Gabby. "Good boy. Now, stay."

The angle made the terrier look huge against the tall pyramid, and she managed several great shots before Charlie got distracted and dashed around the building. Gabby started packing up her things. Maybe by the time she reached California, her heart would stop aching.

Charlie barked, a frenzied, happy bark. The slow *whop-*

whop-whop of helicopter rotors grew in volume along with a black speck that morphed from a dot in the sky to a midsized chopper. A moment later, the machine landed far behind the pyramid, sending a mini tornado of air spinning down the prairie. Charlie tugged on his leash, yanking it out of Gabby's hands, and took off across the ground. Gabby called for the dog but Charlie was already bounding toward the chopper.

The door opened, and T.J. emerged. He gave a wave to the pilot then bent down to greet an overjoyed Charlie, who leapt into his arms and slobbered all over his face. T.J. rose, the dog still cradled in his arms, then slipped off his sunglasses and put them in his pocket. His gaze swept across the flat land and stopped when he spotted Gabby. Even from here, she could see his smile.

Her traitorous heart skipped a beat, even as a part of her still sparked with anger at him lying to her, and him keeping his success a secret, especially after she'd told him about the mural debacle. She wanted to run, to hide, but out here in the middle of the wide Wyoming expanse of nothing, there was nowhere to go. So she stood her ground as T.J. approached. Charlie trotted along at his side, looking up at him every few feet as if making sure his new friend really had returned.

The chopper's rotors whirred a while longer, then whined down to a stop. T.J. closed the distance between him and Gabby. "What are you doing here?" she said. "And how did you find me?"

"After you left, I remembered you said Wyoming was next, so I looked up tourist stops here. I figured there was no way you'd resist seeing a pyramid in the middle of Wyoming."

Maybe it was a sign that there was something between

them—or maybe she was looking for something that wasn't there and never had been. "That still doesn't explain why you're here."

"I'm keeping my promise. I said I'd go with you to California, and I will."

"No, you said you'd go with me because your car was dead and you needed a ride." She shook her head. "I can't believe I fell for that whole job-interview-Grandma-gave-me-a-box-of-stuff-I-need-a-ride-thing. You lied to me, T.J. You're rich. That couldn't come up in conversation sometime in the last, oh, five hundred miles?"

"My grandma did give me a box of stuff. And I didn't lie about my car, it is dead. I've been driving the same Jeep Cherokee for eight years and it finally bit the dust a couple weeks ago. I did need a ride to California, which is where my office is located." He shrugged. "I just happen to own the company, and I lied about the job interview part because I didn't want to lead with my wealth. Too many people only see that, not the real me."

She waved toward the helicopter. "You don't need to go with me. It seems to me you already have a ride."

T.J. took another step forward until only a few inches separated them. "I prefer riding with you."

She refused to let that familiar smile affect her or to be tempted by the woodsy notes of his cologne, the soft ocean green-blue of his eyes. She shifted her gaze to the cold stone pyramid. "I'm fine on my own."

"Are you?"

He wasn't talking about her driving alone. He was asking if she wasn't hiding a couple things herself beneath this bravado.

"You don't get to ask me those questions, T.J." Gabby whirled back to him and all the hurt she'd felt this morning roared to the surface. "You lied to me. What were you trying to do? Show the poor starving artist you have some pity on her? Or did you think it'd be funny to go slumming with me for a few days before you go back to your helicopters and limos?"

He recoiled a bit. "It wasn't anything like that. I was wrong for deceiving you. I'm sorry, Gabby. I really am."

The sincerity in his voice and his features eased the tight hold on her anger. Her voice softened. "Then why did you do it?"

"I wanted a way to spend time with you."

The words sent a little thrill through her but she pushed it away. He had hurt her with the deception and a part of her—especially the part that had been intimate with him—just wanted to climb under the covers until the hurt stopped. "Why me? And why after all these years? And why now, when you weren't there..." She cursed and shook her head. "Never mind."

"...when I wasn't there for you before?" he finished when she didn't.

"Yeah." She raised her gaze and searched his blue eyes. "You didn't answer my emails. Didn't return my call. I reached out to you, T.J., after my grandmother died and that mural disaster happened because I needed a friend. Then this whole week, you lied to me. Now you want me to take a chance, to trust you? I don't think so."

She started to walk away, but he reached out and took her hand. "Don't go, Gabby, please. Listen, I was wrong to do that. It was selfish and stupid, and I'm sorry." He raked a hand through his hair and took a moment before he spoke again. "After graduation, when I told you how I felt, and you made it clear there was never going to be anything between us, I was crushed. All I wanted to do was forget you, move on. But I couldn't." He reached up and caught a strand of her hair, letting it slip between his fingers.

A slow smile spread across his face and she found herself drawn to that smile, to him, again.

"If there's one thing I've learned in the last few days, it's that no matter how hard I try, I can't forget you and I don't want to. Ever."

"Why me? We were just friends, high school friends."

"We were always more than that to me. I was just too scared to push it, because I was afraid of losing you. In the end, I lost you anyway." He released a long breath. Charlie settled at his feet and curled into a tight ball against the wind. "Almost from the day I started seeing a profit from my business, I became Mr. Popular. For a guy who spent most of his life off the radar at school, it was kinda cool, I'm not going to lie. Then I realized no one knew the real me. They were attached to me because I had money. Power. Influence. But there was no depth to those relationships, no meaning, no history. So I came back here to you, to the only person who knew the real me, and the only person I've ever really known."

"But you weren't being the real you when we were together. You kept telling me to take risks, and you didn't."

"Because as soon as we were together, I was afraid of losing you, this time for good. You are who you are, Gabby, without apologies, without limits and to me, that's a pretty brave thing. I admire that about you." He took her hand in his, sending a zing through her veins. "Right or wrong, your attitude has always been take me as I am, with that pink streak in your hair and the zebra boots and all the things that make you who you are. And you know what? Who you are is pretty damned incredible. Strong and sassy and smart, and braver than me."

"Braver? I don't think so." She thought of all the fear of failure she'd felt in the past few years, how long it had taken her to get her career rolling again, to risk rejection by sending work to that gallery in Chicago. She didn't feel brave. Far from it. Those moments of fear had cost her so much. "I wasn't brave enough to tell you how I felt all those years ago."

"How you felt? But I thought—"

She shrugged, giving him a shy smile. What sense was there in keeping the truth from him any longer? "I fell for you in high school but I didn't realize how I felt until you were gone and it was too late."

His grin spread like hot butter inside her. "It's not too late, Gabby. And maybe it's better we waited all this time, because now we've lived our lives and we know what we want. Who we want."

A row of puffy clouds drifted overhead and the soft sounds of passing traffic hung in the air. Winter still held its crisp, cold grip on Wyoming, but between her and T.J. the air was heated, charged with years of unanswered desire. They'd let so much time pass—too much.

"You've always pushed me to take chances," T.J. went on, "to be my own person. That scared the hell out of me because I knew I'd pay the price for every misstep when I got home."

"I'm sorry. I never should have talked you into half the stunts we did."

"You didn't talk me into them. I *wanted* to do those things, even if I argued sometimes. I'm damned grateful for every chance I took, for every single adventure, and for all the consequences. Because that gave me the courage to start my own business. To come after you in a helicopter and make a big statement about how I felt." He took her hands. "Now I'm asking you to do the same. To go after what you want instead of running away."

She gestured toward the camera sitting in the bag a few feet away. "I *am* going after what I want."

"In your career, yes, but not in here." His fingers danced up her chest. "I'm in love with you, Gabby. I have been since that day you ate the chips in the chemistry lab. You confounded me and challenged me and made my life better just by being my friend. I couldn't forget you, and now I know why. Because I still love you. These few days have been some of the happiest I can remember in a long, long time. And now I know I want more than what we shared back then, I want it all. I don't want to spend a single day without you ever again."

"T.J. — " She shook her head, then paused and faced the truth about herself, about the years apart from T.J. He wasn't the one who had deserted her — she had done it to him. And right now, she felt the old familiar fears rising in her, pushing her to run again. Instead, she held her ground. "I've been afraid all my life, of getting close, of trusting, of screwing up. When you told me how you felt that day, I panicked, instead of being honest. And I pushed you away."

"I would have understood, Gabby. We all make

mistakes."

She moved away from him and crossed to the pyramid. The triangular shaped walls offered a break from the wind and a shadow beneath the winter sun. "My biggest mistake was pretending I wanted you and me to be just friends when I really wanted…"

"What?"

Gabby pivoted toward T.J. and looked up into the eyes that she'd first noticed years ago, back in elementary school. "From the day you made that little explosion in chemistry class, I was hooked on you. I invited you along on my adventures because I wanted to spend time with you, to see you. You were smart, funny, and sexy as hell in those glasses."

He grinned. "I can go back to wearing them."

Gabby reached up and placed a palm against his cheek. "I don't know. I kinda like seeing your eyes all the time. I've loved these eyes for a long time, even if I took years to tell you."

"Then I'll make sure you see them every day." He reached in his breast pocket and tossed his sunglasses to the side. Gabby laughed, Charlie barked, and T.J. took the woman he loved into his arms. "What took us so long to finally figure out what we wanted?"

"Life's a journey, T.J. Some of us just take the long road."

"As long as it leads me to you." He leaned down and kissed her, a sweet kiss filled with love and promise and a taste of forever. She curved into him and thought she could stay in his arms for the rest of her life.

But not on this windy plain in Wyoming. After a while, T.J. waved off the helicopter and they walked back toward Gabby's car, arm in arm. "You promised we'd see the world's largest ball of popcorn, you know," T.J. said. "It's back in Iowa somewhere. We missed it."

"Who needs the world's largest ball of popcorn?" Gabby asked. She smiled up at T.J. and held his hand tight. "I have everything I need right here."

Charlie barked in agreement, then pressed his little body against their legs, as content and happy as a matchmaking, career-saving terrier could be.

The three of them hopped in the car, pointed west, and embarked on a brand-new journey together.

About the Author

New York Times and *USA Today* bestselling author Shirley Jump spends her days writing romance and women's fiction to feed her shoe addiction and avoid cleaning the toilets. She cleverly finds writing time by feeding her kids junk food, allowing them to dress in the clothes they find on the floor and encouraging the dogs to double as vacuum cleaners.

THE SHERIFF'S SECRET

SUSAN MEIER

Copyright © 2013 by Susan Meier. All rights reserved, including the right to reproduce, distribute, or transmit in any form or by any means. For information regarding subsidiary rights, please contact the Publisher.

Entangled Publishing, LLC
2614 South Timberline Road
Suite 109
Fort Collins, CO 80525
Visit our website at www.entangledpublishing.com.

Edited by Shannon Godwin and Libby Murphy
Cover design by Libby Murphy

Ebook ISBN 978-1-62266-217-3
Print ISBN: 978-1493783717

Manufactured in the United States of America

First Edition October 2013

The author acknowledges the copyrighted or trademarked status and trademark owners of the following wordmarks mentioned in this work of fiction: Mercedes Benz, American Heart Association, Jack Russell, James Bond

Chapter One

"9-1-1 Operator, what's your emergency?"

"This is Marney Fields. Someone's in my house." Hiding in her master bedroom closet—behind two rows of dresses—Marney worked to level her breathing so she wouldn't hyperventilate.

"Are you at the address you're calling from?"

She turned away from the door and whispered into her cordless phone, "Yes."

"Thank you, ma'am. Someone will be at your house in a few minutes. Stay where you are."

She sucked in a breath and huddled a little deeper into the corner behind her dresses, her heart racing, her knees knocking. All her life she'd wanted to live in the country. But her very first night of sleeping in the mini-mansion she'd built for herself five miles outside of Chandler's Cove, Illinois, every creak of a floor board or swish of the wind had brought visions of burglars and serial killers to mind.

She'd checked her security system eighty times, but her frightening thoughts still ran rampant. So when she'd heard the bang coming from her kitchen, her heart had about exploded. She'd grabbed her cordless phone, run up the stairs, and hastily dialed 9-1-1.

And here she stood. In the closet. Behind her dresses. Shivering.

One minute turned into two. Two became three. Three chugged along to four. With every minute that ticked off the clock, her chest tightened. Her breathing became shallower.

Footsteps sounded outside her door.

Her heart punched against her ribs. The police had scared her intruder upstairs! And he was in her bedroom!

She searched for a weapon but the best she could find was a plastic hanger. She grabbed it and held it up.

She'd finally made it as a jewelry designer. A home shopping network had picked up her line of earrings, bracelets, and necklaces, and she had money pouring in. She'd built this home, could vacation anywhere she wanted. She had a Mercedes on order for God's sake! She was not going down without a fight.

The door burst open. She yelped a battle cry and foisted her hanger like a sword. The man jumped back.

"Whoa! Whoa! Wait a minute! Are you Marney Fields?"

She swiped the hanger at him.

"I'm Sheriff O'Neil." He shoved his gun into its holster and displayed his ID.

That's when she noticed his gray uniform, complete with gray winter jacket to ward off the cold from an unexpected April snow storm.

He eased the hanger out of her shaking hand. "Relax.

I'm your neighbor." He pointed to the right. "I live about two miles down that road. It was quicker for me to come over than send a patrol car."

A mixture of embarrassment and relief washed through her in dizzying waves.

"Are you okay?"

She peeked up at him. "I heard a noise."

He smiled sympathetically. "That's not unusual in a new house."

His sympathy upped her embarrassment to humiliation. She squeezed her eyes shut.

He chuckled. "Come on. Open your eyes. It's smart to call the police when you think you're in trouble."

Her mortification ebbed. She opened her eyes and attempted a smile. "Sorry."

"No need to say you're sorry."

He shoved his ID into his back pocket, drawing her gaze to his trim hips. It climbed up his flat stomach, along his broad chest, to the chiseled features of his perfect face.

Yum.

In three years of living in Chandler's Cove after her divorce, she'd heard about the gorgeous sheriff. She'd seen him walking down the street or driving in his car, but had never seen him up close. His disheveled black hair reminded her of long nights spent making love. His gray-blue eyes probably glowed in the dark. And that body…Wow. Sexy was too simple of a word to describe him. Sensual was better. But rugged and masculine fit. The man oozed masculinity.

Attraction shimmered through her along with a jolt of pure lust. She pulled her bottom lip between her teeth. It had been a long time since a man had turned her on with his looks alone. But this guy definitely had.

"Ms. Fields?"

Her gaze flew to his face. "Huh?"

"I said I'm going to have another look outside, but I'd also like to suggest that you get an alarm system—" He paused. His blue eyes crinkled at the corners as he smiled. "Are you sure you're okay?"

She licked her suddenly dry lips. "Yeah." Who was she kidding? She wasn't okay. She was melting. She saw good-looking guys all the time when she went to the television studio to do the shows for her jewelry. But this guy was different. Broad-shouldered and dressed in a neat-as-a-pin uniform, he could make a nun question her decision to be celibate.

"Do you need to sit down?"

"Um. No." She cleared her throat. "And I have an alarm system."

"Do you know how to work it?"

Confused, she frowned. "Yes, I know how to work it."

He grinned. "Why don't you just let me check it out?"

"Sure."

She followed him out of her soothing gray and yellow master bedroom. Her gaze automatically traveled from his broad shoulders down his torso to his butt, and she almost groaned. Perfect. Of course.

She shook her head. The trick to surviving his visit would be to quit looking at him. Especially his butt.

Their footsteps echoed around them as they walked down the circular stairway of the grand foyer. When he got to the bottom step, he said, "You're going to have to get accustomed to hearing noises in here. A house with a ceiling this high is bound to have lots of echoes."

"Right." More hormones awoke at the deep, masculine sound of his voice. Holding her head high and pretending she wasn't fighting the urge to rip off his shirt, she marched to the control box for the alarm then stepped out of the way.

He walked over, hit a few buttons, and a green light blinked on. Grinning like a Cheshire cat, he faced her. "That might have been the problem."

She swallowed and simply stared, wondering if he knew how lucky he was to have such beautiful eyes, a chiseled chin, and sculpted cheek bones.

A few seconds ticked by before she realized her foyer was silent and he was staring at her. And not the way she was staring at him—with undisguised interest—but with disgust.

He shook his head and turned away. "You're fine." His voice took on a hard tone. "I'll do one more check outside then I'll swing back in to make sure you're okay. But I'd appreciate it if you wouldn't make any more 9-1-1 calls to meet your neighbors."

"What?"

"It's wrong to call 9-1-1 for anything other than a genuine emergency. In fact, it's a crime."

Mortification replaced attraction. "Do you think I called 9-1-1 to get to meet you?"

"Look. I've seen you around town for a couple of years now. Which means you probably knew I lived out here and that I'm the person who'd be dispatched when you called."

"I heard a noise!"

"I'm sure you did. And I'm sure you *forgot* to set the alarm too."

"I didn't forget to set the alarm! I was so afraid to be

living out here in the dark that I kept checking it all night. I must have hit the button and knocked it off one of those times I was messing with it."

"Right."

He didn't believe her! Her breath caught. She pressed her hand to her chest. "I called *the police* — not *you* — because I was terrified."

Instead of the apology she as expecting, the room became incredibly quiet. *He really didn't believe her.* And she was only making things worse by arguing.

She lifted her chin. "Actually, there's no need to come back after you check my yard. I'm fine. You can go."

He walked toward her front door. "I'll be back anyway." He turned and grinned at her. "For one more look."

The double meaning of that statement cut through her like an embarrassing knife. Not only did he not believe her, now *he was laughing at her.*

"I said I was fine."

His gaze rippled from her head to her toes. His lips lifted into a confident smile but he didn't reply.

He walked out the front door and she plopped down on the third step of the stairway.

Get ahold of yourself, Marney!

Oh, right. Get a hold of herself. It was little late for that. She couldn't remember the last time she'd behaved like a teenager in heat. So she couldn't fault the sheriff for making a bad assumption. He was incredibly good looking, and women probably did do weird things like call 9-1-1 to get to meet him. Plus, her situation did appear odd. But once she'd explained that she really had heard a noise and she'd probably accidentally turned off her alarm, he should have understood. Actually, he should have apologized for accusing her of calling 9-1-1 just to get him to her house. Instead, he thought she was some kind of sex starved…idiot.

He returned about ten minutes later, flashlight in hand, but he didn't step inside. As if afraid of her, he stayed on her front porch, telling her not to worry, she was safe now. Then he grinned his infuriating I-know-you're-attracted-to-me grin and left.

Marney fell to her steps again and covered her head with her hands. She'd just made a colossal fool of herself.

* * *

Driving back to his house, Sheriff Dell O'Neil shook his head in wonder. Local jewelry shop owner Marney Fields was a beautiful woman with her long brown hair and dark eyes that flashed when she'd realized he'd noticed her sizing him up.

Lucky for her, he wasn't interested in romantic entanglements or he probably could have taken her on her Italian marble floor.

But her image popped into his brain as he got ready for bed and again the next morning when he drove past her house. He thought about her when he walked by the little shop she had on Main Street and again when he drove home at about three. Worse, he thought about her on the long drive to his parents' house in Chicago to attend a fund raiser for his parents' pet charity.

Since his divorce, he hadn't allowed any woman to rent space in his head and he had no idea why Marney Fields had suddenly set up residence there. But he did know he would get her out.

• • •

After work Friday afternoon, Marney drove to Chicago, grateful to be getting out of town. After her embarrassing encounter with Sheriff O'Neil, she needed the weekend to chill out.

She had a fundraiser to attend that night, an exhibit of the work of several up-and-coming artists. The gallery owner had committed his share of the profits to the Heart Association, one of her favorite charities. But more than that, this was payback for all the people who had supported her exhibits when she was new. Divorced, just starting out as a jewelry designer, she'd appreciated the gallery's support and the money she made from her exhibits. She would definitely buy something tonight.

On Saturday morning, she would visit her parents, endure the cool reception she'd become accustomed to since her divorce from Doug Stover, Attorney at Law, and come home appreciating the fact that she lived an hour away from them.

Carrying the garment bag that contained her glittery red gown, she checked in to her hotel. She luxuriated in a hot bath then dressed carefully. She didn't need the money from any jewelry commission she might get while hob-knobbing, but she had a reputation to uphold. She was Marney Fields now. *Successful* jewelry designer. Several women would be wearing her commissioned pieces tonight. When they pointed to her, she wanted them to be proud they owned pieces designed by her.

As she stepped out of the elevator, Victor, the concierge whistled. "Ms. Fields, if I weren't married, I drop to one knee right now and beg you to be my wife."

She laughed. But men's heads turned as she walked through the lobby to the portico where a limo awaited. Stupidly, Sheriff O'Neil popped into her head. And she wasn't sure why. She didn't want a man. Didn't *need* a man.

And he obviously didn't want her.

She tossed her long dark hair over her shoulder and smiled at the chauffer who closed the door behind her.

The limo ride took fifteen minutes. The driver handed her out, and she headed into the gallery without a backward glance. It never occurred to her to be embarrassed that she was alone. She'd made herself a success. On her own. Plus, she had the love and support of three wonderful friends in Chandler's Cove. That was what life was really all about— connecting with people who liked you just as you were.

She snagged a glass of champagne from a passing waiter and spent the next hour walking from display to display, examining paintings, considering sculptures, and eventually deciding to buy a bronze basket filled with shiny metallic apples for her office.

Satisfied with her purchase, she strolled through the maze of paintings, carvings, and metallic sculptures and figurines, chatting with people she knew. Some were customers. Some were women who wanted her to design pieces. Others were friends, people who had deserted her when she divorced Doug Stover, attorney at law, who —now that she was famous—had decided to forgive her for ending their marriage.

Luckily, she was gracious. She didn't hold a grudge against

them. Doug affected people oddly. He had a charisma that attracted everyone to him. He could get anyone to do just about anything he wanted. Manipulative and controlling, he'd actually thought she should stay after she'd discovered he'd been cheating. He'd dragged his feet along every step of their divorce, and ultimately she'd given him their condo for her freedom.

Her glass empty, she scoured the open first floor for a waiter. Spotting one walking away from her, she turned quickly and ran into a man. Her glass rammed into his very solid chest.

Looking up with a smile, she said, "Oh, I'm so sorry!" Then she froze. "Sheriff O'Neil?"

"Yes. If you'll excuse me." He turned away.

Her mouth hanging open slightly, she let her gaze follow him. Why not? The man was eye candy personified. She might have originally thought that she'd drooled over him because of his uniform, but seeing him in a tuxedo? With broad shoulders filling out his jacket and hair disheveled as if he didn't give a damn what anybody thought of him, he was sex on a stick.

He disappeared into the thick crowd, and, shaking her head, Marney went back to her quest for more champagne.

"Wasn't that Dell O'Neil?"

Overhearing the comment, she stopped walking. Two thirty-something women with big hair and skinny cocktail dresses stared in the direction Dell had gone.

"I wonder how his parents talked him into coming to this event?"

"I thought he'd disowned them."

"Or they'd disowned him."

"Or both."

"I for one don't care what happened. I'm just glad he's back. Chicago society might not have missed him, but I did. He brings more sex appeal to these dull things than three or four of the other guys put together."

The women laughed.

Marney's face scrunched in confusion just as the crowd parted, and she spotted Dell again, standing next to an older man she recognized as renowned surgeon Dr. James O'Neil.

She remembered what the women had said about his parents talking him into coming to this event and she gasped.

Wow. Just wow.

Dell O'Neil was billionaire philanthropist James O'Neil's son.

Dell glanced up, and their gazes connected. She smiled. A look of panic overshadowed his handsome features.

Well, well, well, the sheriff was keeping a secret from the good people of Chandler's Cove.

Chapter Two

He approached her twenty minutes later as she studied a statue of a blue goat done by a new artist.

"Good evening, *Sheriff*."

He winced. "Come on, haven't you ever known anyone who was suffocated by their family?"

"Yeah. Me. And I ran to Chandler's Cove too. But I didn't have family responsibilities. No one was counting on me for contributions and glad-handing. I wasn't rich."

He sighed. "Neither was I when I left Chicago."

"Which implies that you lost all your money, and now you're rich again." She laughed. "Tell me. How does one with family money lose it all when the rest of the family seems perfectly fine?"

He caught her elbow and dragged her to a dark corner, away from the crowd. "He marries the wrong woman."

Though she knew all about bad marriages and bad spouses and should have sympathized, the way he'd insinuated that she'd faked an emergency to get him to her house still rankled. He deserved a little teasing. "Ouch, wife took you to the cleaners?"

"Yes. Now—" He leaned in a little closer. So close she could smell his aftershave and feel the masculinity rolling from him in waves. It seeped into her pores, sending heat shimmering through her.

Her breath stuttered in and out.

"I don't think you're in any position to be laughing at me."

"Why? Because I think you're good looking?" She chuckled. "Like that's a big news flash to anybody. Every woman in the world is probably attracted to you. Outing me for agreeing with them isn't much of a threat."

He stepped away and combed his fingers through his hair. "Come on. Cut me a break. I don't want my identity getting out in Chandler's Cove."

She almost told him that he didn't have to worry. She wasn't a snitch. But she wasn't quite ready to give up the teasing yet. He'd refused to accept that she'd accidentally turned off her alarm. Worse, he'd thought she'd called him just to meet him. A few more minutes of teasing wouldn't hurt. "I'm not sure why. Most people would be proud to come from the family you come from. *You're* the black sheep."

"No kidding."

She feigned innocence. "Oh, *that's* what you don't want to get out."

His pretty blue-gray eyes narrowed. "You think you hold all the cards here because I'm trying to keep my background private?" He stepped close again. "I've got cards you haven't even seen yet."

That made her laugh. For a guy who could dish it out, he sure couldn't take it.

His face turned to stone. "You think this is funny?"

"I think this is hysterical."

Before the word hysterical was fully out of her mouth, he swooped down and kissed her. His lips moved over hers roughly and though a tiny part of her brain told her to be insulted, all she could think to do was enjoy. His mouth was warm and firm, his lips practiced in the art of kissing. He nipped and sipped, then smoothed his mouth over hers, sending tingles of delight careening through her. Her insides warmed. Her body became pliant, boneless.

When his tongue slid into her mouth and the rough ridge sent an explosion of joy straight to her femininity, she didn't even pretend to put up a fight. She melted against him.

Which caused her common sense to return. What was she doing? Dell O'Neil was an arrogant, conceited man. He'd thought she'd called 9-1-1 just to get to meet him. He hadn't listened when she'd tried to explain.

She didn't want anything to do with him.

Her hands flattened on his chest to push him away but they met a solid wall of muscle.

Oh, man. Really? Did her pride have to demand she break this delicious kiss?

She thought of the smug look on his face at her house and her boneless body solidified.

She pushed.

• • •

He stepped backward. He never let a sexual fog go so far that he didn't recognize a "No," but it took a few seconds for him to get his bearings.

The woman could kiss.

Then he realized who the woman was and he remembered why he'd kissed her, and he groaned internally.

Why didn't he just give her a whole arsenal of ammunition to ruin his reputation in town?

"The next time you want me to shut up, just ask."

She thought he'd kissed her to shut her up?

In a way he supposed he had. She was feisty and gorgeous in the shiny red dress that outlined curves so perfect they should be illegal, and, honestly, he hadn't cared to hear her talk any more. His body wanted some action.

Which was stupid. Childish. He had much better control than this.

"Look, let's just forget this happened."

She yanked up the strap of her glorious red dress. "No argument from me."

Turning, she headed out of their dark corner and disappeared into the crowd.

Damn it! He hadn't gotten her promise to keep his identity a secret.

He forked his fingers through his hair. Nothing with this woman went the way it was supposed to.

. . .

The kiss confused Marney so much she decided not to stay at the fundraiser or even in Chicago. Though it was after ten, she took the limo back to the hotel, changed clothes, repacked and drove home. Tomorrow morning's visit with her parents would have to wait for another time.

After Doug, she'd vowed to stay away from demanding, controlling guys—and she suspected that control was exactly what the good sheriff was after—so why had she virtually melted for Dell O'Neil?

She parked her car in her garage, entered her house through the kitchen, and carried her suitcases and red sparkly dress upstairs. She showered, wrestled herself into boxers and a tank top, and just as she slid under the covers, she heard the noise again.

Damn it!

She refused to call 9-1-1 because they'd probably send her stupid next door neighbor to check it out. There was no way in hell she wanted to be at Dell O'Neil's mercy again. She liked it too much.

Of course, he could still be in Chicago—

Oh, yeah, right. Unless he'd told his staff he was going out of town—highly unlikely since he kept that part of his life a secret—they'd call him on his cell phone and he'd know she'd called 9-1-1 again. He might even think she'd called to get him to her house.

She grabbed her smart phone from the bedside table and called her best friend Gabby Wilson—now Gabby Shepherd.

"Who is this?"

"It's me. You'd know that if you ever looked at your caller ID."

"What time is it?"

"Gabby, focus. I'm coming over to get Charlie." She'd kept the pup Gabby was dog-sitting for the reclusive Nicholas

Bonaparte while Gabby had been on her honeymoon, and she knew Charlie was a barker. He would alert her if there really was an intruder.

"The dog?"

"I keep hearing an odd noise in my house."

"Call your next-door neighbor, the sheriff."

She sucked in a breath. She'd told her three friends Gabby, Mia, and Jenny about hearing the noise and about Sheriff O'Neil being her next-door neighbor, but she'd left out the part about him being attractive. She almost told Gabby that he was still in Chicago but she bit her tongue. She didn't owe the man a damned thing, especially not secrecy, but something inside her wouldn't let her spill the beans about who he really was.

So she said, "Please. There was nothing the last time I called him. I don't want to go through all the rigmarole of calling and having him come over and find nothing."

"So you'd rather go through the rigmarole of waking me and T.J.?"

"Thanks. I knew you'd understand."

She clicked off the phone and headed to Gabby's to pick up her newly appointed guard dog.

• • •

Monday morning, Marney had just slid the key into her shop door when Charlie, Bonaparte's adorable Jack Russell terrier, barked and strained against his leash. Her heart sped up out of fear, but when she turned and saw Sheriff O'Neil, her blood raced through her veins for an entirely different reason.

Ignoring him and her body's automatic reaction to him, she inhaled sharply, twisted the key in the lock, and opened the door.

Charlie barked and growled.

"Charlie! Come on now! Stop that!" She hoisted her purse on her shoulder and lifted Charlie into her arms.

Sheriff O'Neil followed them into the shop.

"If you're here to apologize, don't bother. I'm fine." She deposited Charlie on the glass display case along the back wall, disconnected the leash from his collar, and set him on the floor. He raced into her office, where he knew she kept the doggie treats.

She turned from the display case with a smile but Sheriff O'Neil's pretty blue-gray eyes shot sparks of fire at her.

"Apologize? For what?"

"Well, we could start with the kiss. I think you owe me an apology for trying to bully me like that."

"Bully you?" His mouth fell open, drawing her attention. Memories of kissing that mouth and being kissed by that mouth flooded her. She swallowed hard and jerked her eyes to his again.

"You were the one all but threatening to tell everybody in town about my family. If you think you worry about your new house, imagine having a hundred times the money you have. They get death threats. They worry about their kids being kidnapped." He laid his hand on his chest. "I live here in this nice little town without any of those worries because no one really knows who I am. I won't let you ruin that."

"Humph. You'd think you'd be nicer to me then."

"Nicer to a woman who all but threatened me?"

"I didn't threaten you!" Tired of his tirade when there

was no reason for it, she walked over to him. "I was teasing you. But now that I know you have no sense of humor I'll stop. You don't have to worry. I can be trusted."

He snorted a laugh. "Right."

Her chin lifted. "Hey! I had brunch with my friends yesterday. Three women I'm closer to than sisters and I didn't breathe one word of your stupid secret. You could be James Bond for all I care."

"I hope you mean that."

He turned on his heel and stormed out, and she leaned against her display case. Dear God, that man was handsome. Even confronting her, he had left her breathless.

Charlie trotted out of her office and over to her. He blinked up at her.

She reached down and lifted him into her arms. "I know what you're thinking. He's the first man I've reacted to since Doug. I can't just dismiss that. But he's also arrogant and self-centered. He didn't give a damn that he'd kissed me. But he virtually wanted me to sign a blood oath that I wouldn't tell anybody about his real identity. He'd be a handful."

Charlie barked.

"You think that makes him a challenge?" She laughed, loving the way Charlie barked again as if they really were having a conversation.

"And you wonder what kind of woman would it take to break through and find the real Dell?" She ruffled the fur between his ears. "I don't know. But it's insane to even consider it. I married one arrogant, self-important guy. I shouldn't want another."

Her door burst open and Gabby raced inside, her blond hair with the hot pink streak billowing around her. "Oh my

God! I saw Sheriff O'Neil leaving! Is everything okay?"

"It's fine."

She ran over and took Charlie from Marney's arms. "You're shaking." She studied her face. "And your face is red—" she stopped. Her mouth fell open slightly. "Oh, my gosh! You're attracted to him."

Marney stepped away, unlocked her main display case, and dropped her keys into her purse. Damn Gabby and her sixth sense about people. "Don't be absurd."

But Gabby was already on the phone. She said, "Jenny, don't ask questions. Just get over to Marney's shop." She disconnected the call, pushed another speed dial button, and gave Mia the same instructions. Within two minutes, petite, blue-eyed Mia and sensibly-dressed Jenny had joined Gabby in front of Marney's display case.

Gabby didn't waste a second. "I saw Sheriff O'Neil coming out of Marney's shop this morning." She grinned. "I think our Marney has a crush on him."

Marney's face heated. Without being able to tell them that she'd seen Dell at the fundraiser, their morning "meeting" had no explanation. But she absolutely didn't want her friends thinking she had the hots for him. Because she didn't. Not really. He presented a sort of challenge, but she'd already dismissed it. "Dell was just checking to see if everything had been okay at my house over the weekend. I told him it was, and he left."

Gabby laughed. Jenny giggled. Mia, her normally reserved friend, shook her head. "You don't think it's a big deal that our handsome Sheriff checked up on you?"

The conversation would have been so much easier if she could just tell her friends who he was. But she'd promised, so she had to find another way out of this.

"Has any one of you stopped to realize he's bossy—like my ex? Even if he wanted to get involved with me, and I don't think he does, I don't want to get involved with another man like Doug. I followed his every instruction for four years of marriage, and he *cheated on* me. Then because I was the one who insisted on a divorce, he held out until he got the condo. Wouldn't I just be an idiot to get involved with another man like that?"

Chapter Three

The next morning, as Marney walked out of her office to give Claudette a new box of bracelets to display in the main case, a small crowd of people raced by her shop window. She didn't think much of it, until the wail of the ambulance echoed around her. From the sound if it, it stopped only a few feet up the street.

"What the heck?"

Claudette, a university student with brown hair and big blue eyes who worked a few hours every day to earn tuition, almost bounced out of her skin. "Let me go find out what's happening!"

"You're busy." She ambled to the window just in time to see an elderly woman on a gurney being rolled into the street from the little grocery store a few doors down. She stood on tiptoes. "I think it's Mrs. Baker."

"Oh, go find out!" Claudette cried. "Be nosy for once!"

Marney stayed at the window a few minutes but really

couldn't see over the crowd. And she was as curious as Claudette. She pushed open her shop door and stepped onto the street.

"He just dropped to his knees and started giving Mrs. Baker CPR."

Marney listened to the chatter around her, not surprised a Good Samaritan had jumped in to save the town's favorite church lady.

"He always goes above and beyond the Sheriff job."

As she realized it was Dell they were talking about, she noticed him standing by the ambulance.

"You'll be fine," he crooned, patting Mrs. Baker's hand as the crew shoved the stretcher into the vehicle. With an IV in her arm and an oxygen mask over her face, it was clear she'd been in real trouble. "I'll check on you later."

The ambulance doors closed, and Dell turned away. Several people patted his back and offered congratulations. He brushed them off and headed down the street.

Marney bit her lower lip, turned back to her shop and shoved open the door. "It was Mrs. Baker. She must have had a heart attack because Sheriff O'Neil gave her CPR and she's on her way to the hospital."

Claudette sighed dreamily. "He's such a good guy."

She absently said, "Yeah, he is," as she picked up Charlie, who'd trotted over, apparently done with his morning nap. She walked into her office and closed the door.

She scratched Charlie's head lightly. "There is much, much more to that guy that meets the eye."

Charlie barked.

"It's too bad he's so bossy."

Charlie barked in agreement.

. . .

Unable to stop thinking about Dell O'Neil, Marney left work early and indulged in her other passion after jewelry design: cooking. Specifically, making her own pasta.

She worked for hours preparing sauce from scratch and perfect fettuccini noodles. After the first ten minutes of sauce prep, Charlie had deserted her, scampering away, she presumed, for another nap. But that was fine. She needed to be alone, to clear her head, to stop thinking about Dell O'Neil. He might be good-hearted, but he was bossy and controlling. And she'd had her fill of that with Doug. Everything he wanted came first. Everything she wanted came second. She'd be an idiot to give up her freedom for that.

As she finished straining the noodles, her doorbell rang.

She kissed a finger which had gotten in the way of some of the steam and called, "Just a minute!" With a quick wipe of her hands on an available dishtowel, she raced to the front door. She looked through the peephole, and there stood the very man she'd been thinking about all afternoon.

She groaned, but she couldn't very well pretend she wasn't home. The lights were on. Plus, he had Charlie in his arms. She opened the door.

"What's up?"

He scratched Charlie behind the ears. "I think your dog likes me."

She frowned.

"He was on my front stoop when I got home."

"Oh! Sorry. I've been cooking all afternoon by myself,

and I didn't even notice him leave." Fear shot through her. Good Lord, what the devil would they tell Mr. Bonaparte, one of the richest men in the world, if they lost his dog?

Dell smiled, his pretty blue eyes crinkling at the corners. "And here I just thought you'd sent him over to do reconnaissance."

Irritation warmed her blood. Was he always going to accuse her of trying to get him to her house? After the way he'd behaved the day before and especially after *he'd* kissed *her* at the fund raiser, he still thought she was attracted to him?

Okay. The second argument didn't work because she'd kissed him back. But he'd started that kiss. Still, what difference did it make? She'd lived in Chandler's Cove for years and had never known him beyond his name, but suddenly she was seeing him every day.

Maybe fate kept throwing them together for a reason...

"Why don't you stay for dinner?" The words were out of her mouth before the thought had fully formed. Fate or no fate, she didn't want Dell O'Neil thinking she was an idiot. If it killed her, she would prove to him she was just as decent, as nice, as normal—if not more normal, given that he had a secret—as he was.

"I've made enough for an army." She gave him a self-depreciating smile. "Because I love to cook. Made the sauce from scratch and the pasta."

"You made pasta from scratch?"

She presented her hands, wiggled the fingers. "I'm multi-talented."

He frowned. "I am hungry."

"I made extra." She paused then said, "I heard about

you saving Mrs. Baker this morning."

"It's part of the job."

"Some people might say that. But it still takes a selfless person to do the job you do. And even though I'm just a humble jewelry designer, I'm not so bad, either. We got off on the wrong foot."

"And you think spaghetti can fix that?"

"*Fettuccini* with Alfredo sauce that will make you weep and thank your maker."

"Really?" His voice had taken on a more accommodating tone. He set Charlie down and followed her into the kitchen.

She grabbed some plates from the cupboard. "We'll just eat at the center island, if you don't mind."

"I don't mind at all." Shrugging out of his jacket, he sniffed the air. "Smells like heaven in here."

They set the table companionably. He helped himself to a beer from her fridge. After she set his plate of Fettuccini Alfredo in front of him, he took a bite and groaned. "Wow."

"See. Could a wicked, evil, secret-telling woman cook this well?"

He laughed. "Probably not."

She dug into her pasta. "So tell me how a guy who loses all his money decides to become a small-town Sheriff?"

"It's sort of a funny story…on me."

"You've already got me sworn to secrecy."

"When I graduated from college, my father said I had to do one of the four e's … employment, education, enlist, or evacuate the family home.

She laughed. "Evacuate the family home?"

"My dad can get a bit theatrical." He chuckled. "Anyway, being a smart ass and wanting to drive my dad crazy, I enlisted.

After my dad exploded and I'd had my fun, I wanted to take it back, but the army wasn't so accommodating, and they wouldn't let me out of the commitment. They made me an MP and that got me through my time in Afghanistan okay, but it also taught me a lot. MP training was a lifesaver when I needed a new career. Now, I like the life I've built and don't want to complicate it." He caught her gaze. "Especially not with a relationship."

There were so many questions she could have asked him—about his family, his ex—but since they were trying to get on a normal footing as neighbors, she ignored them in favor of a response that would make it clear she wasn't a love-stuck idiot who intended to follow him around.

"Interesting. And fairly normal. Everybody's life has something odd in it."

"Oh, really? What's your story?"

"Pretty much the same as yours. Crappy first marriage. And though we didn't have a lot of property, Doug managed to get the condo. Still, my freedom was worth it."

He laughed and clanked his beer glass against her wine glass. "To first marriages that teach big lessons."

She raised her glass in toast. "Here, here."

The whole conversation was fun until she caught his gaze to smile at him and their smiles faded simultaneously. She wasn't exactly sure why his smile had faded but hers had disappeared because she realized why fate kept throwing them together. She *liked* him. They had enough in common that they understood each other. And unless she missed her guess, he now liked her, too.

Charlie trotted into the kitchen, his little paws making a clicking sound as he ambled over to her chair. He stopped, plopped his bottom on the floor and barked once at her. "Woof!"

Accustomed to talking to the dog as if he were a person, she almost answered him. Luckily, she caught herself and simply rose to get him some doggie treats.

Dell stood, too. "You cooked. I'll clean up."

Handing Charlie a treat, she shook her head. "I can't let you do that. That wouldn't be very hospitable."

"What do you say we do it together?"

They stacked the dishes in the dishwasher, chatting a bit more. He made her laugh a time or two, and Marney's stomach clenched. He was smart, funny, and very good looking. Not only that, but they shared a lot of similar experiences. Families who suffocated them. Exes who'd dumped them. And he really wasn't bossy as much as incredibly sure of himself, confident in a way that was more sexy than manipulative. He really wasn't like Doug at all.

But he didn't want to get involved again. She'd invited him to dinner to rectify their former misconceptions. Wouldn't it be counterproductive to try to start something that might make her look crazy again? Especially since he'd made it perfectly clear he didn't want a relationship?

Of course it would.

Still, when they stood at her front door, close enough to touch, but not touching, her hormones sat on the edges of her skin, breathlessly awaiting a kiss that she knew wasn't going to happen.

"Thank you for dinner."

His soft, sensual voice sent goose bumps down her spine. "You're welcome."

He turned to open the door, but stopped and faced her

again. His gray-blue eyes sparked with confusion. "I meant what I said about not wanting a relationship."

"I know."

"Neither of us should want a relationship anyway after our first failures."

"I think my ex cured me of that." But suddenly she didn't feel like that. Her divorce had been nasty, but she was surprised to realize she was ready for another relationship. Plus, she and Dell had fun together when their attraction didn't make them both nervous. She wouldn't mind exploring where this would go.

He stepped close to her, slid his hand down her hair. "The hell of it is I like you."

The breath that lodged in her throat prevented her from replying. *He liked her?* She'd guessed that but she never thought he'd admit it.

"We'd probably be perfect lovers." He laughed. "God knows I'm attracted to you."

Before she could even think of a response to that, he lowered his head and kissed her. His lips rubbed across hers, coaxing them open. Just like at the fund raiser, her head spun. Her bones dissolved. Her heart thundered in her chest.

His hands slid from her neck to her shoulders and down her back to her butt, sending rivers of molten need through her. He squeezed once, twice, then his hands drifted up her back, massaging until one drifted around front and found her breast.

Her nipples instantly hardened. Her breath stuttered out of her mouth, into his. Their kiss shifted from hot to super nova, their tongues mating frantically.

And then he pulled away.

The world vibrated around her for thirty seconds before she realized he stood there staring at her.

"I want to sleep with you." He sucked in a breath. "But you wouldn't like my terms. No strings. No commitments. It's awfully hard to have that in a small town unless both of us are ready to be so discreet even our friends don't know what we're doing."

Then he opened the door and left.

She combed her fingers through her hair. What the hell was that? How was she supposed to sleep now? Every hormone she had was on red alert. The man was potent. Like a drug. And ninety-nine-point-nine percent of her wanted to throw caution to the wind and spend a glorious night in bed with him.

What was left—a tenth of one percent—saw his point. Basically, they were incredibly attracted strangers, people who lived in the same small town where gossip could ruin a person who wasn't careful. Plus, he didn't want anything beyond a sexual relationship. And she didn't jump into bed just for fun.

No wonder he'd stopped. There was no way in hell they'd be able to have a relationship.

So, if her mind was so sure, why did her body still tingle from that kiss?

Chapter Four

The following afternoon, waiting for Claudette to arrive for her shift, Marney stood behind the display case, rearranging pieces of her jewelry. Like a little bodyguard, Charlie dutifully sat beside her. Gabby had called that morning and told her she could keep the adorable pup indefinitely as she and T.J. would soon be moving T.J.'s office from California.

Marney was abundantly glad to have Charlie's company. She needed someone to talk to. She'd fallen asleep believing Dell had given her a brushoff, but this afternoon her mind had spun off in a whole new direction.

"I want to sleep with you. But you wouldn't like my terms," she recited verbatim what she remembered him saying, as she glanced down at Charlie. "What if he wasn't giving me a brush off, but actually asking me to sleep with him, long-term, like a lover? And he left because he wanted me to think about his terms?"

Charlie barked, as if saying she'd hit the nail on the head.

She laughed. "Of course, you agree with that. You're a man. But I have to think this through. I agree the guy is gorgeous. But he's trouble. Anybody keeping a secret is trouble. I just don't know what kind yet. Worse, I can't talk to my friends because I can't tell them who he really is. It isn't just a matter of my promise to him. I'm not the kind of person violates another person's privacy."

She switched the necklace tray back to the left with a sigh. "No strings attached. No commitment. Basically, sex for fun. I've dated since my divorce, but deep down I've always been looking for Mr. Right. This would just be about sex." She shook her head. "My reputation-conscious parents would be horrified."

Charlie tilted his head.

"Right. They're an hour's drive away. There's no way they'd find out unless I told them…and, frankly, why would I tell them?"

Charlie barked.

She sighed. "Oh, Charlie, you see the world so simply. It's not so simple for humans."

Charlie just looked at her.

"And it's not like me to be so easy." She shifted the display case of earrings back to the right, thinking how childish the term 'easy' sounded. She was an adult. Technically she was considering taking a lover. Not a boyfriend. Not a potential mate. But a lover.

A thrill ran through her at the thought. A lover. It was the ultimate proof of maturity. Of independence. Of stability. She didn't *need* a man. She *wanted* a man.

She squeezed her eyes shut. She *really* wanted this man.

"I wish I knew what he'd meant last night. If he was

making a proposition or giving me the brushoff."

She paced away from the display case, tapping her fingers on her chin. "Even if he was making a proposition, I'd need more time with him, getting to know him, before I decide what to do."

Charlie grabbed the leg of her trousers and coaxed her toward the door.

She laughed. "I'm not going to the sheriff's office to chat. That would be ridiculous."

But when Claudette arrived, she retreated to her office and found herself with nothing to do. The shopping network took care of the administrative work that used to bog her down in red tape. All she had to do was design new pieces, take the plans to the manufacturing plant that now made her jewelry and show up at the studio on the days they were taping her show.

It was no wonder she was overthinking the situation with Dell. She was bored.

She glanced down at Charlie. "I don't have to stay here. With Claudette to handle customers, I could go home. I could cook again. Take supper to Dell's house. He wants no-strings-attached sex. I want to make sure choosing him for a lover is a good idea. Why shouldn't I go to his house?"

Charlie barked approvingly.

• • •

Four hours later, she showed up on Dell's doorstep with homemade vegetable soup and bread. He answered the door with wet hair, wearing only blue jeans that hung low on hips lean hips, as if he'd jumped into them after a shower.

Her mouth watered.

"What's this?"

She had to look down at her crock pot because the sight of him had knocked rational thought out of her head. "Soup. Bread. I made too much for myself and I thought I'd share again."

He opened the door a little wider, granting her entry. She stepped inside, surprised to see how simple his home was. Unlike her grand foyer with its marble and curving staircase, his entry was nonexistent. His front door opened onto his living room. Though nicely decorated with hardwood floors and a modern black leather and chrome sofa and chair in front of a tile fireplace, it wasn't the kind of home anybody would expect an O'Neil to have.

"Set the food on the coffee table and toss your jacket on a chair. I'll get some bowls and spoons."

"You'd eat in your living room?

He laughed. "I do anything I want."

Watching him leave, she swallowed. With a backside like his, she didn't doubt he did whatever he wanted.

Another thing to consider. If she decided to sleep with him, she'd want to be exclusive sexual partners. A guy like him probably didn't do exclusive.

He returned with the bowls and spoons, and she still stood by the door like a ninny. After setting the utensils on the coffee table, he took the crock pot from her hands and set it beside them. She quickly removed her jacket and tossed it to the chair as he sauntered over to her again.

Without missing a beat, he slid his hands to the back of her neck under the waterfall of her hair and lifted her head as his descended to kiss her.

Their mouths met deliciously. Before she realized what was happening their tongues were twining. Her blood raced through her veins. All solidity left her body.

As if realizing she was about to fall into a puddle of desire at his feet, he moved his hands from her neck, down her back. One stopped at her waist. One slid to her bottom.

The intimate touch of his hand sent a shot of need straight to her femininity. As their mouths mated and he kneaded the supple flesh of her behind, his other hand slowly drifted to the spot just beneath her breast.

Red-hot desire exploded in her core. When his hand covered her breast, it was all she could do to control a whimper. He massaged for a second then found her nipple.

"What do you say we get rid of your sweater?"

The words whispered against her mouth were every bit as sensual as the request. He didn't give her time to think, though. He reached for the hem of her sweater and pulled it over her head. Her red lace bra greeted him.

He smiled. Caught her gaze. "Pretty."

Then he kissed her again. One hand held her head. One hand breezed along her skin, to her back, and snapped open her bra as if it were no trouble, no challenge, at all. Her breasts fell free, and he broke the kiss to take one straining nipple into his mouth.

Her knees buckled. He slid his arm around her back to brace her as he moved them toward the black sofa. After that, everything became a blur. As his tongue twirled around her other nipple, he reached for the snap of her jeans. He released her to get rid of her jeans and panties but when he returned to kiss her again, his jeans were also gone. His erection pressed against her thigh.

Nothing had ever felt so wonderful, and she was abundantly glad she was on the pill. Just the thought of him naked above her sent arousal careening through her veins. Through her sexual haze, she felt him push her thighs apart and enter her.

Sweet bliss filled her. Her swollen femininity wept with welcome for him. He moved in and out, intensifying the heavenly tension, and suddenly her insides exploded in an orgasm that sent ripples to her toes.

He cried out in his own release.

They lay there for thirty seconds before Marney came down to earth. She couldn't remember how the seduction began or much of anything about it except that she'd never felt that kind of arousal in her life.

And that she hadn't done anything—hadn't even had the presence of mind to touch him.

He pushed himself off her, left for a few seconds then returned to the sofa and sat beside her. Blissfully naked, he reached for the ladle and dished out a bowl of soup for each of them, and then handed her a spoon.

"Thank you." Her voice squeaked. Every muscle and bone and tendon and ligament of her body felt different. They hummed with life and energy, as if they hadn't really been alive before.

He dug into his soup. She slid her spoon into hers. She wasn't exactly mad at herself. Who could be angry after the best sex of their life? But she hadn't done what she'd come here to do. Find out about him. And she wasn't entirely sure how they'd ended up having sex...except maybe that she'd been ogling him again. He'd known she wanted him, so he'd taken her.

Although, it wasn't as if she'd put up a fight.

She ate five bites of soup. Naked. Sitting on a couch with a guy with whom she'd already made love, but didn't really know.

"This soup is excellent." He finished a whole bowl and dished out another.

Sex obviously gave him an appetite. Who said she hadn't found out anything about him?

Damn it. Stop. You can't be an idiot about this. You have to do what you came here to do.

"So...Um..." She set her bowl on the coffee table, glanced up into his perfect blue eyes, and totally lost her train of thought.

He smiled at her. "So...um...what?"

The little hum she now recognized as acute arousal started up in her again. She had to talk fast if she was going to talk at all.

"I actually wanted to talk a little bit. I brought the soup over to be neighborly, but I came here to talk."

He frowned. "I thought you'd considered what I'd said last night and made up your mind to sleep with me." He pointed at the soup pot. "I assumed you'd used the soup as an icebreaker."

She reddened to the roots of her hair. If that wasn't proof that they had communications issues, she didn't know what was.

He set his bowl on the coffee table and slid his thumb across her chin. "You had a little bit of soup there."

His voice was deep and husky. His blue eyes warm and seductive. Her gaze fell to his chest and followed the trail of soft black hair to his brand new erection. She swallowed. It looked as if he was feeling exactly the same thing she was…a need for more.

She bought her gaze to his and he slid his hands to her nape, tilted her face, and kissed her again.

This time there was no hesitation. And this time she wasn't going to be a rag doll. Her hands fell to his chest and slid down to his navel, simply enjoying the silky feel of the dusting of black hair and firm muscle. As if playing a game of follow the leader, he slid his hands from her breasts to her lower abdomen.

She slid her hands up.

He slid his hand up.

Sweet desire rippled through her. And so did an unexpected burst of boldness. They'd already made love once. Why be shy? Why deny herself?

Her hands moved down again, but this time they didn't stop. She smoothed both along the sides of his erection and back up to the top. She bent down and traced her tongue along the tip.

He groaned and skimmed his hands down her torso. Following her lead, he didn't stop at her tummy, but traced a line to the fluffy mound of hair beneath it. He found her sensitive nub, circled it, then lowered his head and glided his tongue over it.

She about shot off the sofa, but he didn't linger. He shifted and brought both hands to the sides of her face and kissed her again, long and deep. Somehow she ended up straddling him on the sofa as they kissed, her hands at his shoulders, his hands cupping her behind. But one of his hands slipped from her butt to her sex. He slid one finger inside her, then two. When she groaned with ecstasy, he rolled them onto the sofa and entered her again.

· · ·

Two hours later, she sneaked into her house through the kitchen door, not entirely clear why she felt guilty. Not only had the sex been great but they were clearly very good at it. Sure, he'd gotten her to go beyond a few of her inhibitions, but who really needed inhibitions?

She tiptoed to the sink and lowered her crockpot inside. When she turned away, Charlie was at her feet, wagging his tail.

"Don't be so thrilled. We didn't talk, and I didn't care. I really might only want sex from this guy. And what does that make me?"

Guilty and confused?

Or sated and happy?

Really? Was she allowed to be sated and happy over a one-night stand?

Because that's all this was. A one-night stand. They might not have talked much tonight, but he'd made himself abundantly clear. He didn't want a relationship.

Chapter Five

Though the following afternoon was just as boring as the two days before had been, Marney forced herself to stay at the shop. She hadn't just made love with Dell O'Neil on a misconception. She'd done it three times the day before at his house.

And kissed him passionately at his door.

Because he was gorgeous and an excellent lover—but she hadn't made a conscious decision. He'd sort of taken the decision out of her hands by seducing her...because she'd made soup.

So, no soup tonight. No fettuccini. No nothing. She was getting back her bearings.

She locked the shop door at her usual five-thirty quitting time, then drove home determined not to be embarrassed that she'd slept with a man she barely knew and equally determined not to be glad she'd slept with him. Even if she only wanted him for a lover, she should know him.

Tossing her keys on the hall table, she made her way to the stairway, strode to her bedroom, and changed out of her purple pantsuit into threadbare jeans and a ripped pink T-shirt. These were not clothes to be seen in public. They were laundry day clothes. That would keep her home.

Satisfied she'd gotten her wits back, she jogged down the stairs. Just as she hit the last step, her doorbell rang.

Remembering it was about time for the piece of art she'd ordered at the Heart Association fund raiser to be delivered, she swung open the door, and there stood Dell, dressed the same way she was, in jeans and a scruffy T-shirt. The weather had warmed, and even though the sun had gone down, he didn't need a jacket. Sweet spring air wafted into her foyer.

He gave her a hopeful look and held out the pot in his hands. "I made soup."

Soup.

Heat enveloped her, a need so sharp and sweet, she swayed.

Still, she told herself to behave. To get her dignity back. "I hope soup hasn't become our code word for sex."

He laughed. "No. Actually, it's apology soup."

"Apology from Dell O'Neil?"

"We had such a...good time...yesterday that it didn't dawn on me until this morning that the way I handled our miscommunication wasn't exactly gentlemanly."

She remembered every detail of how he'd "handled" things the night before, and she swallowed. Her gaze rose to meet his. "I didn't exactly correct you."

He displayed the pot again. "So, apology soup?"

She laughed. "Yeah. Sure. Why not?"

• • •

Dell forced himself not to breathe a sigh of relief until she turned to lead him to her kitchen. Then he let it out in a slow stream of air.

He really had misinterpreted her gesture the night before, but the second time they'd had sex he couldn't plead that excuse. The third time…well, what could he say? They were good at it. But tonight would be different.

Not that he didn't want to have sex with her again. He just wanted it to be her idea this time so he'd know for sure she was okay with it.

She patted her granite countertop as she passed it. "Put the soup here." Then she reached into a cupboard and retrieved bowls. Setting them on the countertop by the pot of soup, she said, "I have beer, if you want one."

He stuffed his hands in his jeans pockets because he itched to touch her. She'd been gorgeous at the gala in the red dress, adorable in her jeans and sweater the night before. But casual, in a T-shirt with a few holes and jeans so well worn they caressed her ass, she made his mouth water.

She handed him a beer. He pulled one of his hands out of his pocket so he could take it.

"Want to eat here or on the couch?"

The couch had definitely gotten them into trouble the night before. He pointed at the tall chairs by the counter on which the soup sat. "Right here is good."

She ladled out the chicken noodle soup and set a bowl in front of him before she ladled a bowl for herself. She took the seat across the counter from him and heat crawled up his neck. She wouldn't even sit by him. He really had gone too far too fast the night before.

She took a bite of soup and groaned. "This is fantastic. Why didn't you tell me you could cook?"

"I can't. I got the soup from my mother. Her housekeeper is a gem."

Her eyebrows rose. "You went to Chicago today?"

"It was my day off."

Her lips quirked a little. "I can't say I'm not glad." She smiled. "So this means we can talk about your other life?"

He glanced down at his soup then up at her. "It's not really another life. It's part of my life." He shrugged, feeling weirdly okay with this. "I just don't advertise it, and I asked my family not to, either. But you already know about it. So, yeah. I guess if we're going to be friends we can talk about my parents…my past."

"The bad divorce?"

"The abysmal divorce."

She laughed. "Honestly, mine was no cake walk, either. My super-charming husband didn't just end up with our condo, he got custody of our friends, and if my parents weren't bound by blood, I think they would have kept him instead of me."

"Really?" He chuckled. "That's not right."

"Well, he is an attorney. Though my brother, sister and I all went to college, none of us became *a professional.* Mom and Dad loved thinking Doug somehow got them into society or something."

"But you're successful now."

"Yeah. And I could probably get them into more places than Doug ever could…but he was their first. And you know how that is."

He laughed. "You make it all sound so funny."

"Why not?" She shrugged. "You have to admit, my parents' reaction was odd by anybody's standards. Doug getting all of our friends, even mine...? Again, odd. When I began seeing it as funny, I got over it."

"So I should see my wife making off with most of my money as funny?"

"Was it odd?"

"Odd?"

"Was there something unusual about the way she got the money?"

"Actually, she sort of stole it."

"That's promising."

"When we began negotiating, we had to present financial statements, and I discovered she'd been siphoning money practically since our wedding day."

"So you married a thief?"

"Technically, yes."

"And you don't see the humor in that?"

He hadn't, but now that all was said and done, he supposed there was a bit of humor in that. His lips quirked. They rose into a full blown smile. Then a laugh escaped.

"See? Stick with me. I'll show you how to make anything funny."

They finished their soup and drank another beer in her living room, talking for hours about her business, which intrigued him.

"So you basically do nothing now?" he asked.

"I wouldn't say nothing. I outsource the production. There's some monitoring involved. And I still design. I have a new collection for every season."

"So why aren't you busy with that?"

"Designing isn't a nine-to-five job. I design when inspired. But when I get inspired, look out. I could work for days without sleep or food."

"Interesting."

The conversation died. Which also intrigued him. Normally he had about five minutes worth of conversation with anybody and then he didn't want to talk anymore. They'd basically talked for hours. And he would continue talking if he could think of something to say.

Thirty seconds clicked by, and Marney yawned.

He'd accomplished what he'd set out to accomplish. He'd proven himself to be a normal, decent guy, which basically took them back to the place where they were on fettuccini night. Very attracted friends. The decision to have a sexual relationship was back in her hands.

He rose. Just thinking *sexual relationship* had started his engines. Watching her rise, dressed in her scruffy jeans and even scruffier T-shirt, revved them. From this point, he could go from zero to sixty in under five seconds, but this wasn't his call. This was hers. If she wanted nothing tonight, that would be fine. He wouldn't consider the relationship over. He'd be a gentleman.

He headed for the door. She followed him.

Okay. Think date. What would I do right now on a date?

"I had a really nice time tonight."

She smiled. "I did, too." She clasped her hands together and looked up into his eyes. "But we forgot something."

Oh, alleluia. He wasn't leaving after all.

"Your pot."

"What?"

"Your soup pot."

"Oh."

Damn.

"I'll get it."

She turned to run into her kitchen, and he swore her hips swayed more provocatively than he'd ever seen a woman's hips sway before. The foyer got hot. His humming engines revved again.

She returned with his soup pot, smiling as she handed it to him. "Here you go."

Either he had a very vivid imagination or her voice had become incredibly breathy and sexy in the twenty seconds it took to get the pot.

His hand twitched.

She shook her head, and her dark hair shimmered around her. If that wasn't a mating call, he didn't know what was.

As if in slow motion, he took the pot.

Seconds ticked off the clock.

She didn't make another move after the hair, so he was going to have to leave. But the least he should get is a goodnight kiss.

Holding the pot, he leaned down and kissed her. His lips brushed against hers softly at first, but that only left him hungrier than having no kiss at all, so he pressed his mouth against her lips and they opened for him. His tongue drifted inside, and sweet arousal poured through him.

Wanting to draw her closer, he nearly raised his hands, but they were holding a pot. He couldn't remember why, so he stepped away, set the pot on her foyer table, and reached for her. She came into his arms willingly, and that was all the invitation his body needed.

They kissed again, and he made short order of her shirt and white lace bra. This time, though, she lifted his T-shirt off. She also went for the snap of his jeans. He barely noticed. Her soft skin seduced his hands, filled his fingers with curiosity and the need to touch and explore.

So he did. He let his hands glide along her arms, down her back, while his tongue laved her nipples. She groaned and wrapped her arms around him, pulling him close. A few of his more magical moves popped into his head but she shifted seductively against him and instinct snapped inside him. He grabbed her bottom, levered her against the wall and pushed himself into her.

He didn't bother to stop a moan of pleasure. She was perfect, wet and every bit as hungry as he was. He thrust only a few times before her orgasm overtook her. And that nearly pushed him over the edge, but he held on. He wanted her to come again. So he slowed his pace, ran his lips along her jawline, kneaded her breasts until her breath hitched. Then he thrust into her again and again, until she cried out his name.

That, he realized, was what he'd wanted to hear. His name on her pretty lips. He let himself go.

A few seconds later, sated and cockily proud of himself, he began to come back to earth. But when he looked down into her face he realized he'd done it again. The only permission he'd gotten from her was a response to a kiss.

"Oh, God. I'm sorry!"

She laughed. "For the wall?"

"For taking the decision to make love out of your hands."

She ran her fingers up his chest and linked her hands behind his neck. "I sort of liked it."

"I wanted you to have choices."

She shrugged. "I did. I know I can always say no, and you'll hear. But I like it when you take…" she caught his gaze, "control."

Everything male in him stirred to life. "Really?"

She ran one finger along his cheek, down his chin. "You can be bossy in the bedroom." She glanced behind her and smiled. "Or up against the wall any time you want. As long as we're equals the rest of the time."

He kissed her. Long. Deep. Enjoying every sensation.

He'd never before met a woman he liked as much as he liked her. His last coherent thought after he carried her up to her very Zen yellow and gray bedroom was a slight acknowledgement that liking her so much might actually ruin his perfect plan not to have a relationship.

Chapter Six

During the next six weeks, Marney created some of the most spectacular jewelry she'd ever designed. Though she normally worked day and night when she was in creation mode, with Dell coming over for supper every evening, she found it easy to quit when he arrived. Some days he brought food. Some days she made food. Other days they ordered pizza or Chinese food and had it delivered.

She could have given Charlie back to Gabby, but T.J. was still organizing his Chandler's Cove office. Bonaparte had been overseas since January and didn't show any signs of coming home, so Gabby was grateful that Marney could keep sweet Charlie for a few more weeks. With Dell sleeping at her house until midnight every night that he didn't work, she felt totally protected. But, frankly, Charlie was the only one Marney could talk to about Dell.

"Remember how I wondered what sleeping with Dell would make me?"

Charlie barked.

"I've finally figured it out."

He tilted his head.

"It makes me happy."

Charlie barked twice.

She turned off her computer, grabbed her purse, and tapped her thighs twice. Charlie raced over and she lifted him into her arms. "You've been so sweet over the past six weeks that I'm not making you walk ever again." She kissed the fur between his ears. "I'm carrying you everywhere."

At her house, she threw together a simple supper of salad, French fries, and thick steaks to be grilled once Dell arrived. At exactly six o'clock, he opened her kitchen door and stepped inside.

He didn't hesitate. He yanked her to him and kissed her so greedily, her heart about stopped.

Breathless, she pulled away. "Okay. I was going to put the steaks on as soon as you got here, but I'm thinking you might be hungry for something else."

He nuzzled her neck. "I just might be."

She laughed.

"How about sex first and steak second?

"Sounds good."

He kissed her again, then scooped her up and took her to the bedroom.

• • •

Two hours later, he glanced at his watch and groaned. "Damn."

She sat up in bed. "Damn what?"

"I have to be in Chicago this weekend. I promised my mom I'd leave tonight and be there on time for a little gathering with a few out-of-town relatives." He jumped into his jeans then grabbed his tennis shoes and socks and fell to the edge of the bed to put them on. "My niece is making her first communion." He glanced back at her. "A big deal in my family. So I have to be there from the night the out-of-towners arrive until the last glass of champagne is done Sunday afternoon."

"Oh." Conflicting feelings tore her in two. On the one hand, they had a no-strings-attached relationship, and that was working for them. On the other, they were friends as much as lovers. Even if she ignored the slight over his not inviting her, fresh hurt arose over the fact that he'd never mentioned this before now. She told him everything, and she'd thought he told her everything. Apparently, that wasn't true.

He jumped off the bed, bent down and kissed her, then shot out of the room like a rocket.

She stared at the door he'd left open, her stomach tied in knots, her chest tight and a river of tears backing up behind her eyelids.

He hadn't even hinted about taking her...or offered an apology for not asking her along.

He didn't think of her at all.

She slid down on her pillow again, told herself not to cry, and reminded herself that *this* was their deal, but her heart still shattered. The absolute worst had happened.

She'd fallen in love.

She crawled out of bed, put on a T-shirt and jeans, and called Charlie. With a bark, he bolted into her bedroom. She scooped him up with one hand and wiped away her tears with the other. It was stupid to cry. Really stupid.

After slipping on a hoodie to protect her from the cool May night, she slid into shoes, packed Charlie into her new Mercedes, and drove to her shop. In two minutes, she was inside her office, her computer open, Charlie snoozing at her feet. Work was the only way she knew to avoid the pain, so she would work.

An hour went by, then two. She heard something that sounded like someone trying to open her locked shop door, but she ignored it. Eventually, they'd get the message that her office lights might be on, but she wasn't open for business.

She turned back to her computer. The noise went away. A few minutes later she heard the rattle again. Her heart popped. What if it was an intruder?

Normally, she'd have been terrified. Tonight, she chuckled and grabbed her cell phone and an umbrella. She dialed the 9 and 1 as she crept through her office. If this was an intruder he was going to be sorry he picked tonight to rob her. The mood she was in, she would happily swat him around with her umbrella before she'd let him rob her.

She slowly made her way along the display case toward the door. Streetlights illuminated the faces of her three friends, Gabby, Mia and Jenny, pressed against her front window.

She closed the cell phone without dialing the final 1, dropped the umbrella, and opened the door.

They poured in. Mia reached her first. In an uncharacteristically open move, her hand immediately went to Marney's shoulder. "What's wrong?"

She faked a laugh. "Nothing is wrong."

"It's after ten. You're never here after nine."

"I'm designing."

Gabby glanced around. "You usually design at home at night."

"I didn't take my laptop home so I had to come back." She shrugged. Working here was better than facing the memories of Dell in every corner of her house. "Figured I'd stay."

Gabby found glasses and the wine Marney kept hidden for celebrations. She set the glasses on the display case and poured the wine. "You've been weird for over a month. Something's going on. We're not leaving until you spill."

Gabby's determined voice let her know she wasn't kidding, but Mia and Jenny's serious faces sealed the deal.

She sighed. She was tired of hiding this and if anybody could be sworn to secrecy, it was her three friends.

"Promise not to tell."

Jenny laughed. "You want a blood oath?"

She shook her head. "Just a promise."

Gabby touched her forearm. "You always have our promise."

Marney blew her breath out on a tired sigh. "I've been seeing someone."

Jenny gasped. "I knew it!"

"The problem is he doesn't want a relationship. I knew that when we got involved."

Mia frowned. "But you fell in love, didn't you?"

"Head over heels."

Jenny squeezed her hand. "Maybe he fell in love, too."

Remembering Dell's quick exit, she shook her head. "I don't think so."

Gabby handed her a glass of wine. "Have you asked?"

"No, but…"

Gabby sighed. "No buts about it. You have to ask."

Marney sucked in a breath. She knew her friends were right. She had to ask. She should have known better than to get involved only for a fling, but she hadn't. Now she had to pay the consequences of admitting she'd fallen hard and letting him decide if their relationship went forward or ended.

• • •

Dell returned to Chandler's Cove early. He'd missed Marney so much that he'd bowed out at three on Sunday afternoon. He didn't even stop at his own house. He drove directly to hers, jumped out of his car and raced to her back door.

It opened on an empty kitchen. "Anybody home?"

She peeked out of her pantry. "Hey."

He walked over, caught her elbows and kissed her. "Hey."

"I was going to make soup."

"Why don't we go upstairs and make soup?"

She laughed. "Because one of us is seriously hungry."

He tugged her to him and growled in her ear. "How about a glass of milk to tide you over?" He didn't like the fact that he'd missed her. But holding her close, he realized he might not have missed *her* as much as he'd missed this. The easy familiarity. The ability to really be himself with her. Especially sexually. There was no artifice. No game playing. They both enjoyed sex, enjoyed each other. And that's what he'd longed for all weekend. A little unpretentious fun.

He reached for the hem of her T-shirt.

She skittered away, laughing lightly. "All right. Fine. I won't make you wait the four hours it takes to make a good pot of soup. But I will have a glass of milk."

He said, "Good," but he got a strange feeling that squeezed his stomach. The easy familiarity didn't quite feel so easy. Something was wrong. "So what did you do while I was away?"

She met his gaze. "I worked."

He slid onto a stool. "That's good. Right?"

"Yes. It was very good." She paused, took a drink of milk, then her gaze meandered to his. "I also spent time with my friends."

"That's even better."

She smiled. "You're awfully accommodating."

"I missed you." Even as the words came out of his mouth, he hated them, if only because they were so easy to misinterpret. But when Marney smiled, he forgot all about regret.

Her milk finished, she put her glass into the dishwasher then sashayed over. She slid onto his lap. "Now, what were you saying when you first arrived?"

He swallowed. He loved her big brown eyes, loved her pert little nose, loved her kissable lips. "As I recall, I wasn't saying anything." He bent his head and kissed her and his world suddenly righted again. He smoothed his hand under her T-shirt, up her sleek spine and unhooked her bra.

She giggled. "Kitchen? Really?"

"Why not?"

She bumped her forehead to his. "I'd planned on showering." Her voice had dropped to a breathy whisper that sent tingles of delight directly to his groin. "And putting on something sexy for your homecoming."

"I like you in your birthday suit." His hand trailed down her spine again. "Warm and naked."

She laughed, and he deepened their kiss. But the intimacy of her smoky whisper finally hit him. He reminded himself that they were lovers, but there was something more in her voice.

He rose from the stool, taking her with him. "You know what? Maybe we should go to the bed."

She wrapped her arms around his neck. "Sounds good to me."

He carried her up the back stairway to her master bedroom. The pretty yellow and gray room greeted him like a long, lost friend, filling him with an emotion he couldn't quite put his finger on.

He slid her to the floor and she reached for his shirt. After wrestling it over his head, she tossed it across the room and pressed both hands to his chest.

He closed his eyes in ecstasy.

"I'm happy you're home."

His eyes popped open. Why had that sounded different?

Her hands moved down the length of his chest and opened the snap of his trousers. Without finishing the job, they glided back up as her lips met his chest. She sprinkled warm, wet kisses across his pecs, down his abs, and along the waistband of his jeans.

His control snapped. He unzipped his pants, and jumped out of them. He got rid of her T-shirt and jeans, her red bra and her panties and was inside her so quickly the only response he got was breathy moan.

There. That was better.

. . .

He awoke the next morning totally confused. The silken
sheets caressing his naked body reminded him that he was
at Marney's. He glanced at the clock, saw it was after six and
bolted up in bed.

He'd slept over.

He bounced out of bed, yanked on his trousers and shirt,
and ran downstairs. No harm done. He could quickly make
himself some breakfast to eat as he checked his texts and
voice mails, and race home, and get into his uniform before
his seven o'clock starting time. All without waking Marney.

In five minutes he had eggs, bacon, toast sitting on the
countertop.

"You made me breakfast."

His gaze swung to the kitchen entryway. Dressed in
a T-shirt and panties, with her dark hair tousled and her
eyes sleepily sexy, she nearly coaxed him back to bed, but
her comment confused him. When he looked down at the
mountain of bacon, and four eggs, instead of two, four pieces
of toast, instead of two, he came back to the real world.

He *had* made her breakfast.

"I didn't mean to."

She ambled over to him. "Didn't mean to?"

He looked at the toast and bacon again. Why four eggs?
Why so much toast? Where the hell was his head? "Seriously,
I don't know why I did this."

She set her hand on the hand he had leaning on the
granite top of the center island. "You don't know what's

happening here, do you?"

"Not a clue." But the breathy, uncertain whisper of her voice told him what she was about to say.

"I think we've fallen in love."

And from the wobble in her words, she wasn't any happier about it that he was. Except, it didn't matter what she thought. Or what he thought. He had rules. Standing by those rules kept him grounded, safe. And if he had broken a few of them, that could only mean he was comfortable. Maybe too comfortable?

"Marney, this isn't about love. This is about me getting accustomed to you. Too accustomed."

She stepped back.

An arrow shot into his heart at the pain that exploded in her sexy dark eyes. But that wasn't his fault. "Hey, I told you. I don't want to be in love. I like the fact that we're friends. I like that we can talk to each other about anything. But if you think you're in love, I'm out that door."

• • •

Marney licked her lips. Her throat ached with the need to cry. Her heart ached with the pain of realizing she'd never see him again if she told him the truth.

All she had to do was laugh, say she was teasing, pretend she didn't love him…and he'd be back tonight. Heck, they'd probably eat breakfast together.

All she had to do was pretend.

And spend the rest of their relationship longing for him to love her? Controlled by a love she felt but he didn't?

That wasn't how she lived. It wasn't who she was.

Her gaze slowly rose. When it connected with his blue-gray eyes, eyes she could stare into forever, her heart splintered. But she knew what she had to do.

She swallowed. "I love you enough to know that if I let you stay you will really, really hurt me someday."

She turned and walked out of her kitchen.

Chapter Seven

That afternoon, Dell sat at his desk, trying to forget the sad look on Marney's face before she'd turned and walked out on him. With the May sunshine brightening everything, he'd left the main office door open to let in some fresh air, hoping to dispel his mood.

He was not wrong. She was. He'd made his intentions known. She'd agreed to his terms. He wouldn't be upset.

Suddenly, something cold hit the little space between the cuff of his trouser leg and the top of his sock. He glanced down, and there sat Charlie.

He lifted the furry pup and scratched behind his ears. "What are you doing here?"

Charlie barked.

Dell shook his head. "I'm not taking you back." He set him on the floor. "Go. Go back to Marney's."

The dog sat and—if dogs could grin—Dell swore the

little beast grinned at him.

He tried taking him to the door. He tried shooing him up the sidewalk. Each time, Charlie plopped on his butt and grinned at him. Annoyed, he picked up the dog and headed to Marney's shop.

Two doors away, he bumped into Laura Jennings, the first-grade teacher. From her soft yellow hair to her pretty blue eyes, she was the vision of the kind of woman Dell usually liked to woo. In fact, he'd considered asking her out.

Take that Charlie.

She caught his hand. "Dell! I'm so glad I ran into you. I'm having career day right after lunch and I need a solid closing speaker. After the way you saved Mrs. Baker a few weeks ago, I know the kids would love to hear from you."

Dell frowned. He hadn't had a reaction to Laura's touch. Nothing.

Charlie barked. Laura patted his head. "See, even your dog thinks you'd be a perfect speaker."

He might have been attracted before, but he wasn't now. As for speaking to the first graders...Well, he was the chief and these kids were his responsibility. Teaching them was the serve part of *protect and serve*.

"All right. I'll be there. What time?"

After getting the details, he took Charlie to Marney's shop.

Claudette greeted him. "Hey, that's Charlie!" She took him from Dell's arms and hugged him to her. "Bad puppy! How'd you get out anyway?"

Dell said, "I don't know how he got out, but he made it to my office. You might want to put him on a leash. Don't forget we have a leash law."

"He has a leash. Marney only takes it off when she's working."

"Yeah." He glanced at the office door. Closed. His heart stuttered a bit, surprising him. Normally, he didn't have a problem losing someone—he'd learned not to care so much that it hurt. But Marney had been a friend as well as his lover. He had to admit he would miss her.

But this was for the best.

• • •

Even though everyone in town knew who he was, Dell had to sign in at the elementary school and have an escort take him to the first-grade classroom. Gideon Roth, the town vet, was just coming out as he approached the door. He shook Dell's hand. "Tough crowd in there. Good luck."

Dell laughed. As he entered the classroom, the kids saw his uniform and they cheered.

Halfway through his talk—a little speech that was part admonition for the kids to be good and stay on the right side of the law and half description of his job—he noticed a little girl sitting in the back. Her brown pigtails reached her shoulders and her brown eyes could light up a room.

Marney immediately came to mind, and he had to squelch a chuckle. That was probably what Marney had looked like as a little girl. But another thought quickly replaced that one. He suddenly realized that adorable girl in the back looked exactly like what Marney's daughter would look like.

This time his heart stalled. Marney would someday have kids without him.

He went back to his speech, telling himself to forget *that* and stop thinking about her. But two rows over, he spotted a little boy who reminded him of himself at that age. Inquisitive. Funny. Smart. His heart beat out of rhythm for a few seconds. It was odd to see himself as a child — then he realized he wasn't seeing himself but what his *son* would look like.

Confused, he shook his head to clear it. He didn't want kids. He *had*. When he was younger, he'd wanted lots of kids. But he didn't want them now.

"So that's my job. Anybody have any questions?"

Ten hands bulleted into the air. But the little boy who reminded Dell of himself, simply shouted, "Yeah, have you ever shot anyone?"

He laughed. "No. We're lucky not to have that kind of trouble here."

"What about in Afghanistan."

"I was MP. Military Police. And I wasn't about to shoot one of our own guys."

A confirming gasp rippled through the room as if they were little patriots who understood, and his heart lurched. He only ever saw kids at family functions, and usually they were as bored and crabby as he was in his parents' sterile mansion. But these kids were real. Normal. In their own environment, they were fun. Funny.

And they got to him. This was what Marney wanted. Not just sex, but a life. The life *he'd* wanted before his ex had cheated on him. That was why he'd felt so odd the night before and this morning. He might have made rules, decisions, but his heart had always had other plans. He'd tumbled into love without even realizing it.

"Do you have a dog?"

"No, but my friend has a dog. His name is Charlie."

He'd had the dog in his hands that morning as if life—or Charlie—was giving him a second chance.

But he'd dropped the ball. Because he was afraid.

The big, tough policeman these kids looked up to was afraid.

• • •

Marney stared at her computer screen, refusing to let herself think about anything but jewelry. A knock sounded on her door.

Without looking up she said, "Go away, Claudette. I need another six hours with this piece before I'll be happy with it."

Claudette said nothing, but the door opened. She looked up to politely remind her staffer that she didn't wish to be bothered, but she didn't see anyone.

She did, however, hear a bark. Then Charlie scampered over and nudged her ankle.

Claudette's shaking voice came through the crack of the open door. "The Sheriff's here. He wants to talk to you."

Her pulse raced. *He was here?* Oh, Lord. She didn't want to break down in front of impressionable Claudette. And she definitely would break down if he tried to explain again why he didn't love her. "Tell him I'm busy."

Claudette didn't say anything else. She simply closed the door. But Charlie tugged on her pant leg.

"Stop that!"

He barked, grabbed the hem of her pants again and tugged again.

"Stop!"

He barked, grabbed her hem and tugged.

"For the love of pity and peace! Stop, Charlie! I'm not leaving this room."

The door opened a crack. "I know from experience he isn't going to stop until you do what he wants."

Her head snapped up. There was no mistaking the masculine sound of Dell's voice.

Charlie began barking like a crazy dog. With a sigh, she rose, walked to the door and opened it completely. Then walked back to her desk and took her seat again.

Hat in hand, Dell strolled in. "I need to talk to you."

"I think we established this morning that you've already said everything you want to say."

"Yeah, well, that was before I went to first grade this afternoon for career day." He paused. "I saw a little girl who looked like what you probably looked like as a little girl."

"Peachy."

"And a little boy who looked like me...and acted like me." He shook his head with a laugh. "Our kids would be incredible."

She peeked up at him. "Our kids? With me raising them alone because you keep secrets?"

"I don't want secrets anymore. Yes, I'll still be sheriff, but there's no reason to hide my roots—especially if I'm going to raise our kids *with* you."

Her heart stalled and blood rushed to her head. But she'd made wrong assumptions before. She wouldn't make one again. "Are we going to share custody, shack up, or are you asking me to marry you?"

"I'm asking you to marry me."

Shock froze her in place, but the warmth in his eyes quickly melted it. He meant it. He wanted to marry her. And he wanted kids. He wanted a life together.

She burst off her chair and into his arms. "Yes!"

He caught her face between his hands, his gaze searched her eyes. "My heart knew last night that I'd fallen in love with you. It just took those kids to remind me of who I was and what I wanted. A real life…with you."

She squeezed her eyes shut then popped them open again, just to be sure this was actually happening.

He still stood in front of her, holding her.

He laughed. "Having a little trouble believing this is real?"

He knew her so well. She should have known better than to close her eyes.

He reached into his back pocket, pulled out a little box. "Maybe this will help."

He opened the box and presented her with a two-carat diamond surrounded by little diamonds that made a square.

"Oh, my God."

He dropped to one knee. "Since we're doing this, let's do it right. Miss Marney Fields, will you do me the honor of being my wife?"

The tears that backed up behind her eyelids this time

were happy tears. "Yes."

She held out her hand, and he slid on the ring.

The earth shifted. She swore she felt a click. The past was gone. The future was ahead of them. And he was hers.

Forever.

"Wanna go home and make some soup?" She grinned.

He rose and caught her hand. "I thought you'd never ask."

About the Author

A one-time legal secretary and director of a charitable foundation, Susan Meier found her bliss when she became a full-time novelist. She's visited ski lodges and candy factories for "research" and works in her pajamas.

But the real joy of her job is creating stories about women for women. In her over 50 published novels, she tackles issues like infertility, losing a child and becoming widowed with sensitivity and humor.

One of eleven children, Susan is married with three of her own kids and two well-fed cats.

LOVE UNLEASHED

JACKIE BRAUN

Entangled Publishing, LLC
2614 South Timberline Road
Suite 109
Fort Collins, CO 80525
Visit our website at www.entangledpublishing.com.

Edited by Shannon Godwin
Cover design by Libby Murphy

Ebook ISBN 978-1-62266-217-3
Print ISBN: 978-1493783717

Manufactured in the United States of America
First Edition October 2013

The author acknowledges the copyrighted or trademarked status and trademark owners of the following wordmarks mentioned in this work of fiction: Chevy, Chevrolet, Jeep, Dumpster, Victoria's Secret, Kool-Aid, Goodwill, "Love is In the Air"

For my little dog, Pip, who joined our family during the writing of this story. Thanks for rescuing me..

Chapter One

Mia Andale wasn't quick to smile, but she was grinning broadly as she opened the door to Marney Fields O'Neil, who stood on the cottage's tiny porch with a squirming Jack Russell terrier clutched in her arms.

"Hello, Charlie," Mia said.

"It figures you would greet the dog first."

"You know I'm always happy to see you."

Mia stepped back to allow them both inside. As soon as Marney released the dog, he took off like a shot, bouncing maniacally around the cottage's small living room.

"His only speed is fast," Marney mused wryly, giving her brown hair a toss. Then she handed Mia the large canvas tote bag that had been slung over her shoulder. "Here's his leash, bowl, and some food. I tucked T-R-E-A-T-S in there, too."

"Tr—"

"*Shh!*" Marney clapped a hand over Mia's mouth. "You think he's hyper now? You haven't seen anything yet."

Charlie finished inspecting the room and came back to sit at the women's feet. He gazed up at them, the picture of innocence, and cocked his head to one side. Mia's heart melted.

"Aww."

"Don't let his cuteness fool you," Marney warned on a laugh. "He can be a handful."

"Yes, but if not for him, you and Dell might not have kept getting together, and look where that led."

Marney's smile bloomed in full. "You make an excellent point."

Her friend had just married the sheriff after a whirlwind courtship and record-short engagement and was now leaving on her honeymoon, which was why Mia had volunteered to take over dog-sitting duty. This made the third stop for the infamous Mr. Bonaparte's equally infamous pooch. So far during Mr. B's extended trip overseas, Charlie also had stayed with their friend Gabrielle Wilson. Gabby too had wound up falling in love and was now Gabby Shepherd, wife of handsome software designer T.J. Shepherd.

Marney leaned down and patted Charlie's head. "Bye, boy. Don't let her do anything I wouldn't do." He let out a soft yip, almost as if he understood.

Mia, however, wasn't sure she did. "What's that supposed to mean?"

"Nothing. Be good." Marney pointed a finger at the dog.

"Charlie's going to be on his best behavior for me. Aren't you?" Mia said.

Was it her imagination or did the little dog wink?

"You just keep telling yourself that. Well, I'd love to stay and chat, but I have to run." Marney was halfway out the open front door when she called over her shoulder, "Oh, by the way, Charlie has a checkup with the vet at five-thirty today. Don't be late."

The door closed on Mia's shocked expression. By the time she made it to the porch, Marney was already in her car driving away. Tires actually squealed. Mia scowled. The only veterinarian in Chandler's Cove was Gideon Roth, hence Marney's speedy getaway.

Gideon was a prime specimen of a man with a muscular build, thick sandy hair, rich brown eyes that could undress a woman with a glance, and a mouth that could turn her most wanton fantasies into reality. Mia knew all of this firsthand.

Gideon Roth was her ex-boyfriend.

She'd broken up with him six months earlier. Marney and Gabby, as well as Jenny Travolini—the other woman who formed their close quartet of friends—had been surprised. And no wonder. Gideon was a prize. Not only gorgeous and gainfully employed, but smart, funny, and abundantly decent.

Mia's reason for dumping him? He'd said, "I love you."

Three little words that most women longed to hear. Not Mia. Especially when Gid had gotten down on one knee on Christmas Day and backed them up with a diamond engagement ring large enough to have its own ZIP code.

Panic had bubbled up, burning her like lava. God help her, for one foolish moment, hope had as well—a geyser's worth of it had shot up and then rained down on the old, painful memories. But nothing could wash away the past, which was why Mia had come to her senses.

Why did Gid have to go and ruin a really good thing with a declaration of love and a proposal of marriage?

Mia trusted neither.

She didn't trust people in general. With the exception of her three girlfriends, everyone who ever had mattered in her life had pulled a disappearing act. That included her mom and dad, six sets of foster parents, and even the social worker who'd promised she would find Mia a permanent home. Six placements and a decade later, Mia had finally aged out of the system—eighteen years old and completely alone. Now approaching thirty, she was still largely alone. Only this time, it was her choice.

She closed the door and blew out a breath. At her feet, Charlie whined as if sensing her change in mood.

"It's going to be okay," Mia said, feeling anything but.

Forty minutes later, she pulled her car into the veterinary clinic's parking lot. Charlie was riding shotgun, his hind feet on the passenger seat, front paws positioned on the dash just above the glove box. He yipped twice, as if to draw her gaze to the for sale sign that was rooted in the small patch of lawn that ran between the street and the lot. The dog needn't have bothered. Although the sign was an innocuous white with san serif navy and red lettering, it might as well have been blinking in neon. It had her attention all right.

Gideon was selling? When had that happened? Why? Unfortunately, she thought she knew the answer to at least one of those questions.

• • •

Even with the heads-up his receptionist had given him, Gideon felt caught off guard when Mia walked into the examination room with a leashed Charlie in tow. It had been awhile since he'd seen her. He figured she was avoiding him. Given his gut-punched reaction to seeing her now, he decided that was probably a good thing.

She'd always been petite, slim. She looked even thinner now in a plain white T-shirt and a pair of jeans that used to fit far more snuggly over her hips. *Fragile*. God, she would hate that description, as apt as it might be. According to her friends, since the breakup Mia had been putting in a lot of overtime at the flower shop that he knew she secretly hoped to own one day. He hadn't asked Gabby, Jenny or Marney about her, but they always volunteered information whenever he ran into them in town. Then they would stand around in awkward silence—sort of like how he and Mia were now as they faced one another in the sterile, white-tiled room.

Charlie was the first to "speak." At his sharp bark, Gideon crouched to give the dog's head a pat, scratching behind his ears for good measure. Glancing up at Mia, he nodded a greeting.

"Hello, Gid," she said.

Her voice was as soft and sexy as ever. Those wide-set blue eyes every bit as distrustful as they'd been during his last encounter with her, which meant that chip on her shoulder, the one he'd tried so desperately to dislodge, remained firmly in place.

If only…

He let the thought ripple away like rings from a stone skipping over water. The time for if onlys was past.

He undid the leash and straightened. "Come on up here, Charlie. Let's have a look at you."

He patted the exam table, but Charlie didn't budge. In

fact, the dog plunked down his rear end on the floor and whined pitifully.

"No shots today, pal," Gid promised and patted the table again. This time, Charlie leaped onto it. Gideon turned to Mia. "He's all caught up on his vaccinations, but there is the small matter of…" He cleared his throat.

Mia raised her brows and leaned in expectantly, bringing the well-remembered scent of lavender with her. Whether it was from the hours she put in at the flower shop or soap, he'd never been sure.

"Yes?"

When Gideon made a snipping motion with his fingers, Charlie let out of an indignant *woof!* and shook his head. Gid couldn't help chuckling. "I swear he knows exactly what I'm saying."

"So, he needs to be F-I-X-E-D?" Mia's tone turned hushed while she spelled. "Marney didn't mention it."

Gideon shrugged. "Probably because it's Bonaparte's call. I've been after him for awhile, ever since he adopted Charlie. In fact, the deed really should have been done before the shelter handed over the dog. That's the standard protocol. But…"

"Mr. B's not one to follow protocol," Mia inserted wryly. And wasn't that the truth?

No one in town knew much about the mysterious Mr. Bonaparte, other than that he lived in the largest mansion in the area, traveled extensively for business, and was rarely seen in public. Mia thought it odd that he had adopted a high-energy pet since he spent months at a time out of the country. Indeed, he wasn't scheduled to return from his latest trip for awhile. But she could see the terrier's appeal. All of her friends were smitten with the feisty dog.

"Yeah, well given Charlie's penchant for getting out and visiting the ladies, it's irresponsible to, um, leave the family jewels intact. Dogs aren't like us. They don't bother to use protection."

He'd been speaking in general terms when he'd said us, but color flooded Mia's face. She hadn't been shy when it came to sex, so her blush made Gid wonder if she was remembering how good it had been between them. God help him, he was. He cleared his throat.

"If you talk to Bonaparte, you might mention it."

"That's not likely, but sure."

She took a seat on a wheeled stool while Gid finished the checkup. Fifteen minutes later, Charlie was off the table and at the door whining, clearly eager to put the clinic behind him.

Mia stood to go, but Gideon wasn't quite done.

"He's healthy, but I see from his chart that he's gained a few pounds since his last visit." Tapping the clipboard, he added, "You might want to lay off the treats."

At the mention of the T-word, the pooch turned into a canine hurricane, twirling in ever-widening circles as he yipped excitedly. He knocked over the stainless steel trashcan, sent the wheeled stool Mia had been sitting on flying across the room, and was up and over the examining table three times before they were able to corral him.

Gideon lifted the dog and placed him in Mia's arms. One of his hands brushed her breast in the process, the touch so light and brief it shouldn't have mattered. They all went still, even Charlie.

I miss you. He almost said it out loud. He almost leaned

in, kissed those full lips of hers that knew how to drive him insane whenever they left his mouth.

"Why?" Mia whispered softly. Her eyes were clouded with confusion. At Gideon's frown, she blinked and he recognized the walls being erected once more. Her tone was no longer quite so reedy when she asked, "Why is there a for sale sign out front?"

Irritated, he replied, "Because I'm selling."

She frowned at the obvious and a line of impatience formed between her brows. There had been a time when Gideon would have been quick to smooth it away with the tip of one finger before moving on to the other tense parts of her body. He tucked his hands into the pockets of his white lab coat now and allowed them to curl into fists.

"You're selling the clinic?"

"My house, too."

"Why?" she asked again. Her tone was bewildered now. Hurt? He wanted to think so. Hell, his ego demanded it.

"We talked about this before Christmas," he reminded her. "The job offer out west." No small suburban clinic like this one but a big state-of-the-art facility tied to a prestigious university where he not only would have access to the latest research and advances in veterinary medicine, but be an adjunct professor. He'd been willing to pass it up before. Willing—hell, *happy*—to stay in Chandler's Cove. But now...

His tone was hollow when he added, "There's nothing to keep me here, Mia. You made sure of that."

Chapter Two

The spray of freesia refused to cooperate. Instead of simply plucking it out, Mia scuttled the entire arrangement and started from scratch. It was the third time she'd done so in the past hour.

"You do realize those flowers are slated for the afternoon delivery," Loretta Faust said from the doorway. At nearly sixty, the owner of the Posy Peddler remained active and healthy, but she no longer wanted to work the long hours the business required. She left those to Mia, who was only too happy to oblige, since she wanted to call the shop her own one day.

And since she no longer had Gid to spend her evenings with.

"I just want it to be perfect."

"It was fine the way it was."

"Yes, but it wasn't perfect," Mia replied.

Loretta sent her gaze skyward. They'd had this argument

before. "Just make sure it gets on the truck, okay?"

On the floor at Mia's feet, Charlie snorted softly before settling his head on his front paws.

"Not you, too," she told the dog. "There's nothing wrong with wanting things to be just right."

Half an hour later, she was placing the last sprig of greenery when she heard the floor boards creak.

"All done," she announced with a grin, pleased with her handiwork. When she looked up, however, it wasn't Loretta or the deliveryman who stood in the doorway. It was Gideon.

Her smile faded, and just for a moment she regretted that she wasn't wearing any makeup. She dipped her head, allowing her hair to fall forward, partially obscuring her face from view. From behind the long fringe of the bangs she was growing out, she said, "I wasn't expecting you."

Indeed, after their exchange at the veterinarian clinic the previous week, she figured he would go as far out of his way to avoid seeing her as she had to avoid seeing him.

"Yeah, I got that when you frowned." Charlie was on his feet, his wiry, white tail wagging madly as he trotted over to Gid to have his ears scratched. To the dog he said, "At least someone is happy to see me."

"So, what brings you here?" she asked.

Charlie had flopped down on his back, and Gid was down on one knee, giving the dog's belly a thorough rub. Without looking up, he said, "My mom's birthday is next week."

"What? No big family dinner?" she asked before she could think better of it.

Gid's family made the Waltons look dysfunctional. And even as she'd yearned to be part of such a loving, tight-knit clan, every time Mia had been in their company she'd been all the more aware of her own family's shortcomings.

"Actually, Sue is having everyone over," he replied, referring to his older sister. "But I've got to fly to San Diego to finalize some details at the new facility, so I won't make it. I'm taking Mom out for dinner when I get back, but I wanted to send a bouquet to the house."

The new facility. His dream job. The reminder of what awaited him on the West Coast caused her tone to be sharper than she intended when she said, "You could have ordered flowers over the phone."

"I could have." He did look up now. His tone was full of challenge when he asked, "Do you have a problem seeing me, Mia?"

"No. Why would I have a problem seeing you?" Okay, that came out defensive.

He straightened and stepped closer, leaving only the stainless steel prep table to separate them. Even with flowers perfuming the air, she caught a hint of the aftershave she'd given him for his birthday the previous fall. He was dressed in wrinkled cargo shorts and a faded T-shirt that sported the name of his college alma mater. It was just her bad luck that her mind decided to replay a scene from the previous summer when she'd helped him out of that very shirt.

They'd gotten caught in a downpour, after which they'd stumbled into her house, laughing and drenched. Gid had taken one look at the thin fabric plastered against her body and sobered. He'd traced a circle around one breast, causing its already erect nipple to tighten further through her sports bra. That was all it had taken to have Mia yanking off his sodden tee in desperation. They hadn't made it to the bedroom—or even to the couch half a dozen steps away in her living room. In his urgency, Gid had made love to her against the wall in the tiny foyer.

"I can't get enough of you," he'd told her afterward as the breath sawed from his lungs. "Even when we're old and gray, Mia, I won't have had my fill."

They were words that should have made her happy but instead had left her unnerved. Too many people in her life had made promises they could not keep. In a way, such words often had signaled the beginning of the end.

Mia crossed her arms as she shifted her weight to one hip. She couldn't bear to open herself up to the kind of pain she knew firsthand abandonment caused. It hadn't been wise to become so involved with Gid. She'd let things with him grow too serious and go on for too long. Ultimately, however, she deemed it wiser to reject than to wait around to be rejected.

Not that walking away from Gideon had been easy. But it had been necessary. Besides, he was better off without her. He deserved someone who was emotionally healthy and whole. Someone who wasn't afraid to love him back.

"You've been avoiding me," he said.

She shook her head in denial. "I've been busy."

"That's a handy excuse, Mia. Not to mention an overused one."

"It also happens to be true."

His eyes narrowed and she braced for a battle of words, mentally lining up her arguments. Instead, Gideon merely shrugged.

"Whatever."

Nothing got Mia's back up quicker than that one, three-syllable word. *Whatever* said, *I don't care.* It said, *what you have to say doesn't matter to me.* Extrapolated, it meant, *you don't matter to me.*

If she'd been thinking straight, she would have realized that her strong reaction to the word was exactly why Gid used it. He wanted to get a rise out of her. He wanted her to fight back. He wanted to pull out the volatile emotions that she tried to keep under lock and key. But seeing red blotted out the obvious.

"Are you calling me a liar?" she demanded as she came around the prep table.

In her flat shoes, the top of her head barely came to his shoulder. That didn't keep her from poking him in the chest.

Gid eyed the finger a moment before his gaze returned to hers. He replied, "This is a small town and I haven't bumped into you once in the past six months. Not once. Just sayin'."

His lips quirked, and it irritated her all the more that she still found his mouth to be so damned sexy. The man should be out of her system by now. Forgotten. But no matter how hard she tried to banish them, those memories of the two of them together held on stubbornly, pressing to the forefront at the most inconvenient times.

Including right then.

"You're staring at my mouth," he said.

The best defense was a good offense, Mia decided. She offered no apology. Instead, she tilted her head to one side and noted casually, "I've always liked your mouth. It's one of your best features."

"There are others you like even better as I recall."

Heat didn't merely shoot up her spine at his soft-spoken

reply. It flooded into parts of her body that had been stone cold since their breakup.

Still, she managed to keep her tone casual. "That's true. Sex was never an issue for us."

He nodded. "Just commitment."

"I'm not going to feel guilty."

"Is that what you were feeling just now?"

His lips quirked again, telling her he didn't buy it. She ignored the remark and pressed her point.

"I told you going in what my…my limits were — live for the moment, don't plan for the future. I explained everything, Gid. I made it clear. And you said you were okay with it. You" — she poked his chest again for emphasis — "You were the one who changed the rules."

His lazy smile faded as the first licks of anger flared in his eyes. He didn't lose his temper often, or at least he'd rarely done so in her presence. Not since the first argument they'd had after a month into dating when she'd sidled out of reach as soon as he'd raised his voice. The pity she'd seen in his eyes as realization dawned still had the power to mortify.

Well, he was mad now.

"Okay. I did. I changed the rules. But we weren't playing a damned game, Mia. We were in a relationship, and relationships develop over time."

"Or they end." She swallowed, tipped up her chin. "And ours ended."

"Are you over me, Mia?"

She couldn't bring herself to answer the question, in part because saying yes would be a bald-faced lie, and he'd already called her a liar. So she turned the question around.

"Are you over me?"

He snorted before replying, "I want to be."

"It's not the same thing," she murmured.

"Tell me about it."

Gid stepped closer, crowding her personal space in a way only suited to lovers or enemies. She was no longer the former, and didn't want to be the latter. Forget going on the offensive. It was time to retreat.

"About those flowers…" she began.

Before she could step back, though, his head dipped down, and he kissed her. The initial brush of his lips was tentative, the eyes that regarded her unblinking. He drew back a fraction of an inch, waited for her to tell him no or to stop—words she should have had at the ready, but they refused to be spoken. When she remained silent, his mouth covered hers again, and Mia closed her eyes on a sigh.

The kiss deepened. She rose on tiptoe, hands braced on his chest as their bodies drew flush. Underneath her palms she could feel Gid's heart beating every bit as erratically as her own. She remembered this. Oh, yeah. And she missed it. Standing in the circle of his arms, she felt safe, cherished, loved. If those were the only emotions, everything would have been fine. But she also felt sick with fear that he would leave her.

She ended the kiss abruptly. She'd gone down this road once. It was a dead end. And that was for the best.

"Mia—"

She shook her head. When she started to back away, though, Gid grabbed her wrist. Nothing about his action was painful or threatening. His hold was loose and could have been broken easily. Charlie was on his feet and surprised them both by growling, the fur just behind his collar spiking up in menace.

Gid released her. "Looks like you have a protector."

It was on the tip of her tongue to say she didn't need one. She could take care of herself. Gid knew it, too. She could tell by the way his eyes narrowed.

"Don't."

"What?" she asked innocently.

"Don't give me more crap about how you don't need anyone. It's not you against the world, Mia. It might have been at one time but it doesn't have to be that way now. It's okay to let someone else have your back."

Loner. Distrustful. Has difficulty forming meaningful attachments. The assessment she'd spied long ago in her caseworker's file rang in her head.

"I know that." At his raised brows, she added, "My friends have my back."

Jenny, Marney, Gabby—they were the only people around whom Mia felt comfortable dropping her guard and even that had taken a long, long time.

Gid shook his head. His expression was resigned. "I was your friend, too, you know."

She swallowed, both stunned and shamed by the accusation she saw in his eyes. She'd never thought of their relationship in those terms, but it was true, she realized now. They had been friends as well as lovers, which perhaps explained why she missed him so damned much.

"Gid, I'm sor—"

He waved a hand, silencing her. "I don't want another apology. You've offered enough of those. What I want, what I need…" He took a deep breath, let it out slowly. "What I need are two dozen roses."

Flowers. They were back to discussing business. Why did she feel disappointed? She should be relieved.

"Sure." She worked up a polite smile. Stepping around him, she said in her most professional voice, "Let me just grab an order form, and we'll get everything taken care of."

• • •

Gid followed Mia out of the back room, irritated anew when his gaze was drawn to the subtle sway of her slim hips. If it had been only attraction, he might have been able to shrug it off. But it went deeper than that. Much deeper. God help him. He still loved her every bit as desperately as he had the night he'd proposed marriage and had received her "thanks, but no thanks" reply.

Actually, her response hadn't been quite as tidy as that, but the end result was the same. She'd turned him down flat.

He wanted Mia out of his system, but she remained as much a part of him as the air he breathed and was seemingly as vital.

Naively, he'd thought that following through with his plans to sell the practice and move across the country would exorcise her. Then she'd walked into his clinic a week earlier and, ever since, he'd done nothing but think about her. The quasi peace he'd cobbled together had shattered once again.

Coming here had been a mistake. As she'd so annoyingly pointed out, he could have called in his order. For that matter, he could have used a different florist, one closer to his childhood home in Chicago. But he'd gotten in his Jeep and had come here because…because he was a freaking idiot.

Well, even idiots had pride. Gid scraped up what he could find of his while Mia retrieved the order pad and a pen from the front counter.

"So, roses," she said, making a note.

"Two dozen."

"White." They said it at the same time.

She glanced up. "They're your mom's favorite."

"Right. Have the card read—"

"*With love from your favorite son.*" One side of Mia's mouth lifted.

It was a standing joke. It was how Gid, who had three older brothers, always signed cards to his mother.

When he frowned, Mia sobered. "Or did you want it to say something else?"

"No. That will do."

He paid with cash, offered Charlie one last ear scratch, and started for the door. Two steps from it he stopped, turned.

"Did you forget something?" she asked.

Leave it be, he commanded silently. *Just let it go.* But the question that was torturing him tumbled out anyway. "I'm just wondering how it is you can know me so well, Mia, and still not trust me."

"I…I…" She swallowed, glanced away.

"Exactly. You can't say you trust me any more than you could tell me you love me."

With a shake of his head, he stormed out of the shop, irritated with both of them.

Chapter Three

"You're quiet tonight," Jenny noted later that week as she and Mia had drinks at Pablo's Pub. "Everything okay?"

"Sure." Mia reached for her wine. Before taking a sip, she said, "Why wouldn't everything be okay?"

"Come on. We're better friends than that," Jenny remarked. "Tell me what's bothering you."

The reminder of her friendship with Jenny stirred anew the emotions Gid had kicked up during their confrontation at the flower shop.

"I trust you," she said sharply.

Jenny blinked before her eyes rounded. "I...I didn't mean to imply—"

"No, no." Mia shook her head and sighed heavily. "I'm sorry for jumping down your throat. I guess I'm a little... touchy."

"Gideon?"

"How did you know?"

"Because I know *you,* and because Gid is the only person who makes you question yourself and your decisions."

Mia sighed, took another sip of her wine. "He came into the flower shop a few days ago."

Jenny's smile was soft. "He came to see you."

"He didn't come to see me. It was business. He ordered flowers for his mother. Her birthday is coming up."

"And he couldn't have done that over the phone?" A point Mia herself had made. "Or had his receptionist do it? Or have used another florist? Please." Jenny snorted. "He came to see *you*, Mia. And the reason he came to see you is because he still loves you."

As always, hearing the L-word had panic bubbling up her throat.

She swallowed hard. "Well, nothing has changed, so it was a wasted trip on his part."

"Did you tell him that?" Jenny looked sad.

"Not in so many words, but he knew." Mia plucked at one corner of the napkin under her wineglass as she tortured herself for the millionth time with Gid's parting shot. "He said I don't trust him."

"You don't."

She glanced up sharply. "And it's a good thing, isn't it? He's leaving me." She cleared her throat, embarrassed by the telling remark. "He's leaving Chandler's Cove."

"Mia, he's leaving because you turned down his proposal of marriage. Gid would have passed on the job opportunity out west to stay in Chandler's Cove with you. He knows this is your home and where you want to stay."

"They offered him his dream job, Jenny."

"Yes, and what does it tell you about his feelings for you

that he was willing to pass on it to start a life here with you?"

"So he said."

Jenny's gaze turned pointed as she replied dryly, "And you wonder why he claims you don't trust him?"

On her way home later that evening, Mia mulled Jenny's words. Her friend had a point, and it wasn't the first time she'd made it. In fact, Jenny, Gabby, and Marney had made similar points several times since Mia and Gid's breakup. They'd even gone so far as to stage an intervention of sorts right after the holidays hoping to get Mia to re-examine her motives for scuttling a good relationship with a good man.

"You can't let the past dictate your future," Gabby had told her that day five months ago as the women walked to their cars in the parking lot of their favorite coffee shop, The Cuppa Café.

That was easy advice to dole out, but very difficult to follow when one had a past like Mia's.

"Charlie!" she called as she let herself into her house. She needn't have bothered. He was in the foyer, tongue lolling out. He didn't jump up and down and start barking excitedly the way he usually did, though. Rather, he rose on his hind legs, rested his front paws against her thigh, and licked her hand. His welcome, though subdued, was balm for her soul nonetheless.

"Hey, boy." She rubbed his head.

It was nice to come home to someone. Memories of opening her door to find Gid already inside crowded her mind. On days when she worked late at the flower shop, he often let himself in with the key she'd given him and started dinner. Of the two of them, he was the better cook, which wasn't saying much. Scrambled eggs and one-pot meals were his specialties. The food might not have caused her mouth to water, but the man always had.

"I'm not going to miss him," she told Charlie. The dog looked as convinced as she felt.

If she were home more, Mia would have considered getting a pet of her own, but it wasn't practical to take an animal to work with her all the time as she'd been doing with Charlie. Nor would it be a good idea to leave one home alone—even for shorter stretches, she decided, looking past the dog to the mess scattered across the living room floor. In the two hours since she'd dropped Charlie at home to meet up with Jenny, it looked like a tornado had touched down. Neither Gabby nor Marney had mentioned Charlie's predilection for home destruction. Then again, they'd rarely—if ever—left him unattended.

"What have you been into?" she murmured.

Garbage was the obvious guess, since she spotted an empty egg carton amid the debris. But there was a plastic milk jug from the recycling bin, too and...was that black lace? She moved closer to inspect, eyes widening in disbelief. Indeed it was black lace, and some of it still clung to the mauled remnant of what she deduced to be an underwire.

"You ate my bra?" she asked incredulously.

Mia had hand-washed the undergarment that very morning and hung it over the shower curtain rod in the bathroom to dry. She should have known that for a dog with as much spring in his hind legs as Charlie it wouldn't be out of the way.

He belched in response and then threw up on the toes of her shoes. Afterward, he moaned pitifully and plopped down on the floor. Garbage and a side helping of lingerie had taken their toll.

"Oh, Charlie."

In the time it took her to clean up the mess, Charlie continued to whine and hadn't moved. More than anything, his lethargy had her concerned, especially since she'd never found the bra's other underwire. Even though it was nearly ten o'clock at night, Mia debated for only a moment before dialing Gid's home number.

"I'm sorry to bother you at this late hour," she said when he answered.

"Mia?" He sounded surprised, and her traitorous heart kicked out an extra beat when he asked in a voice laced with concern, "Are you okay?"

If she said no, even after everything that had passed between them, would he still get in his Jeep and be over right away? She didn't have the courage to find out.

"I'm fine. It's Charlie. He ate my...um, some stuff he shouldn't have, and now he doesn't look so good." She cast a glance at the dog. Upon hearing his name, not even his tail twitched.

"Has he regurgitated any of it?"

"Yes, but that doesn't seem to have made him feel much better."

"I'll meet you at the clinic in fifteen minutes," Gid offered without hesitation.

"Thanks, Gid. I really appreciate it."

"It's all in a day's work," he replied.

• • •

Was that *all* it was? Gid wondered as he tugged on a pair of jeans and, after giving it the sniff test, pulled over his head the T-shirt he'd found on the floor of his bedroom. He didn't want to see Mia. He wasn't a glutton for punishment. But he knew he wouldn't be dashing up to the clinic after hours to attend another emergency with such a sense of anticipation.

Mia's older model blue Chevy was in the parking lot in the spot closest to the door. She was out of the car, a limp Charlie in her arms, even before he had shifted the Jeep into park. Worry caused her features to pinch.

"Has he thrown up again?" he asked as he unlocked the main door and deactivated the alarm system.

"No, but he was making heaving sounds all the way over here."

In the examining room, she placed Charlie on the table. He whined pathetically and the look he shot Gid said, "Help me," as clearly as if he'd spoken the words aloud.

"Hey, fella." He put a stethoscope against a few places on Charlie's belly and listened. The rumbling he heard was music to his ears. "Things are moving around, which is a good sign." He glanced up at Mia. "What exactly did he eat?"

"What didn't he eat might be the better question," she replied wryly. "He got into the garbage can in the kitchen. I think there might have been some chicken bones in there from last night's dinner. And he hit the recycling bin. He chewed up a plastic milk jug pretty good. And..." She glanced away before mumbling, "He ate one of my bras."

Gid wasn't sure he heard her right. "Excuse me?"

"He ate one of my bras."

"Ah. I see. Which one?"

"An underwire," she mumbled.

"The black lacey one from Victoria's Secret?"

She folded her arms. "That would be the one."

Well, no one could fault the dog's taste, Gid thought. That stingy bit of lace had always looked plenty appetizing to him, too. He forced his mind back to the matter at hand.

"How much of it did he eat?"

"I only found one underwire attached to a piece of lace."

"Ooh. That's not good. The wire could perforate his intestines or cause a blockage. Either scenario would be serious." Gid palpated the dog's distended stomach. Charlie moaned.

"But he's going to be okay. I mean, you can fix him, right?"

Mia looked up at Gid with such hope shimmering in her eyes. With such...was it trust? He wanted to tell her that he could. He wanted to tell her that he would move heaven and earth for her.

But what he said was, "I'll do everything within my power to help him, but I won't make any promises that I'm not sure I can keep."

He wasn't only talking about the dog. Did she understand that? Her brow furrowed a moment before she nodded.

Gideon scooped up the dog. "Let's get some X-rays so we can see exactly what's we're dealing with."

Chapter Four

It was a very long night.

Mia passed most of it sitting on the floor beside the little bed Gid had made up for Charlie out of towels. The tiles were cold thanks to the air conditioning. Even though she hadn't asked for one, Gid gave her a blanket, settling it around her shoulders with the same sort of tenderness and caring he'd exhibited with his four-legged patient.

Thankfully, the X-rays revealed nothing ominous. If Charlie had swallowed the underwire, he'd chewed it up into pieces small enough to pass through his intestinal tract.

Before finally settling down and falling asleep, the dog vomited twice more, emptying his beleaguered belly of an interesting assortment of inedible objects. Both times, Gid had sifted patiently through the mess, unfazed.

"I liked that bra," she thought she heard him mutter as he'd pushed a scrap of soggy black lace to the side with the tip of a pen.

Mia fell asleep not long after Charlie did. When she woke, she was no longer alone on the floor with the dog. Gid was seated next to her, his long legs stretched out. Her head was pillowed on his right shoulder. His temple rested against her crown. The warmth she felt wasn't from the blanket, although he'd apparently tucked it under her chin. The man radiated warmth, inside and out.

She allowed herself to luxuriate in it and breathed deep to take in his scent. She couldn't smell aftershave or even a hint of the soap he'd scrubbed with after tending to the dog. But she recognized his smell. Indeed, everything about this moment was familiar, comforting, compelling. It terrified her how deeply she wished they could stay like that, caught halfway between the dreaminess of waking and the stark reality of day. But that was impossible. Even before Charlie stirred and roused Gid, Mia knew time was up.

"*Woof!*"

Charlie was already on his feet as Gid lifted his head. The little dog stretched. The man yawned. Mia held her breath.

"Looks like someone's feeling better this morning," Gid said.

The hand he pushed through his hair left it a sexy, rumpled mess. She couldn't resist reaching over to smooth it down, just as she had done dozens of times in the past.

Gid's expression grew serious at her touch. He reached for her hand as she drew it away, captured it and held on tight.

"I always liked waking up to you," he said quietly.

Her heart squeezed, the sensation at once painful and pleasing. She'd always liked waking up to Gid, too. These past several months, she'd been so lonely. She missed seeing his face at first light, his jaw rough with stubble, his mouth soft and welcoming. She was leaning toward him when Charlie barked again.

"*Woof*!" The dog padded to the door and continued yipping.

"I think he wants out," Mia said wryly.

"His timing stinks," Gid muttered as he rose. He was still holding her hand, which he used to help her to her feet. "Come on."

Together, the three of them went outside. Even though it was barely past dawn, the temperature was already in the seventies. It was going to be a hot day. Humid, too, at least until the sun was at full strength and the mist burned off. Before opening the door, Gid had slipped on Charlie's leash as a precaution. He needn't have bothered. The dog wasn't moving as fast as he usually did. His steps were slower, more tentative, but as his wagging tail clearly attested, he was on the mend.

Charlie lifted his leg and did his business on the shrub closest to the door.

"Let's try something," Gid murmured before saying, "Hey, boy, want a treat?"

The offer didn't turn Charlie into the whirling dervish of old, but the dog's triangular ears perked up and Mia swore he grinned.

"I think he's ready for a meal. I'd recommend giving him something plain to start and not too much." He handed her the leash.

"Are you hungry?" she asked Gid, her gaze still on the dog.

"That depends."

She chanced a look at him. "On?"

"Are you asking me to breakfast?"

She moistened her lips. "If I say yes?"

He regarded her for what seemed like ages. "Then I'm starving."

• • •

Gid had to close up the clinic before he could get in his Jeep and head to Mia's house. He almost hoped he would change his mind. He was asking for trouble, spending time with her when she'd already made it clear they had no future together. But he couldn't stay away. She was like a magnet that way, always drawing him in. When he arrived at her house fifteen minutes later, he knocked rather than just going in as he would have in the past. He heard Charlie barking a moment before Mia opened the door.

Her smile was uncertain and slightly embarrassed as she invited him inside. "I started the coffee already."

The scent of French roast, which was most welcome after a night of little sleep, greeted them in the kitchen. Gid got two mugs from the cupboard and filled them, adding a dash of creamer to Mia's, while she puttered in front of the stove, cracking eggs into a pan where butter already had melted.

The silence stretched, broken only by the sound of sizzling eggs and Charlie gobbling up the dry dog food Mia had put in his dish.

"So, when are Marney and Dell back from their honeymoon?" he asked, hoping to end the awkwardness.

"Next week." Mia nodded in Charlie's direction.

"Despite last night's excitement, I'm going to miss him."

"You should get a dog."

Her expression softened. "You know I would if I were home more."

"I think Loretta would let you bring one to the shop. She obviously has no problem with Charlie being there."

"That's only because he's Mr. Bonaparte's dog." Mia chuckled. Mr. B.'s reputation for both his wealth and his wrath were equally known around town, despite the fact the man himself wasn't around much. "Besides, she knows it won't be forever. Once Marney is home, she'll take Charlie back. If Gabby doesn't return to town first. She and T.J. are in California right now visiting his office there."

Gid sipped his coffee. "Well, once you own the shop, you can do as you please."

"Yes."

He watched a grin spread across her face and doubted she knew she was smiling.

"Has Loretta made any more noise about retiring?"

"Not exactly, but she comes in less and less frequently these days, and she knows I want to buy the business eventually."

"You finally talked to her?" Before their breakup, Gid had been after Mia to put her cards on the table with her employer and make her desire known.

"More like she talked to me." The smile turned circumspect. "Apparently I'm not as hard to read as I like to think I am."

No, Mia wasn't hard to read. Not since the first time she'd cowered at Gid's raised voice. She'd been abused, abandoned, let down repeatedly. All of that became abundantly clear both in what she said and what she held back.

But knowing what she was thinking and figuring her out were two different things, as Gid had discovered the hard way. They'd met at the flower shop when he came in to order roses for his mother. Mia had waited on him. He'd flirted with her. She'd flirted back the next several times he made excuses to come in and see her. Finally, he'd asked her out, figuring his interest would cool once they'd slept together. The opposite occurred, surprising them both. It felt right, though, destined in a way no other relationship ever had. He'd settled in, aware of her baggage, even if she'd never shared with him a full account of her childhood. She'd seemed happy if still guarded.

She turned the eggs while he put a couple of slices of bread in the toaster. Then he set the table. They worked in the companionable silence of a couple, even if they no longer were one.

Once they were seated at the table, she said, "I can't thank you enough for helping Charlie last night."

Being on call for emergencies was part of his job description but Gid decided not to remind her. Instead, he said, "I'm glad it turned out to be nothing serious."

"Same here. I feel bad enough as it is. I can't imagine having to call Marney or Gabby and telling them something had happened to the dog or, worse still, having to call Mr. Bonaparte."

"These things happen, especially when an animal is in new surroundings. It wasn't your fault, but you might consider partitioning him off in a safe area the next time you're out." He ate a bite of egg. "Speaking of Bonaparte, have you ever met him?"

"No. Even Loretta, who knows everyone in town, told me the closest she's ever come to him was a couple years ago when his butler called the shop to place an order. What about you?"

"Never. The guy's been the town recluse ever since I came to Chandler's Cove right out of veterinary school and opened my practice."

"He doesn't bring in Charlie for appointments?"

"No. The butler again."

Mia frowned. "Charlie must get awfully lonely in that big house with nothing but a crusty old servant and a recluse for company. I guess that explains why he was always running loose when he got the chance—and why Gabby said the servants were thrilled when Mr. B. asked her to dog-sit while he was out of the country."

"If I suspected abuse or neglect, I would report it. But as you can see, the dog is in good health. He's also well socialized and takes to a leash. Someone's worked with him, trained him. It doesn't hurt that he's smart as a whip." Gid cast the dog a look. "Well, even if he doesn't have the enough sense not to eat a bra." Charlie barked in response.

The finished up their meal, engaging mainly in small talk. Even so, the time passed quickly. It was with regret that Gid glanced at his watch.

"I'd better shove off. I want to go home and take a shower before heading back to the clinic."

"You can take one here." From the look on her face, it was clear her offer surprised them both. "I mean, if you want. It would save you time."

In terms of practicality, she was right, but that wasn't why he nodded. He didn't want to leave yet.

Mia's house was built in the 1920s and while a number of renovations had been done to the quaint cottage over the years, the bathroom still sported the original pink and black tile work. She claimed that the period detail added character. She'd teased him once that men who were secure in their masculinity could handle the color, but when she handed him a pink towel just then, secure or not, Gid felt foolish.

Her wry smile told him she knew it.

"I think there's some of your shampoo under the sink. And a razor and shaving cream."

"You kept them?" he asked, a little surprised. Of course, he still had miscellaneous items of hers at his house, too.

"I…it seemed a waste to throw them out."

"I don't suppose I left any boxers behind?"

"Not that either I or Charlie has found."

He shrugged. "Guess I can go commando."

He'd been half teasing but was pleased to see her eyes widen a fraction of an inch. Interest. Need. Desire. One after the other, the emotions flashed there, emboldening him enough to close the distance between them. He dropped the towel, cupped her face in his hands and lowered his mouth to hers.

The kiss lasted maybe thirty seconds, a slow plunder that did nothing to take the edge off his mood. He waited for her to pull back, to step away and remind him their relationship was over. Instead she helped him out of his T-shirt.

They didn't speak, which was just as well. He didn't want to know what was going through her mind just then. For that matter, he refused to heed the warning that was blaring siren-like in his own. Instead, he relieved Mia of her blouse, taking the buttons slowly before peeling the two sides open as if he was unwrapping the last gift of Christmas. Since it was a good bet this would be the last chance he ever got to make love to her, he was going to savor it.

The bra she wore was white cotton and fastened in the front. He found it every bit as sexy as the black lace one the dog had eaten. He nuzzled the soft flesh that mounded ever so slightly from the unadorned cups, before undoing the clasp and brushing her nipples with the pads of his thumbs. Her breasts might be small, but they were beautiful and, best of all, sensitive.

Her moan was all the encouragement he needed to follow up with his tongue. Her head fell backward. Her hands fisted in his hair. Her breathing turned to ragged panting. Gid knew what she liked. That was the advantage of having been lovers. He knew which places to kiss, which to caress, just where to run his tongue to elicit the most pleasure.

He might have wanted to go slow. Mia, however, had other ideas. She reached between them and unbuttoned his shorts. An instant later, he felt the zipper give way and then she was pushing the shorts down his hips, followed by his boxers. He did the same to her shorts and panties. Then, hands on her bottom, he pulled her against his erection and kissed her again.

"Bedroom?" she managed to ask.

He grunted his ascent.

The dog was waiting in the hallway. Gid swore Charlie was grinning. When he tried to follow them into the bedroom, Gid blocked the way.

"Sorry, pal. Find something else to entertain yourself for the next half hour or so."

Gid closed the door and turned to find Mia reclining on the bed. She looked gorgeous, a feast for a man who had been starving for months.

"Half hour?" Mia asked, one eyebrow cocked.

"Or so," he repeated, coming to join her.

• • •

Mia and Gid both wound up being late for work. Since she was the one expected to open the shop, she had no one to answer to. Except herself and on matters that had nothing to do with punctuality.

"Don't look at me like that," she told Charlie as she began work on a hand-tied bouquet of Stephanotis.

The blooms were as expensive as they were fragile. They were for a wedding the following day. He continued to stare at her anyway, and she swore his expression was just shy of damning.

"It doesn't change anything," she went on. "And Gid knows that."

His exit after they'd made love told her so. He'd made no declarations, no promises. All he'd said was, "I really have to leave now."

Then he'd levered off the mattress to find his clothes. The offer of a shower that had started everything was forgotten. Once he was dressed, he came back to the bed, kissed Mia on the forehead, and left.

She still wasn't sure how she felt about that, despite her claims to the contrary to Charlie.

Would Gid call? The question crept past her defenses. Her hand tightened on the bouquet.

"He doesn't need to call," she muttered aloud. "I don't give a damn if he calls. In fact, it would be best if he doesn't."

Charlie settled his head on his front paws, his expression unchanged.

"It was just sex," she told the dog.

But then Mia swallowed and her eyes blurred. When her vision cleared, she knew the delicate Stephanotis wasn't the only thing bruised.

Chapter Five

A week passed and Mia didn't see Gid. Nor did she hear from him. But his scent lingered on her pillowcase and she couldn't fall asleep for wanting him.

The scent would fade and these feelings would pass, she told herself. She would get used to being without him again, just as she had after their breakup. Really, he was doing her a favor by staying away. Which was why it made no sense at all that she scheduled an appointment for Charlie on the very day that Marney and Dell were due back from their honeymoon. As mortifying as it was to admit, the dog gave her the perfect excuse to see Gid.

When he walked into the exam room, he was all business. No intimate glances, no fleeting caresses. After offering a polite smile and the standard greeting, he said, "So, what brings you and Charlie here today? He hasn't eaten any more undergarments, I hope."

"No." Her laughter was strained, laced with nerves. She

could only hope Gid hadn't noticed. "But he seems a little less, well, hyper than usual. Do you think anything could still be in his system?"

Gid studied her a moment before giving the dog his full attention. "Has he been going to the bathroom on a regular basis?"

"Yes."

"Any more vomiting?"

"No."

"How has his appetite been?"

"Good. The same as before, I guess."

Gid palpated the dog's stomach, after which he gave Charlie a playful rubdown and declared, "Everything feels normal. I don't detect any hard spots in his abdomen. I really don't think there's any need for another X-ray at this point since he's eating and voiding as usual."

"Oh, okay. I just wanted to be sure."

Finally, Gid met her eye again. "Playing it safe?" he asked, leaving her to wonder if he meant with the dog or with him. When she said nothing, he asked, "So, when are Marney and Dell due back?"

"This afternoon. The house is going to be quiet tonight," she remarked before she could think better of it.

"Are you going to miss him?"

"I am."

"Nothing worse than a quiet house."

She nodded, not sure of the proper response.

He stuffed his hands into the pockets of his white lab coat. "I'm here till seven tonight finishing up some paperwork. I could stop by Luigi's and bring you a pizza on my way home from the clinic," he said.

She swallowed. "You would do that?"

"I would."

"Thin crust?"

"If that's what you prefer."

Gid, a born and raised Chicagoan, naturally was a deep dish guy when it came to his pizza. Thin crust was for New Yorkers, or so he'd claimed the first time Mia had ordered it while they were on a date.

"You've always been so good at compromising," she murmured. And wasn't that true? Her heart squeezed.

"Thin crust." He shrugged. "It's a small sacrifice to make."

Yes, but they both knew he'd been willing to make much bigger ones where Mia was concerned. California. A dream job at a state-of-the-art facility attached to one of the most renowned schools of veterinary medicine in the country. And a position on its faculty.

Gid's eyes had lit with excitement when he'd told her the details of the job offer the previous summer, even if he'd tried to feign indifference when she'd asked if he was going to take it.

"Nah. It's nice to be asked, but I've got everything I want right here." He'd pulled her close, kissed her breathless.

He'd been willing to stay in the small Midwestern town where Mia had made friends who were her only family and had begun to sink down roots for the first time in her life. He'd never wavered in his decision until after she'd broken off their relationship. She'd been the one with all of the doubts.

Her heart squeezed again, this time painfully. "You know, deep dish sounds good to me."

He blinked in surprise. "Since when?"

She lifted her shoulders. She had no rationale to offer. Compromise didn't come as easily for her as it did for him. Her smile trembled.

"It just does."

· · ·

"Something's different about you," Marney declared the moment she walked through the cottage's door.

"I'm wearing makeup," Mia deadpanned.

"So, I see. But that's not it." Marney tossed her dark curls over her shoulder and tapped her lips. "You look…happy."

"Gee, thanks."

"Seriously. There's a twinkle back in your eyes, almost like you…Oh, my God!"

Mia turned away, but Marney wasn't letting her off the hook.

"You had sex."

Charlie barked, as if responding to Marney's statement.

Rather than deny it, Mia said, "I am allowed, you know."

"With Gid," Marney announced smugly.

"How do you know it was with Gid? The flower shop has a hot new delivery guy. I could be doing it with him."

"Are you?"

Mia huffed out a sigh. "Okay, it was Gid. So?"

"Details. I want details," Marney said, setting her purse aside and taking a seat on the couch. "Are you back together?"

"Not exactly."

"Do you *want* to be back together?"

Mia swallowed. "I want things to be the way they were...
before."

"Relationships evolve, honey. Consider how Dell and I
got started."

Hadn't Gid said that very same thing?

"I don't like change," she said quietly and settled on to
the cushion next to her friend.

"Change doesn't have to be bad. I never thought I would
find someone like Dell. And Gabby can attest that love is
worth the risk."

"Gid took the job in California. His house is on the
market, and so is his clinic. He's leaving Chandler's Cove."

"I know." Marney took Mia's hand in both of hers. The
diamond ring on the left one caught the light and seemed
to emphasize her friend's words when she added, "But he's
not leaving *you*, honey. There's a difference. Gid would stay
if you wanted him to. That man would do anything for you.
He loves you."

Mia swallowed. She didn't feel sick or panicked, which
she supposed a therapist would say was a step in the right
direction. But she was a long way from feeling comfortable
with the idea of commitment and capable of the kind of
trust it entailed. Would she ever?

"What can I do?" she asked.

"That's for you to decide, but I will give you this bit of
advice—don't listen to your head. Listen to your heart."

Marney left not long after that. Charlie stayed.

"I think Dell and I could use a few more days alone, if
you don't mind?"

"You're transparent, you know."

"What do you mean?" Marnie replied, eyes wide with

innocence.

"You think the dog might give me a good reason to go and see Gid."

"That's merely a bonus. I just want time alone with my man."

. . .

What was he getting himself into? Gid was still asking himself that question when he parked in the driveway behind Mia's car and carried the pizza box up to the front door.

A flurry of excited barking followed his knock. Mia opened the door with Charlie in her arms and a sheepish smile on her face.

"Marney and Dell didn't get back?" Gid asked.

"Actually, they did, but Marney asked me to keep the dog for a little longer."

"Ah," he said when Mia's gaze darted away. "The honeymoon continues, I take it."

"Apparently. Come on in. Want a beer?" she asked as they made their way to the kitchen.

"That sounds good."

"I thought we could eat on the back patio, if that's okay? It's so nice out this evening."

Something seemed different about her. He couldn't put his finger on exactly what.

"Sure," he said.

Mia set down the dog and grabbed plates, napkins, utensils, and two long-necked bottles of beer before heading out the back door. Her yard was fenced in white pickets and surprisingly large given how small the house was. Charlie dashed around like a lunatic, lifting his leg on a lilac bush and two other shrubs before returning to the patio. His nails clicked on the red brick pavers that were edged in moss, the sound an appropriate accompaniment to birds chirping and the swelling buzz of cicadas.

It would be a couple of hours yet before the sun set. In the meantime, its rays filtered though the leaves of an enormous oak tree that kept the yard mostly shaded. They sat at the wrought iron bistro set that he recalled Mia telling him she'd received from her friends as a housewarming present.

When he opened the lid on the box, she smiled.

"Half deep dish *and* half thin crust. Another compromise," she murmured.

"Not really. The thin crust is for me. I've become a convert," he admitted, and then narrowed his eyes. "Of course, if you tell anyone I said that, I'll deny it."

"Of course."

He reached for a slice of thin crust. She took deep dish. When he glanced up, she smiled. "I have a confession to make. I sort of like deep dish."

"Yeah?"

"It's not real pizza, mind you. You don't need a knife and a fork for real pizza. But it's good in its own way."

He nodded. "I can accept that."

They ate in silence for a few minutes. Charlie rose on his hind legs and begged until Mia made a shooing motion.

"You know the rule. No people food. Go chase a squirrel or something," she told him.

He plopped down on the pavers and whined instead.

"Your yard looks nice," Gid told her. She had a way

with plants, an eye for arranging them in the flowerbeds to highlight their beauty, which was no surprise given her profession. He pointed to a mound of dirt that broke the flow of pink and white blooms. "Well, except for that spot over there. Charlie?"

Mia nodded. "He uprooted half a flat of impatiens before I got him to stop."

"Jack Russells are diggers by nature. They were bred to hunt and root foxes out of their dens."

"Gee, now someone tells me," she grumbled good-naturedly, and cut off a small piece of pizza. Before popping it in her mouth, she said, "Speaking of flowers, how did your mother like the roses?"

"She loved them. Of course, she would have preferred to have me there but…" He shrugged.

"I guess she'll have to get used to you missing family gatherings."

Gid frowned. He would have to get used to it as well. But he couldn't stay here, so close to Mia, yet separated by a gulf too wide for even love to span. He'd go insane.

"I'll fly in for holidays and such. And Mom is already talking about how nice it will be to visit me in sunny California when the weather turns inhospitable here."

Gid's mother may have lived in Chicago for more than three decades but she remained a Southern girl at heart. And she'd never acclimated to the weather.

Mia laughed. "I can just hear her saying that. Maybe she and your dad will move out to San Diego now that they're both retired."

"Nah. As much as she complains about the wind and cold, Chicago is home. Her roots are here."

Mia nodded. "I can understand that."

He took a bite of pizza, washed it down with a drink of beer, all the while considering the implications of the invitation he wanted to extend. "I'm having dinner with her and Dad tomorrow night to make up for missing the party. You could come. I know my mom would love to see you."

"I would love to see her, too."

"So?"

"Okay."

"Yeah? Terrific. I'll pick you up around four. That will give us time to visit for a little while before we eat."

"I'd like that."

They finished eating as evening fell. It was a pleasant night to be outside. The play of the fading light over her face was mesmerizing.

"God, you're beautiful."

He half expected her to deny the compliment. In the year they'd dated, she'd never learned to accept them gracefully. Instead, he swore her eyes turned bright as she replied, "You make me feel beautiful, Gid."

The thud he felt was his heart. He'd patched it up as best he could since Christmas, but he doubted it would ever mend completely. Especially now.

Chapter Six

It wasn't wise, but Gid stayed the night, and the next night after they returned from dinner with his parents. And he stayed the night after that as well. He never planned on doing so, but he wasn't able to resist Mia, especially when she smiled. She seemed more open, more generous with her feelings. Or maybe he just needed to believe that something fundamental about her and their relationship had changed.

Meanwhile, he felt the ominous press of time as it ticked down to the day of his departure.

Two weeks after he'd stayed that first night, he woke to feel the familiar weight of her arm curved over his chest. Her breathing was deep and even. He levered up on one elbow and studied her. In the meager light that made it through the gap in the curtains, her face looked relaxed, peaceful. Was she happy too? More than anything, he wanted that for her. Hell, he wanted that for both of them.

At the moment, however, he wasn't sure what he was

feeling besides apprehensive. As much as Mia preferred not to think about the future as it pertained to a relationship, Gid needed to know where they were heading. Not only because of the immediacy of his situation, but because that was the way he was wired. She stirred and her eyelids flickered a moment before opening fully.

"Morning," she said. She smiled up at him.

At the base of the bed, Charlie perked up his ears and his tail began to wag. Marney and Dell still hadn't come to claim him.

"She's talking to me," Gid told the dog before returning his attention to Mia. "Good morning."

"I thought you said you couldn't stay last night. Something about having business first thing this morning."

"Yeah, but every time I tried to leave, you threw an arm or leg over me."

"I did not."

He glanced meaningfully at her arm.

"Oh." She laughed. "You're not fooling me. You wanted to stay."

"Yeah. I did." He kissed her forehead. "I don't like skulking out of here in the dark. It's bad enough in the morning. Your neighbors are starting to talk, by the way. They think we're back together."

"Busybodies."

Gid banished humor from his tone when he asked, "Are we, Mia?"

"Gid—"

She started to rise. He pressed her back onto the pillow with an urgent kiss.

"Are we?" he asked again. "After the last time, I told

myself I wasn't going to push, but I need to know."

"You're moving to California, Gid."

He inhaled deeply, feeling the way a skydiver must as he prepared to fling himself out of a plane. Would his chute open this time?

"And if I weren't?" he asked quietly.

"What do you mean?" Her expression had turned wary. He needed to believe that was a good sign.

"Just answer the question. If I weren't going to California, if I were staying here in Chandler's Cove, would we be back together?"

"But you *are* leaving," she persisted. "Your house, the veterinary clinic, they're both for sale, Gid. And you've accepted the job. You start in less than two months."

This time, when Mia tried to get up, he let her. She pulled her legs up under her chin and wrapped her arms around them. The gesture was protective. The dark hair that fell around her shoulders curtained her face from view. She was shutting down, closing herself off. Meanwhile, he was in a free-fall with the ground rising up fast to meet him.

With impact seeming inevitable, he said, "Actually, my house is sold."

Her head jerked around at that, the curtain of hair parted to reveal a pair of wide eyes. "What?"

"A couple made an offer for the full asking price less closing costs."

"When did this happen?"

"They saw the house last week but made the offer yesterday. My real estate agent called while I was on my way over." Gid's meeting this morning was to sign the purchase agreement.

"Why didn't you tell me?" Mia asked. A note of distrust rang in her tone.

"I'm telling you now."

She looked slightly annoyed. "When do you close?"

"The paperwork still needs to be processed and their mortgage approved, but if all goes as planned, we'll close in thirty days."

"Thirty days," she repeated. "That's so soon."

She looked miserable. Perversely, his spirits lifted.

When she ducked her head again, Gid reached over and tucked the hair behind her ears so he could see her face better. "You still haven't answered my question, Mia."

"I...I don't have an answer for you," she replied, which Gid supposed beat the hell out of a definitive no. Still...

"Do you love me?

At one time, he had been sure he knew her answer, even if she'd never said the actual words. Just as, at one time, he'd thought he'd known what her answer to his proposal would be. Now he held his breath and waited. Everything was riding on what she said next.

· · ·

Mia's first instinct was to get up and dash out of the room. When it came to fight or flight, she preferred the latter. It had served her well, or so she'd thought. But running away in this case wouldn't solve anything. Had it ever solved anything? It was time to face life head on. To grab hold of it rather than let go and move on.

"You never asked about my past," she said quietly.

"Wh—what?"

"My past. You've never asked me about it. Even after we first met and I told you that I didn't have a family and had spent most of my childhood in foster care. You never pressed me on how I got there." She glanced up, held his gaze. "Why?"

"I figured you'd tell me when you were ready."

But she'd never been ready. Sharing her physical space, even sharing her body, those were easy. Sharing her past? Her fears? Opening up her heart to the possibility of not only loving someone else but being loved in return? That was the hard part.

Was she ready now?

Marney's advice whispered through Mia's mind, telling her to listen to the very heart she was worried would be broken.

"My parents were drug addicts," she began. When her voice cracked, she cleared her throat and continued. "From what I was told, they started out as just your basic potheads. We lived in a trailer park. They were young. Younger than I am now. Neither one of them had a high school diploma, but they managed to lead a relatively stable existence until I was about four years old. That's when my dad got into meth and introduced my mom to it. Their lives spiraled out of control soon after."

How different Mia's life might be if their lives hadn't.

Gid didn't say anything, but he reached for her hand. It wasn't pity she saw reflected in his eyes, or disgust—had she really believed she would see either?—instead she saw sympathy and anger on her behalf. Bolstered, she went on, unearthing memories she had buried long ago, determined never to revisit them.

"When my mom was high, she wanted to stay that way. Coming down made her sad and desperate. It made my dad...mean. I was in kindergarten the first time social workers came and removed me from my home." The words came out dully, although the pain behind them remained surprisingly sharp, even after all these years. "I showed up at school one Monday morning with a black eye, my clothes filthy. Except for some stale bread, I hadn't eaten since the free lunch the Friday before. I remember my mom crying, promising to change. She and my dad had to get clean and attend parenting classes in order to get me back. They did.

"Six months later, I was returned to them. But it didn't last. One started using and the other followed suit. My dad got better at hitting me in places where the bruises wouldn't show. But I was removed again. I was in first grade that time. I spent Christmas with a foster family. I liked them. The mom smelled like vanilla cookies and the dad had a laugh that reminded me of Santa Claus. I'd just started to feel settled when my parents got their crap together a second time and regained custody of me.

"Once again I had to adjust to a new school and make new friends. I was doing okay. Overall, I was happy to be home. Can you believe that?" Her mouth twisted.

Gid squeezed her hand. "Yes. Children love their parents, even parents who don't deserve it."

"I suppose. They stayed clean for nearly a year. While I'd been in foster care, my mom earned her GED. She was working nights cleaning offices. My dad was doing some construction work, probably paid under the table. I thought maybe this time..." She swallowed. "Then one night while my mom was at work, my dad came in and woke me up.

He said we were going for a drive. He took me to a party store not far from our trailer, and pulled around to where the Dumpsters were in the back. A man was waiting there. I remember being scared, begging my dad to take me home."

Her breathing hitched and a tear leaked down her cheek. Even now, years removed, the fear she'd experienced, the betrayal, cut her to the quick.

"Mia, you don't have to—"

But she did. She understood that now. Not only did she have to say it, he needed to hear it. All of it, every last ugly secret she'd kept from him. She'd never be truly free otherwise. Free to love.

"I do, Gid. I do. My own father would have sold me to some pervert in exchange for a fix if a store clerk hadn't seen us pull in, gotten suspicious, and called police. They got there just as I was being forced into the guy's car. My dad was arrested along with the other man."

"And your mother?"

"She had supervised visits with me for awhile. Then, after my dad was convicted and sent to prison, she got me back. Everything was okay for a while, long enough for me to start believing I was going to have a normal life. Then she hooked up with another loser who used drugs. She died of an overdose when I was eight." Another betrayal, in some ways every bit as painful as her father's.

"After that, I bounced around the foster care system until I aged out."

Her cheeks weren't the only ones damp now. "You deserved a better childhood than that."

"Yes, I did, although for a time, I wondered if I'd been to blame somehow. If something about me made me…" She swallowed. "Unlovable."

"Aw, Mia. No. If I could make up for the past—God!—I would. But I'm not like your parents—"

"I know that—"

But he cut her off with a vehement shake of his head that had Charlie hopping up and padding over the mattress to where they were. "You don't know, Mia. At least not in here, where it counts." The tip of his finger grazed the lace of her nightgown just above her left breast. "Any promises I make, I will keep, but you have to believe me. You have to *trust* me. You have to—"

"Love you. I love you, Gid." She smiled, surprised to find it wasn't as hard to say as she'd thought it would be.

Gid, meanwhile, stared at her unblinking. Another time, Mia might have teased him for the way his mouth had dropped open. But this wasn't the time for jokes.

"Say it again," he said quietly. "Please."

"I love you." The words flowed easily from Mia's heart—the battered heart that Marney had urged her to listen to.

"I love you, too."

He kissed her then. His mouth was soft and sweet for a brief moment before it turned demanding. He pressed her back against the mattress and followed her down, the weight of his body made her feel secure, every bit as much as the love shining in his eyes. But she had to know.

"What about California? Your job? What are you going to do, Gid?"

"The clinic is still mine." He nipped at her lower lip. "As for the rest, I'll tell them I got a better offer."

He didn't say exactly what that offer was. Nor did he propose marriage. But this was enough, she told herself.

When he would have kissed her again, Charlie started to bark and tried to wiggle in between them.

"I think he needs to go out," Mia said ruefully.

"Yeah," Gid agreed and then bobbed his eyebrows in a way that made her laugh and go soft inside at the same time. "I think he needs to stay out for a little while, too."

Chapter Seven

"I'm so glad that you and Gid are back together." Marney raised her coffee in a toast. Gabby and Jenny followed suit as the women sat at their usual table at the back of The Cuppa Cafe.

"If you start singing 'Love is in the Air' again, I'm out of here," Mia groused, but she was smiling, too.

It had been a week since she had bared her soul to Gid, but this was the first time she and the girls had had a chance to get together and talk. On the tabletop were candid shots from Marney and Dell's wedding that Gabby, a talented photographer, had snapped on the big day. Some were black and white, others full color. All of them captured the couple's joy.

"I knew he would stay in Chandler's Cove if you asked him," Jenny said.

"I didn't ask him to stay." If there was one thing that could mar her current happiness, it was the fact that Gid was giving up so much for her. She couldn't help wondering: would he regret it later?

"You know what I mean."

"He's happy to stay here because he loves you," Gabby said. "He wants to be with you."

Marney had said as much before. Still, that was a heady revelation, one Mia had only just begun to trust.

"You're so lucky," Jenny said. Her eyes misted. "All of you. You've found wonderful men to share your lives with."

"You'll find someone wonderful again, too," Mia predicted of her friend. When they all gaped at her, she shifted uncomfortably in her seat. "What?"

Marney chuckled. "You. Ms. I-Don't-Do-Commitment."

"Looks like someone's been drinking the Kool-Aid," Gabby added dryly.

"I love him. And he loves me. He *really* loves me," she said with no small amount of wonder. She had pushed Gid away, broken his heart. Still, he forgave her. Now, even though he knew her ugliest secrets, he still he wanted to be with her.

"So, when's the wedding?" Jenny asked.

"It goes without saying that I'll take some lovely pictures for you, too," Gabby put in, tapping the photos on the tabletop.

"We'll be bridesmaids, right?" This from Marney.

Mia nibbled her lip.

"What is it?" Gabby asked.

"We haven't talked about marriage."

"Are you still afraid to make that kind of commitment?"

"A little," she admitted. Everything was so perfect right now.

"Take it one step and one day at a time," Jenny, always the most pragmatic of the bunch, suggested. "Just because these two hit the fast-forward button to wedded bliss doesn't mean you have to, too."

Gabby raised her hand. "Just to clarify, Mia and Gid have been dating a long time. Taking a stroll down the aisle would hardly be rushing it in her case. But I agree. There's no need for them to set a date and pick out china patterns. I'd imagine Gid is happy enough just hearing the L-word."

Her friends were right. The knot uncoiled in Mia's stomach, only to twist tightly again when Gabby added, "Besides, now that his house has sold he'll be moving in with you. Right?"

"Actually, we haven't discussed living arrangements."

Marney broke off a piece of chocolate chip muffin. They were her favorite, and she'd ordered some for all of them. Before popping it in her mouth she said, "Have you asked him?"

"No."

Gabby reached for a muffin too. "Well, he can't very well invite himself to live with you, now can he?"

"Do you want him to move in?" Jenny inquired.

Mia liked her little house. She liked the permanence it represented. It was a refuge as much as it was a home. She'd never had a problem sharing its space with Gid, but that had been when she'd known that he had his own place to go back to.

"Well?" Marney nudged.

"I do." Mia rested a hand on her chest as soon as the words were out. Underneath her palm, her heart was beating crazily. "Oh my God! I want him to move in with me."

That wasn't all she wanted, she realized with a start that had her heart tapping in triple time. But, as her friends had pointed out, she could take this one step at a time.

Her cellphone was on the table top. Marney pushed it closer. "Call him."

Jenny looked scandalized. "She can't ask him something this important on the phone."

"Over dinner then," Marney said. "And I suggest you make something decadent for dessert."

Gabby had an even better idea. "I suggest you *be* dessert." And all the girls dissolved into laughter

. . .

It was twenty after eight when Gid arrived at Mia's house. She opened the door, smiling, but she seemed nervous. Not the bad sort of nervous that would have set him on edge as well. But the kind of nervous one got before throwing a big party or making an expensive purchase.

Instead of asking her about it, he reached for her hand and reeled her in for a kiss. Patience was a virtue, especially when it came to this woman. Afterward, with her still settled against his chest, he said, "Sorry for being late. I had a last-minute emergency. Mrs. Johnson's schnauzer stepped on a rusty nail."

"Ooh. Sounds painful."

"Probably not as painful as eating an underwire." Gid shot a glance in Charlie's direction. The dog ducked his head at the mention of it. "How was your day?"

"Good. No emergencies unless you count Nina Hoover changing the flower choice for her bridesmaids again."

"That makes, what, the third time?"

"Fifth, but who's counting." Mia chuckled but soon afterward was nibbling her bottom lip.

This time, Gid couldn't resist commenting, "Something's on your mind."

She nodded.

"Something important, I take it."

She nodded again before adding, "But it can wait till after dinner. We can talk over dessert."

Was she blushing?

Intrigued, he followed her to the kitchen. The table was set, plates and cutlery perfectly arranged. Blue hydrangea interspersed with pink roses spilled from a squat vase in the center of the table. He knew she had arranged them herself and, as always, marveled at her skill. She experienced so much ugliness in her life, yet she was capable of creating beauty. A bottle of wine, their favorite brand, was open and breathing near the bouquet. She'd thought of everything, which made him more curious than ever about whatever it was she wanted to discuss over dessert.

To distract himself from dwelling on it, he asked, "Can I do anything to help?"

"Sure. You can pour the wine."

He completed the task while she puttered at the stove. The scent of seasoned beef had his mouth watering. Beside her, Charlie rose on his hind legs as if drawn upward by the aroma. She shooed him away, but he retreated only as far as the table, where he staked out the real estate beneath it. Obviously, he was hoping something edible would wind up on the floor. Despite Gid's professional position against feeding pets table scraps, he couldn't help feeling sorry for the dog.

The skirt steak was perfectly seasoned and broiled to medium rare. She'd sliced it into thin ribbons, which were arranged on a bed of mixed greens drizzled with a tangy vinaigrette. She'd also made a cauliflower puree whose texture was so smooth it felt like silk on his tongue.

"You've outdone yourself," he remarked.

Mia had never prepared a meal like this for him. The open cookbooks on the countertop and the kitchen's overall disarray attested to the effort that had gone into this one.

"Thank you." She pushed around the greens and nibbled a bite before saying, "How's the packing going at your house?"

"It's going. You don't realize how much junk you've accumulated until you have to box it all up. I've got a couple of loads ready for Goodwill, and the garbage man's back is liable to be bothering him after he stops at my house on his rounds this week."

She cleared her throat. "And the house hunting? How's that going?"

"So-so." He waved his hand. "I've looked at a couple of places. One's in town not far from Gabby's studio. The other one is about five miles farther outside town than Marney's McMansion." He shrugged. "Both of them need a lot of work."

"So you want something that's move-in ready?" Mia speared a piece of meat with her fork, but instead of putting it in her mouth, she pushed it and more greens around her plate.

"Yeah. Small projects are fine, but I don't feel like playing subcontractor for months on end this time around."

Gid had put in a lot of work on the house he'd been living in, renovating nearly every room from floorboards to rafters by the time he was done. Mia had joined in on occasion, helping to sand down cabinets and paint trim. She'd even suggested the wall colors and had helped him pick out his couch. Even so, the house had never felt like home.

Mia cleared her throat. "I might know of a place."

"In Chandler's Cove?" That came as a surprise since his agent seemed to have run out of available listings that fit both Gid's criteria and his price range. "Where?"

"It's in a nice neighborhood on a quiet street. It's not very large."

"I don't need a lot of room. Bigger isn't always better. What's the yard like?"

"Very nice. The back is fenced." She smiled. "And the flowerbeds are gorgeous."

"Oh. That's not good."

She blinked in alarm before sputtering, "Wh-why?"

"I don't want to be responsible for killing plants. You know my thumb is black."

"Oh." Some of the tension left her shoulders. "Well, there's no need to worry. I'll tend them."

"Thanks, but I can't ask you to take care of my yard and yours." In the house he'd just sold, Gid had refused her offer to put in more than a few shrubs and some low-maintenance day lilies for the same reason. She was a perfectionist who wouldn't allow plants to languish from neglect.

She nibbled her bottom lip, her gaze glued to her plate. Had she eaten anything, he wondered? "It won't be a problem, Gid." She glanced up then. The smile she sent him wobbled a little before turning steady. "You see, the house

I'm talking about is mine."

"You want—"

"I want you to move in with me." She exhaled sharply, but her smile was wide and sincere.

Gid grinned in return. It wasn't marriage, but it was a huge step for Mia.

"On one condition?"

"And that is?"

"I get the left side of the bed."

Chapter Eight

With only two days to go before Gid closed on his house, his move to Mia's place was well under way. They'd spent the evenings of the past few weeks packing up his belongings and taking them over to Mia's a few boxes at a time, unpacking as they went.

She'd discovered it wasn't hard to make room for him in her home, especially since other than a few key pieces of furniture, he'd sold off or donated much of his. Her sanctuary didn't feel invaded so much as fortified with him there.

She was boxing up his home office when she spied the email. She wasn't trying to snoop but he'd left his laptop on and the file was open. The subject line read: *An offer too good to refuse*. She recognized the sender as the man who had offered Gid the job in California.

The note read:

I know you've said no several times now, but I speak on

*behalf of the department of veterinary medicine when I say
we are hoping you will reconsider when you learn about the
most recent development. A wealthy alumna recently died and
has bequeathed the university nearly thirty million dollars to
be used for research along with endowing a position. That
position would be yours. Better still, you would be able to hire
a full-time assistant. We look forward to hearing from you.*

* -- Norman Fleisher*

Mia wilted onto the chair behind the desk. Gid's dream
job had just gotten, well, dreamier. How could she possibly
compete with this? How could he possibly turn it down?
The old panic bubbled up inside along with a voice telling
her she wasn't worthy of his love, and that the love she felt
for him, as well as the home they were making together,
weren't enough to make him stay with her for keeps. The
voice grew louder, more insistent. It urged her to cut and
run. For a moment, she almost listened to it, just as she had
at Christmas. In the end, she decided to do what Gabby
and Marney had done and trust her heart. Not only was she
going to trust her heart. She was going to trust Gid.

"My Jeep is almost full," he said as he entered the
office. "I've got room for maybe a box or two. Do you have
anything ready?"

"No. Sorry. I got…distracted."

"What's wrong?"

She smiled, touched by the concern she saw in his eyes.
This was Gid, always putting her first. It was time to return
the favor. That's what love was about. Give and take. Unless
one counted her invitation for him to move in, he'd done
all of the giving so far. And, if she were being honest with

herself, the only reason Gid had sold his home was because he'd planned to move after she'd turned down his proposal and broken off their relationship.

"Nothing is wrong. Actually, you might say something is right."

"*Okaaaay,*" he said slowly and settled one hip on the edge of the desk. "And what might that be?"

"Well, you know I love you."

"I do, but I'll never get tired of hearing you say it." He grinned and leaned down to kiss her.

She felt a little dizzy afterward, but more determined than ever. "And you know I'm happy we're going to be living together."

"I'm happy about that, too. I like seeing you last thing at night and the first thing in the morning."

"Me, too." She inhaled. "But we're going to be doing that in California."

He blinked. The grin of a moment ago was gone. "What? What are you talking about?"

She motioned to the laptop. "I wasn't prying, honest, but it was open, and I read it. This is an opportunity of a lifetime, Gid. I can't let you pass it up. I won't."

She'd expected him to burst into a smile, maybe whoop with joy. He studied her in silence instead.

"Would you say something?" she pleaded when she couldn't stand it any longer.

"I don't know what to say."

"How about, yes? And maybe that you're happy?"

"I am happy, Mia." He rose, pulled her to her feet. "I'm happy right here in Chandler's Cove, with you."

"But, the job—"

He bracketed her face in his hands. "Is incredible. But this is home."

Her heart tripped. "You were going to take it before," she pointed out.

"Only because I couldn't stand living in Chandler's Cove without you."

"Gid, it's the opportunity of a lifetime."

But he shook his head. "That's where you're wrong. *You* are the opportunity of a lifetime, Mia. You're what I want, and this is where I want to live, close to both of our families."

She loved him all the more for understanding that Gabby, Jenny and Marney were her kin, not made so by blood but by choice. Still she needed to make it clear that sacrifices went both ways.

"If you ever change your mind, I'll support you. I'll go wherever you go. You're my home."

"Mia."

His kiss was gentle, even as the arms encircling her tightened.

"You're my home, too," he said when it ended.

About the Author

Jackie Braun is a three-time RITA finalist, a four-time National Readers' Choice Award finalist, and a past winner of the Rising Star Award in traditional romantic fiction. She has written more than thirty books that have been translated into more than two dozen languages and sold in countries around the globe. She lives in Michigan with her husband, two sons, and the little dog they adopted from a shelter while she was writing this story.

LOVE IN THE
SHADOWS

BARBARA WALLACE

Entangled Publishing, LLC
2614 South Timberline Road
Suite 109
Fort Collins, CO 80525
Visit our website at www.entangledpublishing.com.

Edited by Shannon Godwin and Libby Murphy
Cover design by Libby Murphy

Ebook ISBN: 978-1-62266-217-3
Print ISBN: 978-1493783717

Manufactured in the United States of America
First Edition October 2013

The author acknowledges the copyrighted or trademarked status and trademark owners of the following wordmarks mentioned in this work of fiction: Phantom of the Opera

To Peter – my real-life hero who never stops encouraging me.

And to Shirley, Susan and Jackie. Working with these three talented women forced me to bring my A-game to the table. Being included in this anthology was an honor.

Chapter One

"You could at least *look* guilty."

Jenny Travolini scowled her best glare, the one that usually made even the wisest of high school asses think twice. Big brown eyes and a tongue-lolling grin looked back.

No remorse whatsoever.

"Let's hope your owner has a bigger conscience."

Fat chance, seeing how Nicholas Bonaparte left his dog in the care of strangers for nearly a year. Nine months since the mysterious "Mr. B." dropped Charlie into the lap of her friend Gabby Wilson without a word. Until yesterday, when an email announced his return. What kind of man adopted a pet only to ignore its existence?

A man who didn't care, that's who. With that thought, Jenny's annoyance with the Jack Russell softened. "You were just looking for love, weren't you fella?" Who was she to lay blame for him trying to find comfort any way he could? After all, people in glass houses…

Squatting, she gave the dog a scratch behind the ears. "Unfortunately, now it's time to face the consequences."

Because, she thought ruefully, there were *always* consequences. Warm beds turned cold, promises made in the dark proved empty, in the harsh light of day. Charlie nudged her hand seeking more attention. The little pooch didn't realize his good fortune. Forgetting his mistakes as quickly as he made them, a fresh start for him was a simple as taking a nap. No need to pull up stakes and reinvent himself in order to face his reflection every morning.

Just then the door opened, and she found herself staring at a man whose scowl could best hers.

"You've come back," he said, looking down on her and Charlie. His unenthusiastic reception didn't faze the dog, who greeted him like old friend, barking and tugging on his leash.

"And you," he said, turning his attention to Jenny, "are not Ms. Wilson."

Jenny pushed aside the upwelling of insecurity his tone provoked. Rising, she wiped her palms on the front of her khaki skirt before extending her hand. "I'm Jenny Travolini," she replied. "I volunteered to watch Charlie while Gabby settled in after her honeymoon." No need mentioning the two previous volunteers were also settling in following their weddings. Somehow she doubted the man cared about the chain of love and marriage that brought Charlie to her doorstep. "Is Mr. Bonaparte available? I'd like to speak with him."

"Mr. Bonaparte is a very busy man. He doesn't meet with anyone without an appointment."

How much did she want to bet those appointments

weren't so easy to get? "I promise this will only take a few minutes."

She didn't think it possible, but the man's scowl grew more humorless. "As I said, Mr. Bonaparte does not meet with unscheduled visitors. I'll let him know you brought St. Clair Osgood Charles back." He reached for the leash.

Jenny moved the leash out of his reach. She had a bad feeling that if she relinquished custody, she'd never get an appointment to see the man, and since Nicholas Bonaparte's carelessness was going to cost her a small fortune — at least it was a fortune to her — she wasn't backing down without trying. "I *am* a scheduled visitor, aren't I? Mr. Bonaparte did ask me to bring Charlie back." Okay, technically, he asked Gabby, and he didn't specify a date and time, but surely her arrival wasn't completely unexpected.

A few bark-filled beats passed. Long enough for the hair to start rising on the back of her neck. Still, she held her ground. She was, after all, a high school teacher. One, if her students were to be believed, capable of being a humorless bitch. Surely she could handle a Mexican standoff.

To her vast relief, the butler blinked first. "Very well, I'll see if he can squeeze you in. You can wait in the foyer." He punctuated the words with a sigh, as though to say she hadn't won so much as he was doing her a favor.

Either way, Jenny was inside the Bonaparte mansion.

The "foyer" as the butler called it, was a space the size of Jenny's living room. As she surveyed the room's looming collection of marble sculptures and antiques, Jenny couldn't help but think of winter. Even the air felt colder. Goose bumps trailed up her sweater-covered arms. Meanwhile, Charlie was desperate to get free. "Being home doesn't mean you're off the hook," she said, as she unhooked his leash. "Someone still has to pay for your indiscretion." She swore Charlie grinned at her right before digging at the thick maroon carpet, the room's lone contribution to color.

Being surrounded by opulence made her feel self-conscious, so while Charlie waged his war on the carpet, she made her way to a large gilt mirror that hung on the sidewall. For the first time since moving to Chandler's Cove, she regretted her newly adapted disinterest in her appearance. Back in Chicago she wouldn't be caught dead without full makeup. Now, her straight blond hair hung lifelessly around her face and her makeup, if you could call the little concealer and blush she wore that, had long worn off.

Quickly, she combed through the strands with her fingers then pinched her cheeks, only to have the butler walk in seconds later.

"I see we haven't changed," the butler said, spying Charlie. By this point, the terrier had grabbed hold of one corner of the carpet and pulled it back. "Still wild as ever. I'd hoped he'd slow down while Mr. Bonaparte was gone," he said to Jenny.

"I'm sure he'll calm down once the excitement of being home wears off," she said. Of course, she was the same woman who thought Charlie had calmed down at her house, only to find he'd replaced furniture chewing with other activities.

They both stared at Charlie, who had moved on from digging the carpet to squirming across the surface on his back. "Perhaps," he said. He turned his dour expression from Charlie's latest gyrations to her. "Mr. Bonaparte will give you exactly five minutes. Follow me."

As she followed the man down a long corridor that was as opulent and foreboding as the foyer, it dawned on Jenny that she could be one of the few, if not the only person in Chandler's Cove, to meet Nicholas Bonaparte face-to-face. Whenever Charlie got in trouble, it was always a staff member who came to bail him out—never Mr. Bonaparte. Occasionally a check would arrive for one of the local causes—the library renovation, the new lacrosse field—but Bonaparte himself remained a mystery. Even when he summoned Gabby to his house back in January and asked her to dog-sit, he did so through the butler and a note. If not for the occasional, distant sightings of him walking the grounds after sunset, she'd think the man didn't exist.

A pair of heavy oak doors blocked the end of the hallway. Before either human could reach for the handle, Charlie, who had apparently decided to join them, cut in front and began pawing for entrance.

The butler gave a weary sigh. "I should have realized you'd need to be first," he said, granting him access.

Whatever Jenny had been expecting based on her brief tour so far, it wasn't the dark, almost gothic atmosphere that greeted her. Heavy velvet curtains covered the windows, killing any trace of the sun. In fact, the only interior light at all came from a pair of laptops that sat atop a gigantic desk. Oddly enough, the monitors pointed outward. Jenny could see the squiggly lines of the screensavers. The angle turned everything else into colorless shadows.

Behind the desk stood the biggest shadow of them all: Nicholas Bonaparte.

Jenny jumped as the door shut behind her, locking her and Charlie inside. She waited for the shadow to come closer, but Bonaparte stayed where he was, shrouded by darkness.

"Cyrus said you wanted to see me." His voice was low and rough like whiskey. Jenny felt another shiver as the sound wrapped around the base of her spine. "He said it was important."

"Um, yes." She swallowed her nerves. Five minutes wasn't a long time; she could handle this. "It's about Charlie. I've been watching him the past month." She looked over at the dog who'd settled in a wingbacked chair by the unlit fireplace.

"What do you mean, *you* have been watching him? I left the dog in Gabrielle Wilson's care." He didn't sound pleased with the change.

The last thing Jenny wanted was to get her friend in trouble. "I'm doing her a favor. She recently married, and I thought she and her husband might like some privacy, being newlyweds and all."

"Hmmm." Again, not pleased. "Well, if this is about payment, you need to talk with her. She was paid in advance."

"I know. I'm here for a different reason."

"Which is?"

He sat down. Jenny found it interesting that the expansive desk managed to dwarf everything in the room except his figure. Meaning he was as tall and broad as his silhouette suggested. If standing toe to toe, he'd best her height by a foot or more. Or so she assumed. The glare off the computer screens made it impossible to see his features clearly.

If he was trying to use the shadows to intimidate her, it worked.

"It's about Charlie. Are you aware the dog was

never..." She paused, a blush creeping into her cheeks. Under the circumstances, spelling out words felt awkward. Unfortunately, Charlie had a habit of reacting very poorly to words he didn't like. "He was never F-I-X-E-D."

Silence. "Your point?" he asked finally.

"My point is that my Lulu's pregnant."

"And when you say Lulu, I assume we're talking about a dog?"

"*My* dog. Lulu is my cavalier spaniel. I had planned to breed her." High school English teachers only made so much and thanks to her misspent youth, she didn't have a lot in the way of savings. "Now I have to wait another year. In the meantime, there's the matter of veterinary care for her and the puppies, until they're placed anyway." She reached into her satchel and retrieved the paperwork she'd tucked neatly in there earlier. "Here's the report from Dr. Gideon Roth." When he didn't reach out to take them, she dropped the papers on his desk. "I'm sure as a businessman, you can appreciate my predicament. Not only have I lost potential income but I have to pay for the cost of carrying and placing the unplanned litter."

"And you expect me to compensate you for these costs."

"It's only fair, don't you think?"

"The world is hardly fair, Ms. Travolini."

Didn't she know it? If life were fair, she wouldn't have traveled down the road of her youth, endangering her physical well-being and leaving her self-respect in shatters.

"That may be true, but I'm hoping you will be."

"I see." A hand reached for the paperwork, and Jenny caught a glimpse of smooth, tight skin in the dim computer light. "All this says is that your dog is carrying a litter of puppies," he said after a moment. "Doesn't say anything about who sired them."

"Doesn't have to. Charlie sired them."

"Assuming Charlie's the only dog she mated with."

Jenny bristled. He did not just poke that hornet's nest, did he? "Are you suggesting Lulu's some kind of doggy whore?" Although she knew it was impossible, she could almost hear his whiskeyed voice in her head. *Like dog, like owner....*

"What I'm suggesting is that taking Charlie from Ms. Wilson provides you with a convenient way to pay your vet bills."

Terrific. So he was simply accusing her of trying to scam him. Like that was so much better. "Did you read the bill? Do you really think, if I were trying to extort money, I'd go for such a modest amount?"

"I think the best con artists know to be realistic, especially when first dipping into your wallet. Best not to take what anyone says at face value or believe a source too completely.

"I'll tell you what." He picked up a pen. "When your dog has her puppies, have the vet do a genetic test. If the bloodline matches, then we can talk reimbursement."

With that, he bowed his head over his paperwork, essentially dismissing her.

Jenny seethed. It was like she was back in Chicago, being tossed aside by another so-called boyfriend who didn't think she was good enough for a real relationship. She felt small and insulted and angry as hell. Only she wasn't twenty years old anymore and she no longer let men take advantage. She'd send Nicholas Bonaparte his genetic test all right, along with the bill for it and Lulu's care — and demand an apology with his reimbursement check.

As she turned to leave, she caught sight of Charlie sitting expectantly in the chair and felt a pang of regret. In spite of the craziness with Lulu, she'd grown fond of the little guy over the past month. He was basically a good dog who, while rambunctious, was also gentle and friendly and wanted nothing but someone to love him. She hated to see him pinning his hopes on the wrong person. How many times had she made the same bad mistake? Ten to one he found his way to Gabby's studio before the week was out.

"No one would blame you if you did, pal."

"What?"

She hadn't realized she'd spoken aloud, but now that she had, she decided to own her words. Someone should let Bonaparte know how neglectful he was being. How badly being tossed aside hurt. "I said, no one would blame him for running away from this place," she repeated, louder this time. "You do know pets need more than food and water, don't you?"

"Is that so?"

"Yes." Bonaparte had unleashed her schoolteacher instincts. Now he would be forced to listen to the lecture. "They need attention and love and nurturing. They need to know they're wanted. It's only when they don't get affection that they turn destructive. They tear up the house." *Or run around from man to man hoping to find love elsewhere.* "Did you ever think that maybe the reason Charlie's so out of control is because he wants you to notice him?"

When she finished, Bonaparte sat back in his chair, sending him deeper in the shadows. The movement was so deliberate, Jenny felt a spark of hope that her words sank in.

"Thank you for your insight."

So much for making her point. He clearly found her insight unwelcome and unnecessary. Jenny gritted her teeth. Poor Charlie. How on earth was she supposed to leave him? This wasn't a home; it was a marble mausoleum. He deserved better than to be stuck here with a grumpy butler and a hardhearted owner.

To hell with returning him today. "You know what?" She scooped the squirming Jack Russell into her arms. "If you want to wait until you get the genetic testing; you can wait for your dog, too. Come on, Charlie. Let's get out of here."

Chapter Two

"Are you seriously just going to let her march out of here with your property?" Cyrus asked, his eyebrows raised.

Nick stared at the car driving away from the house. She *had* marched, hadn't she? He didn't think the term applied to anyone outside a drum and bugle corps but it fit Jennifer Travolini's exit perfectly. He could still hear the heels of her flat shoes slapping against the marble.

"Yes, I am," he answered, letting the drape fall back into place. Not only would he let her march out, but he planned to let her keep the damn dog if she wanted as well. Wasn't as though he'd win a prize for pet owning anyway. Truth was, he never should have indulged Megan in the first place. But then, he'd always indulged Megan, so when his fiancée fell in love with the purebred puppy, he'd said yes. He should have realized she'd lose interest in the animal after a few months. And, when she walked out, leaving the terrier behind, he couldn't bring himself to punish the animal for her thoughtlessness, or his, by shuttling him off to a shelter. After all, in a way, the two of them were kindred spirits. Both were dumped after she stopped finding them attractive. In retrospect, keeping the dog was the bigger punishment. Ms. Travolini was right; the dog deserved more attention than he could give.

"Do you know why the dog wasn't neutered?" he asked, turning his attention to the reason behind Jennifer's visit.

The guilty expression on his butler's face answered his question. "Miss Megan canceled the surgery. Said she might want to breed him in the future. I assumed you knew."

"I didn't." But then, Megan failed to share many things during their engagement. Starting with the fact that she didn't love him.

"But you told Ms. Travolini otherwise."

"Your eavesdropping skills are rusty, Cyrus. I neither confirmed nor denied knowledge. Besides, aren't I allowed to save some face?" He managed a wan smile. "No pun intended."

"Of course the pun was intended. You have a warped sense of humor." The butler's lips curled into a cross between a grimace and a sneer. During the ten years he'd worked for him, Nick had come to recognize the expression as the closest thing Cyrus had to a smile. He was also the closest thing Nick now had for a friend.

Sometimes he wondered if Cyrus would be as loyal without the sizeable paycheck he received every week. Nick wasn't about to test the theory. Even if he was only staying for the money, at least he stayed. Megan couldn't manage that much. Right now, the older man was looking at him with concern. "You look tired. Maybe you should lie down for a bit. The doctors in Europe did say you needed to take it easy."

"The doctors in Europe don't have a multi-billion dollar empire to run. And I was gone too long as it is. I'll lie down before dinner."

"I'll have the cook make you some tea then." Nick hated tea, but he nodded anyway. Truth was, the fatigue was setting in, along with the painful stiffness in his shoulder. Three years ago, he could work sixteen hours straight and not bat an eye. Now everything took longer and zapped his energy. He hated it. It was one of the reasons he'd gone to Europe. Hoping the doctors and their miracle cures might help built his stamina.

God, how he hated the way the whole damn world walked on eggshells around him. Constantly worrying whether he was tired, whether he was in pain. Whether they would say or do the wrong thing. Everyone except Cyrus.

And Jennifer Travolini. Turns out his dognapper was quite the study in contradictions. At first blush, she looked as steely as a wood sprite in a potato sack. In fact, that shapeless jumper she wore wasn't much more than a potato sack. She either had lousy fashion taste or she was purposely trying to hide her attractiveness. Didn't work. Potato sacks didn't hide shapely legs or slim wrists. Same way her avoiding makeup didn't hide her delicate cheekbones or the spark that found its way into her brown eyes when she started lecturing.

The man in him couldn't help wondering if they lit up at other moments—even if such thoughts were a waste of time. Whatever bravado Jennifer Travolini displayed, she did so while he was in the shadows. Like everyone else in the world, her impression would change once she saw the real him.

Still, the challenge was nice while it lasted. And the dog was in a better home. Something he should have arranged a long time ago.

He made a note to have a check delivered to Ms. Travolini in the morning.

• • •

"You did what?"

Jenny held the phone away from her ear to keep Marney's shriek from bursting her eardrum. "What were you thinking?" her friend asked.

"The man called me a con artist."

"So you decided to prove him wrong by stealing his dog?"

"I didn't steal anything. I simply postponed returning him until the puppies are born."

She was arguing semantics, something that, if one of her students tried to do it, she'd shut down in a second. Truth was, it wasn't until she was halfway home that Jenny stopped to think about her actions. Bonaparte made her so mad she just acted.

What was it she said to Charlie about facing consequences? She looked over at the terrier prancing around the kitchen, trying to roust his sleepy playmate. The chubby King Charles rubbed her nose with her paw every time he poked her. The two of them were definitely a pair. Too much so, apparently.

On to other end of the line, she could almost hear Marney shaking her head. "I still can't believe you dognapped Charlie. It's so not like you."

"I know. I know."

Actually, the behavior was more in character than Marney realized. Far as her circle of friends was concerned, she was dependable, practical, and unassuming. What she liked to call the proper, improved Jenny Travolini. They'd never met the other Jenny. The reckless girl so desperate for love she'd do anything, give herself to anyone. *That* Jenny came to her senses five years ago. Learned the hard way, she might add. From now on she was going it alone. Much better to have no love at all than a whole bunch of bad love.

Which was the real reason she dognapped Charlie. She could claim it was for protest reasons all she wanted, but she knew damn well the real reason she acted so impetuously was that she couldn't stand the idea of leaving the poor little guy in that cold house. Struck too harsh a nerve.

She wasn't going to tell Marney that, though. Far as her friends were concerned, this was all about the money.

Tucking the portable phone under her ear, Jenny left the kitchen to retrieve from her car the large bag of dog food she purchased on the way home. She had a half a mind to bill Bonaparte for the increased food costs, too.

"Question is, what do I do now?"

"You're asking me?" Marney chuckled.

"Of the four of us, you do have the most legal experience."

"Being married to the sheriff doesn't make me a legal

expert. It's not like you gain knowledge through osmosis."

"But you could ask him a hypothetical question."

"Which he'll immediately figure out is code for 'it involves one of my friends'. You forget, he's met Charlie. Besides, I don't have to ask him. I can make a decent guess all on my own. You took a valuable purebred dog without permission. I'm pretty sure that counts as larceny. Mr. B. could press charges."

Groaning, Jenny dropped the bag of dog food by the back door. She leaned back against the frame with her eyes closed, cursing whatever got her in this situation. Why couldn't Gabby have kept Charlie the entire year like she was supposed to? Why did she and the others have to fall in love?

"From the sound of that groan, you're worried Mr. B. might," Marney's voice said in her ear.

Worried wasn't a strong enough word. If Bonaparte balked at paying a tiny vet bill—tiny for him anyway—she could only imagine the stink he'd throw over someone taking his property. "I'm screwed."

"He's that bad?"

"Did you forget the part where he called me a con artist?"

"Too bad. We've spent so much time speculating about him. Shame to think we wasted our time on a jerk. Is he at least as handsome as those pictures we found?"

"Hey! Isn't it a little early in the marriage to develop a wandering eye?"

"I'm just asking. Is he?"

"I don't know." She'd forgotten their Internet search.

One night, after a pitcher of tequila, they'd taken their Mr. B. speculation online and searched for images. The ones they found showed an attractive man with a mop of dark curls and deep blue eyes. "I didn't get a very good look. The room was dark."

"Dark?"

"Yeah, like really dark," she said, recalling the drawn curtains and reversed laptop screens.

"Maybe he's a vampire."

"Very funny. I'm sure it was some form of intimidation tactic." For that matter, she bet he used his voice in the same manner. The husky growl had to be put on. No one's voice actually sounded that way. Gravel-laced yet smooth. Like sandpaper being dragged across silk. She shivered as the memory of the sound wrapped around the base of her spine. Definitely staged. She considered herself an expert on disingenuous voices. After all, she'd fallen for some of Chicago's best.

"Perhaps you'll get a better look on the second visit."

Lost in thought, Jenny almost missed Marney's comment. "What second visit?" Oh. "Never mind." Marney meant when she returned Charlie. "He called me a con artist," she repeated for the third time, pretending her voice did not have a whiny tone.

"I know he did, but I doubt a judge will care when you're dragged in on larceny charges. I looked it up while we were talking. Theft of property over $500 is larceny, and seeing how Charlie is probably worth—"

"I get your point." *Damn.* This wasn't fair. Charlie was more than property. "What about the fact he owes me money? Doesn't that count for anything?"

Marney paused. "Might change the crime from kidnapping to extortion."

"That's not what I meant." Jenny leaned her head against the crown molding. Much as she hated to admit it, Marney was right. Bonaparte refusing to reimburse her expenses without a genetic test wasn't illegal—her refusing to return his dog was. What's more, if word got out about her stealing Bonaparte's property, she'd have to answer to the superintendent. School boards were pretty sensitive about their teachers having criminal records. Her best was to return Charlie and hope Bonaparte had a sense of humor. "I'll take Charlie back tonight."

"Now there's the sensible school teacher we all know and love. Let me know how things go."

Jenny already knew how they would go. Awful. Having clicked off the phone, she stood in the kitchen doorway with the receiver pressed against her stomach, hoping to stem the nausea. Just the idea of facing Nicholas Bonaparte jumbled her insides. She didn't tell Marney, but something about this afternoon's visit unnerved her. Not in a frightened way, but rather a confused, exposed kind of feeling. In five minutes he'd managed to unlock a side of her that until now, she'd successfully buried. She didn't like how he pushed her buttons, caused her self-control to slip. If a simple argument could drive her to dognapping, what else might she be driven to do?

If only he'd shown Charlie a little affection. Then she wouldn't have felt such a kinship for the damn dog.

Kinship or not, nothing was worth losing her job and

reputation over. She took a couple deep cleansing breaths to prepare her herself, then opened her eyes. "Come on, Charlie, we might as well get this over with."

The house was strangely quiet.

"Charlie? Lulu?"

She looked around the kitchen. Nothing but Lulu's empty dog bed, a pair of empty food dishes, and the new bag of dog food propped next to the back door. The *open* back door.

Dammit.

Chapter Three

It was shaping up to be a moonless night. As he walked the woods off the base of his driveway, Nick was beginning to think the weather patterns were coordinating with his moods. Ever since the schoolteacher's visit, his temperament had been darker than usual. He could hear the doctors now. *Bad days are to be expected, Mr. Bonaparte. Healing takes time.* He'd been listening to their condescending comments for close to three years now. Far as he was concerned, the only thing time did was pass by. Neither he nor his disposition were going to heal any more than they already had.

He knew the exact cause of tonight's moroseness. Jennifer Travolini, that fiery sprite, had stirred his libido, and his arousal only reminded him how empty his bed was these days. How empty it would be for the rest of his life. God, but he ached to feel a woman's body against his. Oh sure, he could pay someone. The world was full of indiscriminating women who would sleep with anyone for a price. He wanted more than sex, however. He wanted a woman who wanted him—all of him, scars and all. Who looked forward to seeing his face every morning as well as share his bed every night.

Then again, he couldn't find such a woman even before the accident. Why should circumstances change now?

And he'd thought he and Megan were kindred spirits. Hell, maybe they were. Selfish, driven, superficial kindred spirits. No wonder she couldn't look at him anymore. Now that the outside matched the inside.

In the distance, he heard the faint jingle of metal. He must have walked closer to the road than he realized. As the noise grew closer, he stepped back, into the trees so he wouldn't be seen.

Cyrus considered all this insistence on dark and shadows dramatic. He was forever reminding Nick that his wealth and reputation provided plenty of compensation, even if by some rare chance a nosy paparazzi snagged a photograph. But of course, Cyrus would feel that way. He never had to endure the looks that flashed across people's faces. Pity and revulsion, followed by the smug hint of satisfaction.

This latest effort, the trip to Europe, had been the last. He was done trying to fix what couldn't change. If that meant living alone in the shadows, then so be it. At least in the dark, he could still feel a little bit in control.

The jingling grew closer. Oddly enough he didn't hear footsteps. Nick looked up the path. Thank goodness for daylight savings time. Though dark at dusk, it was still light enough for him to make out shapes. Up ahead, he spied a pair of two-foot high silhouettes trotting toward him, one particularly bouncy and hyperactive while the other followed demurely behind. A moment later, a wet nose could be heard sniffing in his direction.

"Broke out of the big house, did you?" Funny how he instinctively knew his visitor. Guess he paid more attention to his dog than he thought. Kneeling, he extended his fingers. Charlie sniffed them cautiously then began wagging his tail in greeting. His enthusiastic and unreserved acceptance brought a shift in Nick's chest.

"Maybe I'll take you back after all," he said, giving the dog's ears a rub. The short fur was coarse against his skin.

He felt another wet nose nudge his skin and turned to look at Charlie's companion. Though he couldn't make out the coloring, he saw the outline of long curly ears and a small round face. "The infamous Lulu, I presume." He stroked her ear, the strands slipping through his fingers like corn silk.

Made him wonder what her owner's hair felt like.

Her owner. Jennifer would no doubt be looking for the animals. In spite of himself, his blood stirred at the prospect of seeing her again.

"Charlie! Lulu!"

Speak of the devil. A second later, Jenny's silhouette came into view. At some point, she'd put a jacket over her cardigan, another bulky layer hiding her body. Didn't matter. Nick's body still stirred in appreciation. As he looked her up and down, he found himself actually cursing the darkness. It kept him from seeing her features clearly. She had such an expressive face. But if he couldn't see her features clearly, then she couldn't see his.

• • •

"What do you two think you're doing, taking off like that?"

Jenny gave the dogs a stern look, though she doubted the scowl would do much good. First off, she wasn't sure the dogs could see her face, and second, they didn't look the least bit sorry for running away. The two of them were sitting on the edge of the path, tails wagging like they'd won a game. "Your bad habits are rubbing off," she told the terrier. She swore his responding bark sounded proud. "I turn my back for two minutes…"

By the time she'd searched her condo and determined that the two dogs had indeed run outside and weren't simply playing upstairs, Charlie and Lulu were halfway up the street. She'd been playing stop and start with them ever since, with the pair only letting her get so close before taking off down the street again.

"And did you have to come here?" She'd cursed aloud when she saw them dash onto Bonaparte's property. "What if someone sees you and tells Mr. Bonaparte?"

"Too late. He already knows."

Jenny jumped. The gravelly voice seemed to come out of nowhere. Looking around, she finally spied him leaning against the trunk of a sprawling oak tree.

"Did I startle you?" he asked.

He knew damn well he did. She'd brought a flashlight to help her spot the dogs. Now she moved the light so she could see him better, only to have him hold up his arms and step back. "Don't."

"You have a problem with being in the light?"

"I have a problem with light shining directly in my eyes."

A reasonable explanation had he not also hidden in a dark office earlier that afternoon. "Better?" she asked, lowering the light.

"Seeing how I'm no longer blinded, yes. Thank you."

"You're welcome." She noted he didn't carry a flashlight of his own. Either he knew these paths by heart or Marney was right; he was a vampire. "Tell me, do you always skulk around the woods at night?"

"I do when I own the property. And, it's called walking. I find the solitude helps me to think." He shifted his position, his shoulders scraping against the bark. "I'd ask what you're doing here but the answer's obvious."

Thankfully the night hid her red cheeks. "They snuck out while I was unloading the dog food." A small lie, but she wasn't about to admit the dogs escaped while she was thinking about him.

"Interesting how Charlie chose to come here, don't you think? Almost as though he were being kept someplace he didn't want to be."

Ouch. "Except he didn't come alone. How do you explain Lulu tagging along?"

"Maybe he thought she'd enjoy a moonlight stroll."

"Right. Because dogs go on so many dates."

"Do you have a better reason?"

Unfortunately, she didn't other than Charlie's penchant for wandering, and she didn't want to start that conversation again. She was here to return the dog, not come up with a reason to dognap him again.

Charlie trotted over to his owner and stood on hind legs, nudging his hand. To her surprise, the man actually appeared to scratch the dog's head. Taking advantage of the moment, Jenny pulled a pair of leashes from her pocket and clipped one of them to a distracted Lulu's collar. Soon as Charlie made his way back to the path, she corralled him as well.

"Gotcha," she murmured. Not that he put up much of a fight. Must have used up his energy getting here.

"If I'd known you were going to let him roam all over town after dark, I'd never have let you take him."

"Excuse me?" She looked up from leashing Charlie. "Did you say *let* me take him?"

"You don't think you would have gotten off the property otherwise, do you?"

She thought back to her departure. She'd been so annoyed, she didn't give it a second thought, but the security guard barely gave her a second glance now that she thought about it. One would think a billionaire like Nicholas Bonaparte, with his money and access to technology, could have stopped her with the push of a button.

And here she'd been driving herself crazy for the past hour worrying he was going to call the police. She couldn't help herself. She started to laugh.

"Something funny?"

Yeah, her. "I thought—never mind." If the man hadn't thought to call the police on her for taking Charlie, far be it for her to put ideas in his head.

The fact that Bonaparte didn't do anything, however, did beget a question. "Why did you let me take him?"

He shrugged and Jenny really wished she could see his expression to know if he looked as unaffected as the shrug implied. Her gut wasn't so certain. "I never set out to own a dog in the first place. Getting him was my fiancée's idea."

He had a fiancée? "She must be upset I took off with him."

"Doubt it. She departed first."

"I'm sorry." Although why, she wasn't sure. For all she

knew, the man broke the engagement happily. Again, her gut said otherwise. "How come Charlie isn't with her?"

"Simple. I kept him out of spite."

Jenny blinked, unsure what to say. She must have made a sound though, because he gave a humorless laugh. "You believe me, don't you?"

"I don't—" She was confused. "Should I?"

"You can believe what you want to believe, Ms. Travolini."

"Telling me what I can believe and what I should believe are two different things." And she got the distinct impression, based on his tone of voice, that there was a sharp difference in this case. Despite his cavalier behavior. "Which one is the truth?"

A beat passed. "You really want to know?" he asked, pushing away from the tree. "She decided she didn't want him anymore, so she walked away and left him."

"Just like that?" His words stabbed very close to home. No wonder she bonded so strongly with Charlie. It was a case of one abandoned soul recognizing another. "People can be so heartless," she murmured, giving Lulu's neck stroke.

"Present company included, I assume."

Jenny's cheeks grew hot. "I—"

"Don't worry. You aren't the first person to make the suggestion."

Charlie and Lulu were yanking on their leashes, eager to start moving again. Jenny felt herself being tugged forward. "I'd better—"

"Of course." To her surprise, he fell in step beside her. Then again, maybe it wasn't so surprising. Certainly not as surprising as her walking with him. Having found the dogs, she should be turning around instead of heading deeper into his property.

They walked in silence for several feet. If Jenny thought Bonaparte imposing while sitting behind a desk, he was downright huge walking next to her. Her head barely cleared his shoulder. Through her years as a teacher, Jenny had encountered a lot of students larger than her; size usually didn't intimidate her. But with him, she felt... Intimidation wasn't the right word. Intimidation implied fear. Being next to Nicholas Bonaparte made her feel...delicate, female. Very, very female. She hadn't felt this way in five years. It made her stomach flutter.

"So let me get this straight," she said, needing to break the silence. "You won't pay my vet bills until you have proof Charlie sired Lulu's puppies, but you let me drive off with your purebred dog. Isn't that a little odd, logic wise?"

"Your total vet bills will end up larger than Charlie's assessed values. Plus, if you remember, I didn't plan on giving you Charlie. You ran off with him."

"You suggested I was trying to rip you off."

"To which you retaliated by kidnapping my dog. You have an interesting way of proving your honesty." Something about the way his low voice pronounced *interesting* made her insides turn soft.

"My friend Marney made the same point." Much to her chagrin. "Although," she added, "I'd like to remind you that you *let* me take Charlie, meaning I didn't steal anything. I can't kidnap my own dog."

"No you cannot." She heard him chuckle. Walking in the dark the way they were, the throaty sound had a bedroom-like quality. It was the laugh she always imaged a lover to have, intimate and sexy. The flutter in her stomach moved lower. She squeezed her fist before the awareness could take hold.

"Thank you," she managed to say.

"Of course, that also means you're responsible for medical expenses he might incur," he added.

Or had caused. Son of a gun! He'd outmaneuvered her. "You think giving me Charlie gets you off the hook, don't you?"

Another chuckle. This time she was prepared and steeled herself against the reaction. Sort of. She managed to press her fist tight against the fluttering.

"Well, he *is* your dog now," he replied.

Jenny looked over at Charlie who, despite the leash she held, was walking in step with his former owner. "I wouldn't be so sure."

Before Nick could retort, she tossed the leash at him and jogged a few feet ahead. Lulu picked up her pace as well, which caused Charlie to run after them. Bonaparte had no choice but to pick up the leash dragging behind.

"I'd say he's your dog now. Again." She felt only a tiny kernel of guilt, mostly at leaving Charlie behind. "You know what they say. Possession is nine tenths of the law."

God, but she wished she could see his expression. Especially after his teeth flashed white in the darkness. "Well played. Is this how you keep your students in line? By tricking them?"

Jenny stumbled at the question. "How did you I was a teacher?"

"Wasn't too difficult to learn. After you walked out, I made a few calls."

"Really?" The warm feeling began to fade. What else had his investigation turned up? She'd worked damn hard for her reputation. If he thought he could throw her past in her face... She geared for a fight.

Her tension was unwarranted. "You're very well respected in town," he said. "I was impressed. Clearly Ms. Wilson made a good choice when she left Charlie in your care."

When he didn't say any more, Jenny's nerves relaxed. "Does that mean you no longer think I'm trying to con you?"

"I'm willing to concede the point."

"Thank you. And the vet bills?"

"The check is already on my desk."

"It is?" She didn't quite get it. "You said—"

"I know what I said. You have backbone, Miss Travolini. I noticed soon as you marched your way into my office. I like that."

"Jenny," she corrected. She ignored the way his compliment caused her stomach to flutter.

"Jenny," he repeated. The word came out a rough whisper. "Call me Nick."

At that moment, the atmosphere shifted. Jenny couldn't pinpoint an exact change. Only that suddenly the afternoon's adversarial encounter seemed very far away.

"There's something I meant to ask you this afternoon," Nick said once they'd resumed walking. "How exactly did you end up with Charlie anyway? I know you said Ms. Wilson got married, but that was months ago. Her husband's done some work for my company," he added before she could ask.

"Long story. It started when Gabby decided to take a road trip with T.J." She relayed the entire story, from when

Gabby and T.J. fell in love, through Marney needing a guard dog, to their friend Mia marrying Charlie's vet. "Three weddings later, here I am dog sitting while they bask in newlywed bliss."

"Aren't you the good friend."

"More like the single one. By choice," she added, in case he thought her bitter about her friends' good fortune. "Marriage isn't really on my radar."

"Why is that?"

"Little personal, don't you think?"

"You're the one who made the statement."

Yes, she did, only she'd hoped he wouldn't ask her to elaborate. How did she explain?

"Let's just say some people just aren't meant to have relationships. They are…" *Unlovable.* "Not cut out for them."

Nick didn't reply right away and Jenny wondered if she said too much. If she did, it was his fault. He asked the impossible question.

Finally, he nodded. "I understand."

"You do?"

"Sure. Some people are meant to fall in love and get married, others are meant to be alone. Though I have to admit, I find it hard to believe a woman like you could ever be in the second category."

His compliment washed warm over her. "You don't even know me," she said, looking to the ground.

"True. And I haven't always been the best judge of character."

Did he mean his fiancée? Jenny noticed he suddenly sounded very weary, like his shoulders bore the weight of the world. Perhaps she'd been wrong to think him coldhearted.

"One of the reasons I like dogs is because they don't ask for anything but for you to love them," she found herself saying. "They don't care who you are or where you came from. Love them, and they're yours forever. Unconditionally."

"Now I'm definitely keeping Charlie."

"Looking for a little unconditional love, are we?"

"Something like that."

"Aren't we all?" Jenny recognized the loneliness in his answer. It reminded her of the longing she kept tucked deep inside her heart. All her life she'd wished for someone to want her, truly want her, and it was when that longing grew too unbearable that she made her most questionable decisions. Was Nick lonely, too? Was that the reason she found herself suddenly wanting to reach out and hold his hand? To connect?

Ahead through the trees, Jenny could see the lights of the main house shining through the branches. "I didn't realize we'd walked so far," she remarked. "Lulu and I have a hike back ahead of us."

They stopped at a split in the path. It was, Jenny noted, one of the darkest points on their journey. Nick was more enveloped by shadows than ever. They both were. And yet, rather than eerie, the setting felt oddly intimate. They were alone, with nothing but the sounds of the dogs rustling in the leaves and their own breathing. Jenny's body began to hum with an anticipation she hadn't felt for years. What now? Would he invite her back to the house? Would she go? Even as the notion caused her insides to flutter, her body screamed *bad idea*. Only a few hours ago she was verbally sparring with the man over Charlie's care, and now she was reacting to...what? Emotions she thought she heard in his voice. Emotions she had no way of knowing were real, or even existed for that matter, despite the loving happiness her friends had found. She'd been fooled way too many times before.

But, oh, what if those emotions weren't her imagination? What then?

"Would you like my driver to take you home so you wouldn't have to travel alone?"

She told herself it was relief, not disappointment, falling heavy in her stomach. "I wouldn't want to put you to any trouble."

"You're not putting me to any trouble, and my driver does what he's told. Besides, it's the least I can do. It was nice to be able…to have the company."

"I enjoyed it, too." She wondered what he was originally going to say before changing his words. "Plus you got a dog out of the bargain."

"So I did." Again, she caught the flash of a smile in the dark. "Thank you for bringing Charlie back."

"Thank *you* for not pressing charges."

"I wouldn't have anyway. You made some valid points this afternoon. I'll see to it Charlie gets more attention."

"He'd like that," she replied with a smile.

A thick silence settled between them. Jenny wished she could see Nick's face. She swore she could feel his gaze searching hers. His eyes zeroing in on her lips. Why else would her mouth run dry?

"Jenny…"

"You really should install some outside lighting," she said, swallowing hard. "I can barely see my hand in front of my face."

She didn't need to see to feel his body come closer. The air around her hummed with his presence. "That so? I can see just fine." His voice was rough, intimate.

"That's because you like the dark," she told him.

"Who says I like it?"

"Oh, I don't know, maybe the fact you're out here without a flashlight or the fact you insisted on meeting in a dark room this afternoon.' She tipped her face upward. "Why did you act all mysterious today? Were you trying to frighten me?"

She figured he might dodge the question; she didn't count on his hand reaching out to caress her jaw. "You have such pale skin," he murmured. "I bet in the moonlight, it would glow silver."

"I—I—I wouldn't know." Jenny suddenly couldn't think. The seductive growl in Nick's voice *should* frighten her. She was alone in the woods with a man whose wealth and power allowed him to take and do whatever he wanted. The realization should not send a thrill shooting through her body. But it did, and that scared her. His feathery touch left her trembling. Had her wanting more. Dear God, if he were to close the gap between them, she would… She would…

She gasped as his arm reached out and yanked her close. Her flashlight and leash tumbled to the ground. Knocked off balance, she had little choice but to grip the front of his jacket with her free hand, fingers twisting in the worsted wool. She felt his erection against her hip. Instead of setting off warning bells, the knowledge he was aroused fueled her own arousal. The hunger unfolded from a place deep in her soul, as though the lessons from five years ago never happened. She was once again wanton, needy.

"So long," she heard him whisper. He might as well have been reading her mind. When his lips brushed hers, she sighed and allowed him access.

His tongue swept into her mouth without warning. Jenny moaned. He tasted of mint and coffee. She clutched his jacket tighter, pulling close, her hips seeking friction. In the back of her mind, she knew this was a mistake, but the voice of reason couldn't be heard above the rush of blood in her ears. Unable to stop herself, she mewled and clung to him as his hands slid down her back, cupped her bottom.

From far off, she heard a dog barking. Lulu. Charlie. Their baying reached where common sense couldn't and she came back to earth. What was she thinking?

She broke free of Nick's grasp.

"I—I—"

Unable to form words, she turned her attention to fumbling for Lulu's leash. If it was any consolation, Nick appeared to be as dazed as she was. The minute she pushed away, he'd stepped to the edge of the path. He stood there now, silently watching her while Charlie weaved around his legs. Jenny could hear his ragged breath mixing with hers.

What had she been thinking? For years she'd managed to behave herself, to keep the needy, desperate side of her personality in check, and now here she was, practically climbing up a stranger in the woods. She couldn't get off the property fast enough.

Finally, she located the end of Lulu's leash. Forget getting a ride from his driver. Calling him would take too long. Grabbing the leash as well as her flashlight, she stood up. Her legs were still shaking, and she had to hold her arm out to steady herself. This caused the light's arc to swing wide. The beam shone straight at Nick. For the first time, Jenny saw the face of the man she'd so wantonly kissed.

She gasped.

Chapter Four

It was like looking at one of those cartoon villains with two different faces, only this was no cartoon. The right side of Nick's face was marked by a thick darkened blotch that started at his hairline and continued downward, beneath his collar. A thick cord of a scar divided the discoloration into two. It, too, looked like it ran from hair to jaw; its route interrupted by a black eye patch.

The right side of his face, however... The photos she and her friends discovered online didn't do him justice.

His good eye stared at her with such heated blue intensity, it sucked the air from her lungs. What upset her the most, however, wasn't the scarring he'd so clearly tried to hide. It was the renewed ache between her legs. Seeing the flashing heat in his gaze and knowing the passion with which he kissed, she was more aroused than before.

"I..." Dear God, would she ever be able to form a coherent thought again?

No. Not so long as they were here alone in the woods, and he was looking at her like that.

She dragged Lulu down the path before she did something foolish.

• • •

"You just left?" Mia Roth gave her a look from over the rim of her coffee cup. "Without saying anything?"

"I blanked," Jenny told her. "I didn't know what to say."

She, Mia, and their friend Gabby Wilson-Shepherd were in Mia's kitchen the next morning. They were there to look at photographs from Mia's wedding. Jenny had told them about her encounter with Nick. How, as a result of dropping her flashlight, she'd discovered Nick's disfigurement. She left out the reason she'd dropped the flashlight. Bad enough Nick's touch haunted her all night. The way she lost herself in the kiss horrified her. Like some animal starved for affection. Had Charlie and Lulu not barked her back to reality, he could have taken her then and there.

"Found it," Gabby announced. Having heard the story, her friend had borrowed Mia's laptop to find more information. "I can't believe we missed this the first time."

"Because we were looking for photographs, not news articles," Jenny said.

"Not to mention we'd had a pitcher of margaritas," Mia added. "I'm surprised we effectively searched for anything. What does the article say?"

Gabby turned the computer.

"Industrialist injured in lab explosion," Mia read out loud. "Oh, the poor man."

The article described how the heir to Bonaparte Industries had been touring a recently-acquired facility when an explosion tore through the laboratory. Nick was attempting to pull one of his employees to safety when a section of the burning wall collapsed on them.

"Wow," Gabby murmured when they got to that paragraph.

Wow indeed, Jenny thought. She skimmed the rest of the paragraphs until she reached the part about Nick's injuries. Didn't say much, other than the fact Nick suffered extensive burns to his face and body.

"No wonder he's a recluse," Gabby remarked. "I would be, too, if I had half my face burned off."

"The scars aren't that bad," Jenny replied. Then again, she'd been turned upside down by his kiss. Maybe she wasn't seeing straight.

"T.J. has business with him," Mia said. "How come he's never mentioned the scars?"

"Actually," Gabby replied, "they only met in person once and T.J. said Mr. B. sat in the shadows."

"So no one could see his secret," Jenny murmured, pulling at her cardigan sweater. And she'd run off like a scared villager soon as she flashed a light in his face. He'd have no way of knowing her fleeing had nothing to do with his appearance.

"The article doesn't mention a fiancée," she noted. *Speaking of women who ran away.*

Mia set down her coffee. "Mr. B.'s engaged?"

"Was," Jenny replied. "And like I already told Marney, can we please stop calling him Mr. B.? The nickname so doesn't suit him."

On the other side of the table, Gabby and Mia exchanged looks.

"What?" Jenny asked. "It doesn't."

"Not when you can call him Nick," Gabby teased.

"Just look up his fiancée, will you?"

"Yes, *Miss Travolini*." Gabby grabbed the mouse. "This article is from the wire service so they might not have known about the fiancée at the time the stringer filed the story. Other sources probably added information later in the day."

They searched through several more articles, mostly reprints of the original article, before settling on one from a weekly tabloid. The main photograph featured a perfect-looking Nick with an equally perfect raven-haired beauty clinging to his arm.

"She certainly doesn't look like the dog owning type," Gabby remarked. "Hard to picture her breaking a nail—let alone dealing with Charlie's rambunctious side. Can you imagine her spelling out words so he doesn't go crazy?"

"More likely she's one of those types who get a puppy because he makes a cute fashion accessory, then loses interest once they become work," Mia replied. "Gideon hates those kinds of people."

"Yeah, me, too," Jenny replied, although she was only half-listening. Her attention was too focused on studying Nick's face. His blue eyes seemed to reach through the computer screen, brash and confident. So not the gaze she saw last night. Last night she saw fear, a desperation even that matched her own behind the sparkle. Those painful emotions didn't belong in eyes like his. To see them touched a chord deep inside her.

"He sure was gorgeous," Mia said.

"Is." The correction was automatic. "I told you, the scars aren't all that bad."

"Well, he must think they are," Gabby said. "Why else would he pull all this *Phantom of the Opera* stuff?"

Why else indeed? Did Nick think of himself as some kind of marked monster? Jenny's gaze traveled back to the computer screen, to the breathtaking woman on Nick's arm. *The type who loses interest once they become work.* Wasn't that how Mia described her? Had the ex-fiancée bailed on Nick the same way she'd left Charlie, walking away when things became hard? Jenny's heart bled a little at the thought. Not all scars could be seen on the surface, as she knew all too well. The marks of abandonment ran far deeper.

And, last night, she'd run from Nick without explanation, leaving him to think her horror was about him. He couldn't be more wrong. No way he'd know that though.

She owed him an explanation. An apology.

"I have to go," she announced.

Both Mia and Gabby looked up. "Right now?" Mia asked. "Marney hasn't gotten here yet, and we still have to sort through the photos."

"I'm afraid so." Her guilty conscience wouldn't let her put it off. "I need to clear up a misunderstanding."

"Must be some misunderstanding," Gabby noted.

"It is. A big one," she replied. "And it has to be fixed right away, before there's too much damage."

She could practically hear Mia and Gabby speculating as she pulled out of the drive. Even though she tried to cover her odd behavior by blaming a work dispute, she could tell from their shared glances they didn't believe a word. Oh well. Let them speculate. The moment she shared with Nick in the woods was too intimate to share, and while her behavior had shocked her, the magic she'd felt in the moment held a special place in her memory.

She didn't stop to think about why she felt such urgency to set the record straight. Nor did she want to analyze the emotion that clutched at her chest when she thought how her behavior must have hurt him. She only knew that Nick needed to be told he wasn't the reason she ran last night. As shameful as telling her story would feel, allowing Nick to add another layer to his demons would be worse.

She only hoped her courage would last when she got to his front door

. . .

"Cyrus!"

Nick limped his way to the library door and called again, getting nothing but Charlie's bark in response. What the hell good was paying employees if they weren't around when you called for them? He looked down at the terrier who'd followed him. "Nice to know someone isn't afraid to stick around," he said, the words weighing heavy on his shoulder. Charlie grinned and ran back inside where he promptly dragged the throw pillow off the chair. He considered Nick's comment an invitation to play.

"I wish I could." The dog had way too much energy this morning. Unlike Nick, whose back was torturing him. He'd pushed himself too hard working and walking, and as a result, his muscles had tightened up. That was the reason he was looking for Cyrus. Someone should take Charlie for a walk since he couldn't. But the butler was nowhere to be found. Neither, it appeared, was anyone else on his staff.

That's right, he'd given people the day off, to catch up on affairs. Because some people had lives outside this house. "Looks like you're going to have to roam on your own again," he told him. "Just don't tell Jenny."

Jenny. The name stabbed him in the chest. What on earth made him think she'd be different from anyone else not on his payroll? At least the dark spared him seeing the expression on her face when she finally saw him. The fact she ran away was cutting enough.

The rejection wouldn't be bad if he hadn't spent the night reliving the feel of her body against his. Masochistic, yes, but how could he not? After years of solitude and celibacy, he'd gotten to experience physical contact. For a few glorious seconds, he'd been his old self, holding a beautiful woman who wanted him. The memory of those moments would be a long time in fading. Even now, he could recall the taste of her kiss, the way her hips ground against his erection. And, the sounds she made... He'd almost come in his pants from the sounds alone.

Jesus, he was getting hard again. No woman had ever aroused him like this. Much as he wanted to blame celibacy alone, he had a sad feeling his attraction had as much to do with the woman herself. She was smart and quick and perceptive. Talking with her was the best foreplay he'd ever experienced.

"I must have gotten used to being in pain these past couple years to insist on torturing myself like this," he said to Charlie. "I'd be better off walking the dog than indulging in useless fantasies."

Barking his agreement, Charlie tore off toward the

foyer. Nick did his best to keep up, his back aching with each step. This kind of pain, however, he could handle. Physical pain could be managed. Or it could be pushed to the point where he collapsed in oblivion. Either way, the results were better than thinking about a woman who clearly found him abhorrent.

"As long as we stay out of the woods," he called ahead. If he wanted to keep thoughts of Jenny at bay, last thing he needed was to return to the scene of the crime. "We'll stay near the garden." Being Saturday, no one would be arriving to surprise him.

Charlie was already rolling on the Persian carpet. In less than twenty-four hours, he'd turned the priceless object into doggy central. Cyrus was furious. Nick considered it an apt reward.

"Come on," he told the terrier. "You can dig up the mums the gardener planted yesterday." Grabbing a wide brimmed hat to protect himself from the sun, he opened the front door only to come face to face with the woman he'd been thinking about.

The hat slid from his fingers.

Chapter Five

"Hey," she greeted.

She stood on the threshold, bright and gorgeous, the sunlight crowning the top of her head. Desire and tension overtook his tired limbs. His fingers itched to comb through her hair, to feel the golden strands as they slid like silk through his fingers while his blood pulsed hot and needy in his groin. Why was the universe doing this to him? Sending him another woman to want, unrequited? What did he do to deserve such torture? He glared straight into her eyes, waiting for the inevitable pity to flash in their depths. Instead…Was that a blush?

"Are you heading somewhere?"

"Taking Charlie for a walk," he replied, not trusting what he thought he saw. "Since letting him roam free has branded me irresponsible."

He could tell from the way her eyes widened his

comment surprised her. "My injuries left me with physical limitations early on. I wasn't able to walk him myself, and there wasn't always a staff member available."

"So you let him loose, trusting he'd come wandering back."

"On the contrary, I figured he'd find someplace better."

"Why didn't you say something yesterday? Oh." Understanding broke across her face.

"In my position, the fewer people who know my limitations, the better." Crossing his arms, he leaned against the doorframe. That she looked as appealing as ever annoyed him. Today's outfit was more layered than yesterday. Baggy beige cardigan over a heavy brown turtleneck sweater and ankle-length skirt that looked like she was trying to blend with the fading foliage outside. Unfortunately for him, Nick knew the bulk hid a sweet set of curves. He'd mapped them with his hands.

"How did you get past security?" he asked her. The guard at the end of his driveway was the one employee he hadn't given the day off.

"Lowell," she replied. His scrutiny must have been getting to her because she wrapped the cardigan tighter. "Your guard. I had his son for twelfth grade English." She offered a half smile. "Kid wouldn't have graduated if I hadn't given him extra credit. He owed me. Please don't be angry with him," she added.

The pleading in her brown eyes was too much to bear "Lord, you really do think I'm a monster, don't you?"

"No," she rushed. "Not at all."

"Nice recovery. Don't worry. Lowell's not in trouble. I'm

sure you charmed him quite admirably." No doubt, using her wood sprite features without mercy. "I'm afraid your efforts were for nothing. I took care of your veterinarian bill this morning. Instructed Dr. Roth's office to send any further bills directly to me."

"I — Thank you."

"It was obvious from last night that Charlie and Lulu are mates, and I always live up to my responsibilities. Now, if you don't mind, Charlie and I were on our way out."

"I think Charlie beat you to the punch."

Sure enough. The foyer was empty. Dammit, he couldn't even count on his dog today. "Then if you don't mind, I need to catch up with my dog before he winds up at your friend's art studio." He stepped forward, hoping she'd take the hint, but to his surprise, she stayed put.

"Actually," she said, "I'm here about last night."

Nick refrained from letting out a sigh. Since Jenny had stayed her ground, his movement merely closed the distance between them. He stood close enough to smell her floral soap.

"From where I stand, there isn't much to talk about," he told her.

"You're angry with me."

"Me? I'm not angry with you." It was true. He felt a lot of emotions: frustration, hurt, self-admonishment. If he felt any anger at all, it was toward himself for being stupid enough to buy into his own fantasy. "You didn't do anything that other people haven't done before."

"Does that include your fiancée?"

Nick winced. Megan was the last person he wanted to

talk about, especially with Jenny. Since it was obvious she had some point she needed to make, he folded his arms and leaned against the threshold. "What do you want?"

"I—" She started to fidget. Never a good sign. Fidgeting implied discomfort. The toe of her shoe traced patterns along the base of the doorframe. Her gaze seemed immensely focused on this activity as well, unless it was simply an excuse to avoid looking at him. Habit made him want to shrink back into the shadows so she'd be more comfortable.

To hell with her comfort, he decided. She saw him last night, she could look at him in the light of day. "Do I make you nervous?" he asked, leaning forward, challenging her.

"Yes." To her credit, she looked him in the eye when answering. Score one for honesty, even if her words punched him in the gut.

"I see." He backed away.

"I'm sorry."

"Don't." He held up a hand. "I don't want your sympathy, apologies, or explanations. I would, however, like you to leave."

"No."

"No?" Yesterday, he'd found her stubbornness amusing; not so this afternoon. Every second she hung around reminded him what a mistake it had been to kiss her. Especially since he really wanted to kiss her again.

"You don't understand." Her hand reached out to touch his arm. He pulled away. "I know you think I ran because of your injuries, but that's not the case."

"It isn't?"

"No. Sure, they shocked me at first, but you act as though

you're some repulsive monster."

Wasn't he? Megan had said… No, he didn't need Megan's mocking words to know how awful he looked; the mirror told him every morning.

And yet Jenny hadn't looked away. Her eyes remained locked with his, emotion swirling behind the moistness. Nick studied the depths. To his amazement, he saw not pity or fear, but regret.

"I didn't run because of how you look," she told him. "I ran because of how you made me feel." She cleared her throat. "How you *make* me feel."

· · ·

That she got the words out at all amazed her. She thought she had her apology all worked out—Lord knows she practiced enough on the drive over—but then Nick had opened the door and she'd found herself yet again pinned down by his sapphire gaze. He was trying his best to glare but the hurt bled through, muting the chill he was working so hard to cast.

In the light of day, she had a better view of his injuries. The darkened skin was raised and brownish pink, the scar a shade lighter. Both traveled below his collar. She realized the eye patch didn't matter. His remaining eye was brilliant enough to compensate. In fact, the Internet pictures failed to do him justice. What the fire hadn't touched was more than unblemished—it was perfection. Jenny grew weak in the knees.

She knew her comment wouldn't make sense to him.

Sure enough, he folded his arms across his chest and waited for her to continue.

Swallowing hard, she tried. "Last night, w-w-when you kissed me, I…" God, this was more difficult than she thought. "I lost control. I shouldn't have. People in town see me, that is, I have a reputation. If my students—not to mention their parents—thought that I went around… well, I'd lose all their respect."

"I see." He shifted his weight. "So you ran away because people might gossip?"

"Yes. I mean no." She was handling this badly. "Do you think we could do this somewhere besides the doorway?" Talking might be easier without him glowering over her like a sentry.

"What about Charlie?"

Jenny wasn't sure if he was kidding or being sarcastic. Hard to tell from his expression. "I'll take responsibility if he shows up downtown," she said. "Please."

A couple seconds ticked by, and then Nick stepped aside. "We can talk in the library."

He escorted her down the corridor opposite the one she travelled the day before. This time, the artwork and décor passed by unnoticed. Jenny was too focused on what she would say when they reached their destination.

The 'library' she discovered was not unlike Nick's office, only instead of a desk, an oversized sofa dominated the room. He motioned for her to take a seat before walking over to a small bar set up in the corner. "Water or stronger?" he asked.

"Whatever you're having is fine."

He grabbed two water bottles. "So," he said, handing one to her, "you're worried about your reputation."

"Not really. Sort of. It's complicated." She set her water down, bottle unopened. Where did she begin? "Last night, in the woods, you made me feel things I hadn't felt in a long time. Things I didn't want to feel."

"Go on."

"When I came to Chandler's Cove, it was to be a certain kind of person. I wanted to be in control of my life again. Things had gotten chaotic in Chicago."

"What do you mean, chaotic?"

"I mean I was out of control." She looked to her lap so he couldn't see her shame. "My father took off when I was in first grade. One day he just disappeared. My mom use to tell me it was my fault."

"I'm—"

She held up a hand to cut him off. "You didn't want sympathy, and neither do I. What happened, happened. Anyway," she took a deep breath, "long story short, I developed 'issues'. I took affection from wherever I could get it. Whoever. I wasn't always discriminating in my choices."

She heard stirring and the sofa sagged next to her. Nick had moved closer. Exactly what she didn't want, because even when she was filled with shame, his proximity stirred her awareness. Skin burning, she turned her face away. "By the time I graduated college, I'd lost track of how many nights, how many false promises. All I wanted was someone to hold me and make me feel like I was wanted. So long as I didn't spend the night alone."

"Jenny…" Tenderness had crept into his voice. Her

stomach ached at the sound. Kindness had been her biggest downfall. A few kind words, and she was done.

"I had a health scare." She blurted the words out fast as she could.

"A scare?"

Jenny nodded. No need explaining. He was smart enough to figure it out. "Fortunately, it was only a scare but it was enough to make me realize how messed up my life had gotten. I promised myself then and there I would change. That I would stop being some needy, desperate creature who let men use her.

"So I moved here and I reinvented myself. It was hard but I created a new kind of life. For the first time in my life, I had real friends. Supportive, female friends." Gabby, Marney, and Mia didn't know it, but they'd been her lifeline. She grew stronger because they were in her life.

"Do they know about…about your life before?"

Now who thought who was a monster? Jenny shook her head. "No. I buried the old me when I left, never to be resurrected again."

"Then why—"

"Because I owed you an explanation for last night. I couldn't let you think my fear was your fault." Why she gave him such a lengthy explanation, however, she didn't know, any more than she understood why she had to rush here to confess. Who knows, maybe it was his scars that made her feel like she should share her own in such detail.

Or maybe this was another example of how easily he could affect her behavior.

Having heard her out, Nick rose and walked to the

fireplace. He stood with his back to her, staring at the unlit hearth. Jenny prepared to leave.

"So when we kissed last night, it reminded you of Chicago?"

"Yes." There was no reason to say more. He'd been in the woods with her, saw how she reacted. "I swore I would never go down that road again."

"What road?"

Did he really expect her to explain?

Of course. Lost in her shame, she'd forgotten the purpose of her confession was to soothe his demons. He was looking for reassurance that her fear wasn't because of him. Taking a deep breath, she plunged forward. "I promised myself I would never get so caught up in physical pleasure that I forgot reality." She convinced herself lust equaled love one too many times. Another reason last night scared her so damn badly. The arousal that kissing Nick awoke inside her was stronger than anything she'd ever felt before.

Nick turned and though he was trying to hide it, she caught the spark of pride in his eye. Had it been someone else, she'd been furious, but knowing his own fear of rejection, she couldn't fault him his small satisfaction. To his credit, he blinked the reaction away as quickly as possible.

"I'm sorry," he said.

"I already told you, I'm not looking for your sympathy."

"Then why did you tell me?"

"So you'd understand."

His mouth formed a thin line. "In other words, out of sympathy for me." He stared at the floor for a second before crossing the room and perching himself on the coffee table.

A long, thick-legged piece that looked created for that exact purpose. The new position placed them knee-to-knee. His pants leg brushed against her khaki skirt, the contact somehow reaching through the material to touch her skin.

"You didn't have to say anything, you know," he said. "You could have gone your separate way and never said a word. Let me believe whatever I was going to believe. I wouldn't have known."

Instead, he would have continued to see himself as a repulsive monster. "It wouldn't have been fair to you."

"Who says life's fair?"

His words were eerily similar to ones he'd said the first time they met. Was that really only yesterday? It felt like they'd known each other so much longer. "You're right, life's not fair." She knew that as well as anyone. "All the more reason to right the wrongs we can. I know what it's like to feel unwanted. I couldn't allow another person to feel that way when it's not true."

"I can't imagine anyone not wanting you," he said softly.

"I've got a long list that would prove you wrong." Too long a list.

Jenny's eyes burned. Throughout the entire conversation, she kept her tears in check, refusing to embarrass herself further by crying as she confessed her past. She had the situation under control; By God she would act like it.

At least she had it under control until Nick chose to cup her cheek with his hand. "Thank you."

She raised her eyes to look at him. Even with the burns and scars, he remained one of the most handsome men she'd ever seen. What could he ever want with someone as broken and used as her anyway? A tear slipped out and made its way down her cheek. Nick swiped it away with his thumb. The gesture was simple yet so comforting. She could feel her body melting toward him. "I should go," she said, forcing herself to break the contact.

"Do you have to?"

Did he have to speak with such a sultry whisper? "Yes." If she stayed, she'd only compound last night's mistake. From the way her heart raced, she was already in danger of falling too deeply.

That is, if she hadn't fallen already.

Chapter Six

Nick wished she would stay, but walked Jenny to her car without protest. As he watched her car disappear down his drive, he mentally replayed her confession. Frankly, her story left him unsettled. Shouldn't he feel relieved that he hadn't been the cause of her running? Why then did his chest still feel like there was a hole in the middle of it? Certainly, her story answered some of the questions he'd had. He now understood the reason behind the baggy clothes and purposeful plainness. She was hiding herself, same as he was. She was as damaged as he was too, just in a different way.

Perhaps that was the reason for the aching sensation—his heart recognized a fellow sufferer. It humbled him that she shared her history with him. Filled him with shame as well. He didn't deserve her kindness. Jenny believed him to be a wounded soul. She had no way of knowing his wounds were punishment for the vain, arrogant bastard he used to be. Maybe even still was, because after everything Jenny told him, one thought kept coming back again and again: *she'd wanted him.*

Jesus, was he any better than the men from her past?

Someone was sniffing around his feet. "Stuck close to home, did you?"

Charlie didn't answer other than to look at up at him expectantly before trotting toward the back yard.

Nick followed. "What do I do now?" he asked. The decent thing was to shove his own ego aside and pretend he never heard her admit her attraction. That, of course, meant ignoring the damn kiss. Pretty near impossible. Even the most passing memory had him hard as a rock. What kinds of idiots were those men who had treated her so poorly? Didn't they realize they'd been given a goddamn gift? A woman worth savoring? Worth holding on to? Imagining a naked Jenny sprawled across his bed, her lips puffed and eyes glazed, he groaned. God, he wanted her so badly, one fantastical image had him ready to come.

Making him no different than the other men she'd met in her life. Jenny was right to walk away.

The hole in his chest grew larger. A strange desperate sensation nagged at him, as if there was a thought he couldn't quite form or an object he couldn't quite hold on to. Like sand slipping through his fingers. *She wanted you,* the voice whispered in his head. And he wanted her. Worse, he had the sneaking suspicion that beneath the wanting lay the potential for more. For a great deal more.

Puh-lease, who could love you? Megan's ghost taunted.

Who indeed?

"Jenny deserves a lot better than a guy who lives in the shadows, that's for sure," he said to Charlie. Not to mention a man so insensitive, he continued to contemplate sleeping with her after hearing her confession. "Right, Charlie?"

The terrier barked. Nick pretended they were in agreement.

• • •

Lulu didn't like her whelping bed. Jenny followed the recommendations to the letter. She found a quiet, warm corner and filled the space soft blankets. Still, Lulu wanted nothing to do with the thing.

"Lots of dogs ignore the bed until they actually go into labor," Gideon said when she called him Friday night. "I wouldn't worry too much. "

"I suppose," Jenny replied. "Just that's she's been listless all week as well."

"You'd be, too, if you had a bunch of near-term babies in your stomach. Lulu will be fine. Dogs have been having puppies on their own for centuries."

He had a point, although Jenny couldn't shake the feeling Lulu's malaise involved more than pregnancy. The spaniel's lethargy seemed to increase the longer she was separated from Charlie.

Or maybe she was simply projecting her own misery onto the canine. Lord knows, she'd been in a funk since saying good-bye to Nick a week ago.

Stupid thing was that a part of her kept hoping he'd call or come by. Anything. Nick, not Charlie. She really hadn't learned a thing, had she? One kiss and here she was hung up on the guy.

"My guess is she's getting near delivery time," Gideon

was saying. "Keep an eye on her, and if she's been in labor for more than twenty-four hours without a pup or if she starts vomiting or releasing a discharge, give me a call. Have Mia track me down if you can't reach me."

Jenny smiled at the last part. "Thanks, Gideon. I appreciate the personal service."

"A friend of Mia's is a friend of mine, you know that." He disappeared while whispers sounded on the other side of the phone. A second later, Mia popped on the line. "Hey Jenny, don't forget margaritas and karaoke tomorrow night. I'm making Gideon join me on 'Paradise by the Dashboard Light?'"

"Can't wait." Jenny hoped her enthusiasm sounded real. She loved her friends more than anything. but she wasn't looking forward to playing seventh wheel at the moment. Just thinking about it left her with a lonely, heavy feeling.

"Great. Hold on, Gideon needs you again."

The vet's deep voice returned. "I forgot to mention about your bill…"

"Gid!" Mia could be heard admonishing him in the distance.

"It's not what you think," he shot back. Returning to Jenny, he continued, "I meant to say something at your appointment the other day but forgot. Bonaparte called and said to send the bills to him. Said it was the least he could do. Then he made an appointment to have Charlie fixed. Turns out I was wrong about him ignoring my suggestion—he thought the dog had been neutered a long time ago."

Nick had led her to believe he simply didn't care but once again, she discovered that when it came to Nick Bonaparte, the story wasn't as it first appeared. He seemed determined to be viewed as cold and callous when, in fact, those two words couldn't be further from the truth. Another way to keep people at a distance. If only the opposite were true; if only he *were* a cold-hearted bastard. Every sympathetic facet she saw in him made her miss him a little more.

She thanked Gideon for the information and hung up, feeling more alone than ever.

Was she being overly dramatic, refusing to have anything to do with him? Six days and she could still remember his touch on her skin. If she licked her lips, she could almost taste his kiss. Worse was the nagging whisper in the back of her mind telling her this time might be the real thing.

Then Jenny remembered all the times growing up she'd listened to that same whisper, only to find herself tossed aside in favor of someone better, and those had been men nowhere near Nick's class.

Lulu heaved a squeaky sigh and stretched her chin on the sofa. If she intended the move to make Jenny feel guilty, it worked. "Sorry you got caught in the middle, girl," she said, patting the dog's swollen belly. "Looks like we're both paying the price for meeting the Bonaparte men. We'll get over them eventually though, and things will be fine. We'll be fine. I promise."

The last words weren't louder than a whisper. That was all right. Jenny meant them for herself anyway. Lulu gave another whimper and went to sleep.

"We'll be fine," Jenny whispered again.

• • •

The next morning was Saturday, her day off. Jenny slept

in. When she woke, Lulu wasn't on the sofa. She wasn't on Jenny's bed, the overstuffed easy chair, or any of her other haunts. Nor was she using the whelping bed. Jenny tore the house apart trying to find the animal—looking in closets, under beds—but Lulu was nowhere to be found. A walk into the kitchen confirmed her worst nightmare. The back door had blown open during the night. In her distracted state, Jenny had forgotten to shut it tightly. Again. *Idiot.*

Ignoring the growing sense of dread in the pit of her stomach, she headed into the backyard, calling Lulu's name and hoping the dog was simply relieving herself in the bushes. She wasn't. The bushes, the garage, and every potential birthing location were untouched.

Jenny felt sick. She'd done enough research to know pregnant dogs sometimes dragged themselves off somewhere to give birth. Fine if you were talking summer, but it was October and the weather reports were forecasting a killer frost as well as possible snow flurries. She could already feel the cold blowing off the lakes. Even if Lulu did manage to find a sheltered location for her puppies, there was no telling if the little ones would survive the cold. And what if there were complications?

She knew something wasn't right last night. Who cared if dogs had been giving birth for a million years; her dog hadn't. And why hadn't she double-checked the doorway? Now Lulu was God knows where, alone, pregnant, and missing her mate.

Charlie. Jenny tugged her cardigan tighter. Wasn't possible, was it? She'd just finished worrying the dog wasn't bright enough to protect her puppies from the cold and now she was wondering if Lulu went searching for the puppies' father? How would the spaniel know which way to go?

Again, Charlie. The terrier had been in the process of taking her to his house when she found him last week. *The night she kissed Nick.*

Oh God, she so wasn't ready to talk with him yet. She needed time to shake free of whatever spell he had over her.

On the other hand, if Lulu had dragged her pregnant self to his house, or wandered some place with Charlie, she needed to know.

Nick's business card, the one he gave her the day they'd met, lay on the desk. Jenny grabbed her phone and began punching the numbers before she could have second thoughts. *Please let the butler answer, please let the butler answer..*

"Hello?"

As usual, her wish wasn't granted. Nick's greeting rolled through her, making her knees weak.

"Hey."

"Jenny?"

His note of expectancy made the reaction worse. Swallowing her fluttering nerves, she forced herself to sound casual. "I wasn't expecting you to answer the phone," she said.

"This is my private line."

Of course it was. Because a house line would have made things easier for her.

"What can I do for you?"

"Lulu's not there by any chance, is she?"

"Why would your dog be here?"

"I can't find her, and I thought maybe she and Charlie..." Hearing her thoughts out loud made Jenny realize how idiotic they truly were. "Never mind."

"No, wait. Lulu's not home?"

"No. I woke up this morning, and she'd disappeared."

"Isn't she supposed to have her puppies any day now? Gideon told me," he added.

When he'd called about her bill. "That's what has me concerned. I'm afraid she might have gone looking for somewhere to have her puppies. And to be with Charlie. Do you know where he is?"

"Unfortunately, yes. I let him out earlier this morning, but he returned about an hour ago. He's been curled up in his chair ever since."

"So much for that theory. I guess I'll have to come up with another." Jenny gripped the phone tighter. Having heard Nick's voice again, she found it difficult to say good-bye. "If she does show up, will you let me know?"

"Of course. I hope you find her soon."

"Me, too."

"Will you call me when you do? So I know?"

"Sure."

"Thank you. And Jenny?" He called through the receiver, catching her before she could hang up. More than anything, Jenny hated how her heart sped up soon as he said her name.

"Yes?" she asked.

The line was quiet. If not for the sound of his breathing, Jenny might have thought he'd ended the call. Instead, she imagined him gathering his words. To make the most of regaining her attention.

"Good luck," he said finally.

Jenny's heart sunk a little. They weren't the words she'd

hoped to hear, but they were the words she expected. "Thank you," she whispered in reply. She disconnected.

• • •

Since Lulu wasn't anywhere around the house, nor in any of her neighbor's yards, Jenny headed out on foot to search. Given the spaniel's swollen belly, the little gal couldn't have gotten too far. That is, unless she went out at dawn, Jenny amended, an unsettling thought since foxes and coyotes also roamed around at that hour. She could only imagine how tasty a slow, fat spaniel would look to one of them. To that end, her first instinct was to cover the path Lulu and Charlie had taken last week.

Did all roads have to lead back to Nick Bonaparte? she asked herself as she entered the woods boarding his property. Why was it that every blessed thing she did this week brought back memories of their one evening together? Her longest, most pathetic relationships hadn't affected her as much. Johnny Woods had strung her along all through high school, and she got over him the day after graduation. But one kiss in the woods with Nick had given her an ache in her chest the size of the Grand Canyon for more than a week. Granted, Johnny didn't kiss like Nick. No one kissed like Nick. Nor had she met anyone with whom she felt so drawn to in so short a time. She didn't just mean sexually, either. She was drawn to the emotions hiding behind his blue stare.

And then there was that voice inside of her, still whispering how she might be passing by on "the one." She was beginning to really hate that voice.

Up ahead, right before a turn in the path, she noticed a small clump of branches curled in on one another to form a small hollow. The perfect place for an animal to crawl under? "Lulu?" she called, hoping the spaniel might bark in reply. "You there?"

There was a rustle of leaves and Jenny knelt down, hoping to see beneath the clump.

"Lulu?"

A bundle of white and brown burst around the corner, barking excitedly. There was only one problem: it was the wrong bundle.

Charlie danced about on hind legs trying to lick her face hello. "What on earth are you doing here?" she asked him.

More importantly, if Charlie was roaming here in the woods, did that mean…?

"Looks like we had the same idea."

Nick came around the corner. Jenny tried not to react to how rustically handsome he looked in his jeans and barn coat. She failed. Even the floppy brimmed cowboy hat looked good. It was going to take another six days before he was out of her system. Probably more, she realized, awareness pooling in the pit of her stomach.

"After you hung up, I realized Lulu might be en route," he said. Lord, his voice still sounded like honeyed gravel, even in the daylight. "Figured of anybody, Charlie had the best chance of sniffing her out. So far, we haven't had any luck." While he spoke, he moved around the brush.

"You're limping," Jenny said.

"It's nothing."

No, it was very much something. She hadn't forgotten that when she called him, Nick mentioned having let Charlie out for a walk. He told her he only did that when he was in pain. That he would then turn around and go hiking in the woods to help her look for a lost dog... Her awareness shifted, changing from something intensely female into a fullness lodged in her heart.

"I didn't mean to make you walk all this distance. If you want to turn around—"

He cut her off. "I wanted to."

He did?

"Afraid you'll have paid all those vet bills in vain?" The sharp comment was unfair, but she said it anyway, needing something to combat the shift in her feelings, not to mention drown out that damn voice.

"Because I know how important Lulu is to you."

Oh dear Lord, how was she supposed to resist statements like that? She turned away before her expression could betray her thoughts.

She heard the sound of leaves crunching beneath Nick's feet, and suddenly he was behind her, his hands settling on her shoulders. The proximity, after days apart, felt too good. "I've missed you," he murmured.

Yeah, right. "Then why didn't you—?" She caught herself, but the damage was done.

"You made it abundantly clear you didn't want me to contact you. And, truth be told," the back of his hand skimmed her cheek so tenderly she had to close her eyes to the sensation, "I couldn't help but think your decision made sense. That is, once you realized..."

Realized what? Jenny didn't find out because at that moment, her cell phone rang cutting him off. It was Gabby. "I should take this. I called her earlier about Lulu." With her eyes, she tried to convey her regret.

"You need to get down to the studio right away," Gabby said when she answered.

"Is something wrong?" It wasn't like Gabby to issue blunt commands. "I'm still looking for Lulu."

"I know. She's here."

"She is? Where did you find her? Is she all right?"

"I really think you need to come to the studio," Gabby repeated.

Any relief she might have felt faded at Gabby's cryptic response. "All right, I'll be there as soon as I can."

She could feel Nick watching her as she hung up the phone. "Everything all right?" he asked.

"I don't know. She said she had Lulu and I needed to come down to the studio. Do you think it's bad news?" Gabby's studio was near a busy intersection. Chances were very real that an early morning driver might not see a small dog darting into traffic. Charlie had always made it down there safely, but her dog wasn't used to escape the way Nick's independent terrier was. The thought of her little Lulu...

Jenny started to feel sick. Eyes watering, she looked to Nick for an answer.

"Wouldn't she have told you if something was wrong?"

"Not necessarily. Not if it were really bad."

"I'm sorry." Nick's hand settled on her shoulder. Jenny leaned into the touch.

Just being close to Nick made her feel better. What would she do when she had to tear herself away from him?

For the moment, however, she burrowed a little closer, sighing when Nick's other arm wrapped her close. "Thank you," she whispered against his jacket.

"For what?"

He truly didn't know, which made the moment that much...*more*. To be held by a man without expectations. There were no words.

"You know there's a chance you're overreacting, right?" he offered.

Her face buried in his jacket, Jenny couldn't help but smile. "I definitely seem to get emotional around you, don't I?"

"Yeah, you do," he replied in a faraway voice. He pulled her closer and they stood there, quiet. For a brief moment, it felt like they were the only two people in the world, the only noise being the sound of Charlie stalking chipmunks in the leaves.

• • •

Nick breathed in her scent. He'd spent the last six days telling himself that he wasn't right for a woman like Jenny—that he wasn't right for any woman, for that matter—and that his decision to let her drive off was a good thing. Holding her close, however, sent all those arguments flying out the window. Hell, they flew out the window soon as she telephoned him and he heard her voice. So what if they'd only known each other a few days? Instinct told him there was something between them. Call it a connection, a bond, whatever, but it was real, and this moment proved it. Holding Jenny close, he felt complete for the first time in days. Years really, if he was truly honest with himself. Only a fool would let such an opportunity go. And since when was he a fool?

The time had come for him to make a choice. He could

let this wonderful opportunity slip through his fingers or he could step out of the shadows he'd been hiding in and for the first time since the accident, act like a man who'd been given a second chance.

"Come on," he said breaking their embrace. The matching reluctance in her eyes sealed his resolve. "Standing in the middle of the woods worrying isn't helping anything. Only way we're going to know what's going on is if we go to Gabby's."

"We? You're coming with me? To the studio?"

Nick couldn't blame her for looking confused. There was so much he needed to explain when they had time. Right now, he settled for reassurance.

Cradling her face between his hands, he pressed a kiss to her forehead. "Yes," he told her. "I'm coming with you."

It was time to stop living in the shadows.

Chapter Seven

They pulled up to find Gabby pacing the sidewalk. Soon as she saw Nick in the driver's seat, the gallery owner's eyes widened. "Mr. B? I mean, Mr. Bonaparte?" She looked at Jenny then back at him. "I – I wasn't expecting you to come to the gallery."

"Jenny and I were looking for Lulu when you called."

"Really? I didn't realize." She shot another look in Jenny's direction before extending her hand. "It's nice to finally meet you in person."

Nick took in Gabby's welcoming smile. If the woman found his scars repulsive, she hid her reaction well. Was it possible that all this time, his worries had been in his head? The byproduct of a selfish woman's insults?

"Same here. Gives me a chance to thank you for taking care of Charlie. Hope he wasn't too much trouble."

"Nothing the four of us couldn't handle. If anything, he seemed to bring us all good fortune."

Yes, thought Nick, *he certainly did.*

"Not to interrupt the greeting or anything…" While he and Gabby had been talking, Jenny had gotten out of the car. She and Charlie bounced impatiently by the entrance, waiting to be let in. "You called about Lulu. Is she all right?"

Gabby grinned. "Oh, she's fine. Come see for yourself."

With Charlie leading the way, Gabby directed them through her front showroom and into the back office.

"I had no idea she was back here or I would have called sooner," she told them. "I opened the door to grab some paper for the printer and there she was. I still don't know how she got in here. I didn't even know she knew where the studio was."

Gabby swung open the door. On the floor, nestled in some old rags lay Lulu, four tiny brown and white bodies asleep by her belly.

"Oh my God, will you look at them?" Jenny exclaimed. She ran a finger over each of the four backs.

Charlie barked and licked Lulu's nose before settling in next to her. "If I didn't know better, I'd swear he was proud of himself," Nick said.

"Can you blame him? Look at how adorable they are!" She frowned. "Wonder what made her come here?" Jenny said. "I didn't think she knew how to get to the studio."

"Me neither," replied Gabby. "Only dog that ever visits is Charlie. I called Gideon, by the way. He said he'd be over to give her a check soon as the clinic closed, but until then she's fine where she is."

"Thanks. I'm sure he'll happily remind me how he told me she wouldn't need help delivering her puppies."

"Looks like he was right," Nick remarked.

"Which I'm sure he'll remind me about, too. Good job, Lulu." Jenny rubbed Lulu's ears. "Good job."

Seeing Jenny's face glow with such obvious pride and affection brought a lump to Nick's throat. And when she turned and that same emotion was aimed in his direction, the lump nearly doubled. That one smile was worth every stare, every whisper, and every risk he'd ever face. He smiled back, hoping she recognized similar emotions reflecting hers.

Her fingers entwined with his. *Definitely worth the risk*, thought Nick. *Definitely*.

. . .

"Lulu seems happy enough with her whelping box now," Nick pointed out later that afternoon. Following Gideon Roth's proclamation that mother and babies were one hundred percent healthy, Jenny and Nick had brought them from the studio back to Nick's house. The entire family, Charlie included, was now asleep in Nick's library. Lulu and the puppies were resting in the box they picked up from Jenny's apartment, and Charlie slept by their side.

"She certainly does," Jenny replied. "Something else Gideon will be able to gloat about."

"Well, the man is a veterinarian. One should hope he knows what he's talking about when it comes to our pets."

Our. The word inspired thoughts of future that she did her best to tamp down. "You know, Gabby, Mia, and Marney have already made claims to three of the puppies."

"Hope they cleared that with Charlie. He seems pretty darn protective."

Yes, thought Jenny, *Charlie did*. The dog hadn't left

Lulu's side since they'd discovered her. Funny how, when they arrived at Gabby's shop, he ran straight to the back room. Almost like he knew where Lulu was hiding out.. Canine instinct, she supposed.

Nick was limping his way back into the living room. Seeing his uneven gait, Jenny felt a stab of guilt. He'd been on his feet most of the day. As a result, his limp was more pronounced, and he kept rubbing at his right shoulder.

"You let your muscles stiffen up, didn't you?"

He waved off her concern. "It's nothing."

But Jenny could tell it was not nothing. He was obviously hurting. "Sit," she said, pointing to the living room sofa.

He stood and watched her.

"I said sit." She waited until he'd done what he was told, then settled on the cushions behind him. "You spent the day helping me. It's time for me to do something for you."

"You don't have to," he said as soon as she touched his shoulders.

His concern made her smile. He was offering her space, a chance to protect herself through distance again. His giving her the choice made her decision all that much easier. "Let me do something nice for you," she told him.

Slowly, she began kneading the muscles between his shoulder blades, her smile growing when he groaned and let his head fall forward.

"Feel good?"

"Mmm."

"Good." Beneath his cotton shirt, Nick's muscles tensed and released. She was enjoying his pleasure. So much so, it surprised her. A slow familiar heat began to curl through her.

She still couldn't believe Nick had come to Gabby's studio with her. The ladies, of course, thought he was amazing. She knew they would. Especially when he used his coat to swaddle Lulu and the pups.

"Do not let him get away," Mia had whispered.

Jenny had to admit, his behavior was swoon-worthy. She wanted to tell Mia it wasn't a case of letting Nick get away.

Now, with the day's drama behind him, the familiar insecurities rose up to taunt her again. *As if a man like this could care about you.*

And yet today, when Lulu went missing, he'd been there for her. Not just by helping her look for the missing dog, but by understanding and holding her hand. He didn't have to go into town when Gabby called. He could have stayed in his mansion, safely ensconced in his darkened room. Instead, he drove into town – into the public eye - without a second thought. *For her.*

A lump found its way to her throat. What Nick did today took courage. Maybe it was time she showed a little courage herself and trust Nick might stick around..

Taking a deep breath, she leaned forward and whispered, "This might be easier if you took off your shirt."

She felt his body tense. He was waiting. To see if she truly meant what she said. Not every fear of his had been conquered today. "It's all right," she told him. "Let me see you."

When he didn't move right away, she reached out and slowly pulled his T-shirt over his head.

Based on the newspaper descriptions, she expected scars. And there were. There was also a body that looked carved from marble. The burns formed a granite like mosaic, dark on pale, across his defined skin. Covering his arm, the marks spread over his shoulder, and down his right side. Starting at the top, Jenny let her index finger trace the pattern edge down to his rib cage. The texture was rough, but not overly so. Splaying her fingers, she slowly ran both hands back up along his spine. The sigh that Nick breathed out was soft and laced with gratitude. Made Jenny want to drape herself over his back and hold him tight.

"She called me a monster," he said in a soft voice.

She, meaning Megan.

"It was after the accident. I heard her on the phone. She said there wasn't enough money in the world for her to want to wake up to my face every morning."

"Oh, Nick." She wanted to say she couldn't imagine hearing such awful things, but she could. She knew that kind of pain all too well.

"Sometimes I think she was right. I used to be a selfish bastard. Sometimes I wonder if the accident didn't just take the ugly from the inside and move it where people could see."

Wow, they really were two scarred peas in a pod, weren't they? No wonder they found each other. Was he "the one" like the voice in her head kept saying? Who knew? He might be, he might not. But what she did know was that right here, right now, she felt closer to him than any man she'd ever known.

"I don't think you're ugly," she whispered. "Inside or out."

"That's because you're looking at nine months of state of the art skin grafting." It was a feeble attempt to make light of her comment. A defense mechanism she knew well.

Hearing this man fighting the same insecurities dissolved the last of her fears.

Arms slipping around his waist, she leaned forward and pressed her lips between his shoulder blades. "Not ugly at all," she repeated.

Nick's hand rested over hers. "Jenny…"

Again, offering her the chance to change her mind. Jenny answered by kissing a path down his back, her tongue flicking across each knob on his spine.

Down his back, across to his rib cage, until he swiveled around. Hands finding her shoulders, he pulled her toward him. "Jenny," he said again, this time the word sounded like a groan. They came together in a need-fueled kiss. Nick's tongue licked her lips, demanding entrance.

Jenny obliged without hesitation. He tasted as wonderful as she remembered.

"God, what you do to me," Nick groaned. "Ever since that night in the woods… It's like I was dead, and now I'm alive again." Jenny gasped as he took her hand and pressed it to erection pressing at the front of his jeans. "Feel what you do to me?" He thrust up against her hand. "How hard and desperate you make me? I need you, Jenny. You and only you."

Jenny shocked herself by whimpering and fumbling for the button at his waist.

"Shhh," he said, stilling her. "Not yet. We've just started. I want to make sure you want this as much as I do."

He ran a hand down the inside of her thigh, and Jenny whimpered, "I do." Dear God, she wanted him so badly she could barely breathe.

His fingers danced across the juncture between her hip

and thigh. "Are you sure?"

"Yes." Why was he still holding back? His consideration was sweet at first, but now she needed him. It was her turn to show him. Grabbing his wrist, she moved his hand upward, so he could feel how badly. "Please."

There was no need for words after that. They barely made it to his bedroom. Somewhere along the way, Jenny's cardigan dropped to the floor, along with her turtleneck. As they tumbled to the bed, and Nick's fingers skimmed the underside of her bra, she arched her back in anticipation, causing him to chuckle. To her frustration, he stopped there, instead pausing to rain kisses on her neck and jaw. She shivered as his incisors grazed the sensitive spot on her throat.

"That's right, sweetheart," he whispered. "Let go. I'm going to make you feel so good."

His fingers were on her skin again, fingering their way beneath her bra straps, pushing them downward. Feeling his hot breath find its way to her collarbone, she arched again. Her nipples hardened, as though knowing only the thinnest of layers separated them from the touch she craved. It seemed an eternity, but at last his hand cupped her breast, his thumb swiping across the peak. Jenny twisted with pleasure. Finally! She let him mark her with his hands and his mouth, each touch, each swipe of tongue turning her skin to gooseflesh.

Her fingers dug into his shoulders. She ached to feel his hands back between her legs, a need she communicated by grinding her hips against his. A soft pop of a button, followed by the rasp of her zipper, and his hand was there, shoving her slacks below her hips. Lifting up, she helped kick them free.

Her panties followed. By this point, she was wet, throbbing with the need for release. When he finally touched her, it didn't take long for the melting sensation to start.

Nick ran a tongue across her breast. "Spread your legs for me, sweetheart."

She would have stood on her head if he asked. It'd been so long since a man had touched her, and she was so close. So very, very close to coming. Maddeningly gentle, he eased one finger deep inside her. She ground herself on his hand, needing more. Slowly, he pulled out and added a second before thrusting back in hard. Jenny cried out with pleasure. This was what she needed. Over and over, he drove his fingers into her, his thumb passing across her clitoris with each stroke. Nails digging into skin, she rode his hand, letting the pleasure build. Still it wasn't enough. She needed the fullness that came from him being inside her.

As though reading her mind, Nick reached out with his free hand to undo his zipper. Jenny helped him shove his jeans from his hips. The motion helped return a piece of her sanity.

"Please tell me you have protection?" she asked breathlessly.

He kissed her with a smile. "Top drawer on your left."

A few ministrations later, Nick slid inside her. Jenny gasped at the fullness. She couldn't believe how wonderful having a man inside her could feel. Never...never had she felt such...completion.

Looking to the man hovering above her, she saw from his expression Nick felt the same emotions. Fingers trembling, she brushed his scarred cheek.

"More," she whispered. She didn't know if the command

made any sense, but she knew she needed him deeper, as deep as a man could bury himself. Amazingly, Nick understood and he obeyed, rocking slowly at first, then building, each snap of his hips bringing her pleasure to a crescendo. When she came, it wasn't the rough hard pleasure she thought she'd feel, but a long, slow melting that lasted and lasted. Crying out, she wrapped her legs around Nick's waist and drew him deep. His hips stuttered and stiffened, and a moment later he joined her, calling out her name with his release.

The air filled with the sounds of their breathing as they slowly floated back to earth. "That," Nick murmured. He didn't finish the sentence. He didn't have to. Jenny knew exactly what he meant.

"That indeed."

Rolling off her, he pulled her back tight against his chest in a spooning position, but Jenny had a better idea. She turned and nestled into him, her hand splaying over his heart. A soft sigh could be heard from his lips. Raising her eyes, she saw his gaze wet with emotion.

"See you in the morning?" he whispered.

It was both a question and a promise.

"In the morning," she repeated, kissing the back of his hand. "There's no one I'd rather wake up and find."

Nick smiled. "Me, either."

She closed her eyes and floated away on the sound of Nick's deep, easy breathing. Just as sleep was about to claim her, she felt the mattress sag with added weight. A smile curled her lips. She knew exactly who joined them. Funny how one furry little creature could bring so much happiness to so many people. Somehow, he'd managed to bring Gabby, Mia, and Marney the loves of their lives.

As for her…Well, it might be too soon to say the word love aloud, but the voices in her head—and her heart—told her to trust that love was definitely on the horizon. Nick Bonaparte wasn't walking away anytime soon.

She gave the furry little head one last sleepy tussle.

"Good night, Charlie," she said. "Thanks for everything."

About the Author

An award-winning author Barbara Wallace lives in Massachusetts with her five great loves – her husband, their teenage son, and three very spoiled pets (as if there could be any other kind). When she's not writing you can find her rooting for the Red Sox and messing around in her kitchen. She loves hearing from readers. You can follow her (mis)adventures on Twitter (@BarbaraTWallace), and on Facebook.

Indulge in more books from Entangled...

NOT THE MARRYING KIND
Nicola Marsh

Who said marriage had to be convenient?

LA party planner Poppy Collins has kept her side business—planning divorce parties as the Divorce Diva—under wraps, but keeping her sister's company afloat is proving tougher by the day. When a new divorce party prospect gives Poppy the opportunity to save the day and boost her bottom line, she can't pass it up. But this time, she's about to get way more than she bargained for...

Vegas golden boy Beck Blackwood knows Poppy's secret, and he's not afraid to use it to get exactly what he wants—a wife. With his reputation and corporate expansion plans on the line, the only way he can repair the damage is by getting hitched, and fast. And if blackmail is the only way to get Poppy to the altar, then so be it...

But they're in the city of high stakes, and Poppy has a few aces up her sleeve. Now it's time to find out if they're playing to win...or if they're playing for keeps.

Taming the Tycoon
Amy Andrews

Real estate tycoon Nathaniel Montgomery is one deal away from making his first billion and fulfilling a promise to his dying father. Nothing will stop him from tearing down the decrepit St. Agnes hospital and erecting posh condos in its place. Not even the crystal-wearing, health food store owner whose publicity stunt lands him in the hospital.

After her brush with death five years ago, child prodigy Addie Collins learned what's truly important--health, happiness, and the two-hundred-year-old rose garden at St. Agnes. To make amends for the accident, she agrees to pose as Nathaniel's girlfriend at his eccentric grandmother's birthday party.

But Addie has an ulterior motive. To repay her debt to the universe, she must show him there's more to life than making money. Nathaniel hates to lose, but as she breaks through his defenses, losing himself in Addie's arms might be exactly what this tycoon needs…

THE BILLIONAIRE'S CHRISTMAS BABY

Victoria James

Jackson Pierce didn't make his fortune entertaining every half-cocked idea, especially one involving diaper changes. Not even the cute brunette who links him to the baby in her arms can crack his icy heart. A baby on the doorstep is the least of Hannah Woods's problems—she has to find the baby's uncle, or the child will end up in foster care. She sleuths her way to the reclusive CEO's doorstep only to find six feet of holiday sexy—and a door slammed in her face. But when Jackson comes around and urges they marry for little Emily's sake, Hannah finds herself falling for the jaded billionaire and wishing for a holiday miracle of their own…